BREAKING CHAINS

BOOK 8 OF THE SEAL TEAM HEARTBREAKERS

Teresa J. Reasor

This is a work of fiction. Names, characters, places, and incidents are the product of the author's imagination or are used fictitiously, and any resemblance to actual persons, living or dead, business establishments, events, or locales is entirely coincidental.

BREAKING CHAINS
A SEAL TEAM HEARTBREAKERS NOVEL

COPYRIGHT © 2019 by Teresa J. Reasor

Contact Information: teresareasor@msn.com

Cover Art by Tracy Stewart
Edited by Faith Freewoman

Teresa J. Reasor
PO Box 124
Corbin, KY 40702

Publishing History: First Edition 2019

ISBN-13: 978-1-940047-16-4
ISBN-10: 1-940047-16-1
Print Edition

TABLE OF CONTENTS

PROLOGUE

Iraq 2011

*G*ODDAMN CUTTER. HE'D taken the Iraqi kid's side against him. That ungrateful little turd hadn't given a shit that they were saving his bacon, getting him out of a dangerous area of the city He hadn't even wanted to return home. He'd take off again first opportunity he got, and they'd be chasing his ass down again *Damn him.*

So he grabbed the little shit. So what? There were worse things a kid could suffer. He knew all about them.

Derrick braced his feet against the turbulence that rocked the CH-47 Chinook. He turned to Brett, unable to stifle his fury. "We'll be facing him down the barrel of an AK-47 in less than a year. He's probably working for al-Qaeda already."

Brett pinched the bridge of his nose. Maybe the asshole had a headache. Serves him right.

The Chinook bounced and Derrick swore. With anger still riding him, he only half heard Greenback's complaint about the ride and Bowie's smartass remark.

Brett leaned close, and Derrick tipped his head so he could hear him above the whomp-whomp of the propellers. "You need to talk to Hawk about what happened or we'll be up to our necks in shit. The kid's bound to talk."

Fuck that. "It's his word against ours, Cutter." *Or was it? Was*

Cutter turning on him?

Cutter's jaw tightened. "I want you to put in for some counseling, Strong Man."

Jesus Christ, he couldn't believe it. Brett *was* turning on him. His teammate. His brother. Blood rushed into Derrick's head and his heart hammered inside his ears. This was happening more and more lately. More and more lately he could feel his anger crawling around under his skin looking for a way out. It took all his control not to punch Brett in the face. "That little bastard spent twenty minutes pissing on us and our country, and I'm the one who needs counseling? That's bullshit."

"Did you get another letter from Marjorie?" Brett asked.

The change of subject gouged at his control. "What the fuck does that have to do with anything?"

"Every time you get a letter from home you get fucked up. If her letters make you—"

He shoved his face close to Brett's. "Leave it alone, Cutter."

Marjorie said she loved him, but she was busy with her work, up for a promotion, all sorts of other shit. Every time he got a letter from her, she wrote about all the things she was doing without him. Then he started thinking about what else she might be doing... Just the idea of her being with some other guy... His pulse skyrocketed and his breathing with it.

Jesus, he wanted to go home. Everything would be fine once he was home.

"Ten minutes out." The controller's voice came over the bitch box.

"COM systems on," Lieutenant Hawk Yazzie ordered.

Derrick adjusted his throat mike, his attention on the other five members of their team. Thanks to the noise from the props, the chances of any of them hearing his discussion with Brett were slim to none. Greenback was trapped in his own thoughts, his face emotionless. Derrick had seen him like that before every mission. Flash had been in a weird mood for days, seeming to be off in his own world, too. Maybe he was also having dreams.

Hawk looked over the map one last time, folded the schematic, then tucked it away. Bowie and Doc were giving each other shit, as always.

He jerked as Cutter squeezed his shoulder.

"Forget about the shit that happened this morning and get your head in the game. Everything else needs to stay on board this chopper."

For the first time, Derrick's trust lay on a shaky edge that threatened to crumble. "As long as you have my six, we're good, Cutter."

Cutter nodded, his eyes steely.

Brett was a vault about most things, but Derrick bet he'd talk to Hawk about that damn kid as soon as the mission was over. He'd be worried about repercussions to his career if he sat on it.

A vein began to pulse at Derrick's temple and he rubbed at it. But what about his own career?

Brett had a family. All Derrick had was the team. He couldn't afford to lose them.

"Fall in." Hawk's voice came across the COM.

Derrick dragged his thoughts back to the mission, but the anger simmered under the surface like a fever that wouldn't break.

Everyone took their position, one behind the other.

Wind whipped through the cabin as the bay door lowered. A crew member threw out the rappel rope while another manned the machine gun mounted at the bay door.

The Chinook couldn't hover in one position too long, otherwise they'd draw attention.

Hawk gripped the rope and stepped off the platform. Darkness swallowed him. Greenback, Bowie, Doc, and Flash followed, then Cutter. The rope slid through Derrick's gloves like butter, and as soon as his boots hit the ground, he dogged Brett's footsteps while they double-timed away from the drop site.

Ten minutes later they regrouped and started the mile-long trek into the town.

The darkness was so intense it had a texture to it. Without their night vision goggles they would have been blind. The almost inaudible whisper of cloth brushing cloth was the only sound as they spread out but kept each other in sight.

He knew when they were getting close to town because the air hung stagnant and hot, clinging to the rank smell of raw sewage as though reluctant to let it go. They fell into single file again and hugged the shadows while they leapfrogged through the battle-scarred area. Electricity had been knocked out, and the darkness was both a comfort and a threat. The high-pitched squall of a baby close by carried to them. The hum of an engine followed from the east.

Through his night vision goggles, Derrick homed in on Hawk's hand signals. They'd reached their destination. The building housing the al-Qaeda armory sat in the midst of similar structures housing families. The mission was to collapse the armory inward to keep from taking out the buildings around it. Although if the terrorists were really harboring any kind of explosives besides C-4, it might make things interesting.

They split up and searched for cover. Three of them would enter from the east, three from the west.

Derrick hunkered down in the shadows not far from Brett. On the periphery of his mind he worried at the earlier situation, gnawing at it like a piece of tough steak. What would Hawk do if Brett told him he'd roughed up the boy? He just grabbed him and scared the shit out of him, didn't smack him around or anything, but he'd threatened to. Hawk had already chewed his ass about his temper. What if he lost his place on the team because of the Iraqi guy's son?

His breathing went ragged on a rush of rage. They were trying to help these people throw off the terrorist assholes, help them build a better government, and what did they get? *Nothing but grief.*

To try and relieve some of the pressure, Derrick clenched his fists until his knuckles hurt. He needed to concentrate on what was in front of him. But it was like peering through a green fog to see through the night vision goggles. He had to get his shit together.

His vision cleared when he heard clicks over his COM system. Hawk was inside the building and he reported no movement. He drew a deep breath.

The idea that something might be wrong with him flitted through his mind, but he stomped it flat. He'd deal with this shit once he was back home.

They were close. They just had to get through this mission and they'd be home in a few weeks.

He forced his attention on the top of the building. Through the blurry green goggles, he watched the guards wander from corner to corner. At the first hint of a gap in their surveillance, he hunched over and shot out of the shadows, silently crossing the distance between the alley he'd hidden in to the lower level window he'd targeted to climb through.

An itchy feeling between his shoulder blades dogged him like someone had him in their crosshairs. It drove him into the shadows close to the building. He quickly slid the window up, slung his assault rifle across his back, and wiggled inside. For a few seconds he rested on his hands and knees, allowing the itchy feeling to ease and his breathing to calm before he rose. He clicked his COM, drew his service weapon, then in four easy strides reached the door and cracked it open.

The hall was clear. He stole out of the room and moved east toward the area he was to wire. At the sound of footsteps coming his way he darted into one of the rooms and eased the door shut. The space was empty but for four pallets on the floor where the terrorists were sleeping. The room smelled of old sweat and gun oil.

Two men argued in the Kurdish dialect of the region, their voices growing louder as they closed in on his position.

Every muscle in his body tightened. He jerked his K-bar free and rolled back against the wall behind the door. If they entered the room, he'd have to take them out as soundlessly as possible.

Their voices dwindled away as they turned a corner, and his tension eased. The heavy beat of their feet sounded hollow as they climbed the stairs. He cracked the door, looked both ways, then eased silently back out of the room.

Voices came from the top of the stairs, and he pulled back

against the wall until they moved deeper into the building, then hustled across the back hall. His target was the southeast corner of the building's interior wall. They wanted to knock out the supports on the main floor and collapse the structure inward, so he should have entered the building from the back, but there were no windows low enough to gain entry.

His booted steps sounded loud even though he placed each foot as carefully as he could. Standing outside the door to the room he was supposed to rig with explosives, he took a breath and listened for any sound behind the barrier. Everything remained still.

He opened the door, slipped in to one side, and shut it. Aside from a table, the room was completely empty. He released his pent-up breath, holstered his sidearm, set his assault rifle to one side, and shrugged free of his pack, removing the C-4 and blasting caps and setting them out in an orderly fashion.

Five minutes later he had the room rigged to blow. He glanced at his watch and set the timer. Shouldering his pack again, he swung his assault rifle up and cracked open the door.

As he checked the hall for hostiles, a dark, unwanted thought crept into his mind like a bad dream. Without Brett, there'd be no inquiry into what happened with the kid.

He and Brett went through BUD/S together. *He's my best bud. He has to keep his fucking mouth shut about the kid.*

But he knew Brett, knew he wouldn't. Rage and fear pulsed inside him like a second heartbeat, and a mist of sweat slicked his skin.

God, he was tired.

How many nights had it been since he slept? He'd lost count.

He was a SEAL, and sometimes he had to get tough to keep going. He had to keep going. Tough...

Sometimes you had to get tough in order to get info. That's what he'd go with.

But which one of them would they believe?

He couldn't lose his place on the team! He might be transferred to another, but these guys were the closest thing to family he had.

Derrick went through the schematic of the building in his head. He knew where Brett was. He had to talk to him. Brett needed to see reason.

He eased out into the hall, shut the door, and moved stealthily in the direction of the northwest corner.

The trip back through the building was surprisingly easy. Security was surprisingly lax, but the al-Qaeda were in the heart of the city surrounded by sympathizers. Why bother with a guard at the door?

This was the room where Brett was supposed to be. What if he'd already finished rigging it to blow and bugged out? He hadn't heard his clicks on the Com.

If Brett was gone and working his way back to his cover, he'd deal with him later. He'd try to reason with him again. If he was still here… He turned the knob and ghosted into the room.

Fast and slick, Brett drew his sidearm and pointed it at him. Recognition lit his eyes, and, after a moment of tension, relief followed. He shoved the pistol back in its holster.

Derrick put a finger to his lips and pressed his ear to the door. He signaled all clear and for him to hurry.

If Brett talked to Hawk…

He'd spill his guts. Derrick knew it.

He couldn't let Brett take away his place on the team. He just couldn't.

His girl would think he was a loser. She'd leave him. And she had to stay. She was all he had.

His father's voice, derisive, bitter ate into his brain, "You'll always be nothing, boy. Fucking nothing." He shook his head to rid himself of the voice permanently embedded in his brain.

He waited for Brett to set the timer.

Derrick stepped toward him, reaching for the anger that propelled him here to this room. Panic and regret echoed back.

Brett was turning on him, he knew he was. Had he told the others what he'd done?

Being a SEAL was everything. Without it he'd be nothing.

He'd have nothing. The pressure inside his head intensified until it was unbearable.

He gripped his rifle with both hands. Sensing his movement, Brett shifted to the side and started to look up. With a half-growl, half-sob, Derrick brought the stock of the weapon down against his teammate's temple. Brett slumped sideways to the floor.

The numbers on the timer raced on.

CHAPTER 1

Seven Years Later

T HE SMELL OF bacon frying dragged Derrick out of the nightmare. Sweat-soaked, his heart pounding in his throat, he shoved aside the comforter and sat on the side of the bed while his stomach pitched and his hands shook.

He rested his elbows on his thighs, gripping the back of his head, then ran his hands over and over the short stubble covering his scalp.

He always ended up back in Iraq, in that room. Even after seven years he couldn't leave it behind, might never be able to leave it behind. Probably shouldn't be able to.

He could pretend some other man had attempted to murder a friend, but he, Derrick Armstrong, was the one who had done it Would he be capable of doing something like that now? He hoped not. He didn't believe so.

It haunted him. And he deserved to have it haunt him. Yet he still couldn't muster the courage to face every emotion, every action he'd taken during those moments. Not yet. He was finally too distant from how raw his emotions had been then.

His mind was clear now, not clouded by the high peak of emotion he'd ridden for weeks while in Iraq. The fog of sleepless nights, four before the mission, had put him in an adrenaline-fueled haze. He'd been paranoid, angry, confused. His mind racing from one thought to another. And even after he was back home the nightmares continued. He'd still felt the walls closing in on him.

And right here, right now, there were other things, just as hard, he had to deal with.

He was leaving today. As soon as his eyes flew open, he made the decision. In fact, he should have gotten up at three or four in the morning and just left.

He scanned the bedroom, feeling a little disoriented. No pipes or supports ran across the ceiling. No low-level hum of voices vibrated through the air like the murmur of a radio turned down low. No loud male chatter of guys shooting the shit, or the slam of the cage doors inside the brig.

It felt strange to have so much space around him, and so much color.

Battleship gray was the standard color on every bulkhead in the brig, then blue-gray on doors and a darker, duller gray on the chairs and tables in the common areas. There were times he thought they'd painted everything drab to make certain the prisoners suppressed their emotions. It was certainly depressing enough to do that.

But this room wasn't depressing. The walls were a bright blue, and the comforter on the bed a red, white, and blue geometric pattern. The curtains were the same, but a bed, dresser, and nightstand of better quality had replaced the cheap bedroom suite he used while growing up. The original set had probably fallen apart.

He'd stowed his gear in the closet, what little there was of it. All his BDUs were in a footlocker in his storage unit. He wore them during his time in the brig, but no longer.

His dishonorable discharge was the icing on the cake of those seven long years. He'd never again be allowed to own a gun or shoot one. He'd never be able to serve in the military or use any of the training he'd received while in the teams.

He'd be a convict for the rest of his life.

At least he'd served his entire sentence and didn't have to deal with parole, but if he got into any kind of trouble again, he'd end up back in prison. They'd look at his past and that would be it. No questions, no benefit of the doubt, no nothing.

No one would ever again take his word as truth.

The deep rumble of his father's voice, muffled but clear, traveled from downstairs. It had already started.

He'd been advised to avoid physical confrontations and alcohol. But no one had advised him to avoid his family. Which is what he should have done.

His father was on his ass constantly and had been since Derrick walked through the door. Every meal was a gauntlet, every momentary meeting an ordeal. He didn't think he could take it much longer.

He'd only wanted to spend a week with his parents and siblings, to feel like he wasn't alone. But he'd never felt more alone in his life.

He walked quietly across the hall to relieve himself and splash some water on his face. He'd rather go hungry than sit across the table from Dempsey while he made snide remarks about all the mistakes he'd made, so he decided to sneak downstairs and go for a run before he hit the road.

He made the bed and got his running shoes out of the closet. When someone knocked on the door, he braced himself as he said, "Come in."

His mother opened the door. He'd gotten his muscular build and height from Dempsey, but his hair color from her. The small bit of gray scattered through the blonde strands at her temples blended in well.

"I have bacon and pancakes fixed downstairs."

"Thanks, Mom. I think I'll do my run first since I can't run on a full stomach. I can heat everything up in the microwave when I get back."

"I'll tell your father you're already gone, then."

Melba Armstrong had run interference for him more times than he could count growing up, not that it ever made any difference. "Thanks, Mom."

She hovered a moment longer. "He's hurt, Derrick."

"No he's not, Mom." He gripped the edge of the dresser and walked back to stretch his thigh and calf muscles. "All he ever feels or understands is anger. He washed his hands of me back in college when I lost my football scholarship, and he wasn't able to relive his glory days through my accomplishments anymore. Then he rebounded from that when he could tell everyone I was a SEAL. Now he just wants me gone so he doesn't have to acknowledge that I'm still alive."

He straightened. "I know I'm a disappointment to you both. I can't take back what I did. But I've paid with seven years of my life for what happened, and I don't need him to punish me for it, too."

"He's still your father."

Derrick controlled the urge to shake his head. A father didn't withhold his love as a punishment. He didn't demand perfection in order to earn it. He didn't show his love with a slap, a punch, a dislocated shoulder or a broken arm. His throat felt tight. "He stopped being my father the first time he hurt me when I was a kid. I just didn't realize it until I ended up in prison."

He glanced away from his mother's stricken look. It took him seven long years to realize a lot of things. "I'll never be perfect in his eyes again, so I'll never be worthy of his love again. That's the way he worked when I was a kid, and he hasn't changed. I don't want or need his love anymore."

The price he'd paid as a boy was too high, and it was damn sure too steep now.

"I'll be back to pack in a little while and start back to San Diego after breakfast. I need to find a place to live and a job."

"That's so far away, Derrick. I thought that now you're home you'd want to stay nearby. You have family here."

"I love you, Mom." He wrapped his arms around her and rested his chin atop her head. "I love that you want me close by. But I can't be this close to him."

Besides, his sister Tina was nervous about him being around her kids. She tried not to show it, but he'd felt it and kept his distance. And Carter was all wrapped up in his job with a computer software company and his girlfriend Elizabeth. Neither of them had visited him in prison, and the few letters they'd written ended after the first year.

He was glad Tina and Carter had somehow escaped their father's legacy. They'd both grown up and moved on with their lives, but both of them would be relieved when he left.

But he couldn't say that to his mom.

"There's too many people here who know me, and the rumors and gossip will make things more difficult for me to fight my way back to a normal life. And more difficult for you, Tina, and Carter too. I'd rather be in a place where no one knows me and I can have a small chance of starting fresh."

She pressed her face against his chest while her shoulders shook and breath hitched. "I love you, Derrick."

She was the only one who did. The only one who had written him every week. She'd been his lifeline. His arms tightened around her as he fought back the emotions threatening to overwhelm him. "I love you too, Mom."

His chest tightened. "You'd better go down and eat with Dad. He'll be wondering what's keeping you. I'll go for my run."

He tried to shut off his pain and guilt as he went silently down the steps and out the front door, but they still ripped at him.

He started out slow, finding his rhythm and pacing himself. Being in the brig had given him a true appreciation of freedom. Every meal, every round of exercise, every counseling session was scheduled to the nth degree. Even work. And now he was out from under the military thumb, he set his own schedule, but he maintained some of the things that had worked for him inside. Exercise made some of the pain easier to deal with, helped him control the anger.

He chose the route he'd taken four times since he'd come home. Because it was summer and none of the kids seemed to be out in the early hours, so he didn't have to worry about school bus pickups and parents clogging the roads or sidewalks.

Between the houses he caught glimpses of the lake the neighborhood bordered, then caught a whiff of the water's earthy smell. He would have liked to jog around it, but it would be trespassing on private property and someone was bound to call and report him.

He put on some speed to drown out the thought. Thirty minutes later, thigh muscles burning, his chest working like bellows, he stopped at a four-way intersection and walked around in a circle to cool down for a minute.

When his breathing had slowed, he backtracked the same route at a slower pace. Two blocks from his parents' house, he passed a group of women sitting in lawn chairs on the front porch of a southern-style house. As he jogged past, all five stood up. A couple of them whistled, and two or three shouted out playful invitations.

He laughed and waved to them, their small, flirty playfulness giving him the boost he needed to leave some of the darkness behind. He was still smiling as he rounded the corner to his parents' house.

His pleasant feelings died when he spied his Dad sitting on the front porch, so he paced back and forth on the sidewalk, cooling down and taking a few minutes to shore up his self-control.

The man he faced as he climbed the steps wasn't the one who'd beaten and berated him as a kid. That one had been strong, muscular, and dangerous. This one had a tire of fat around his middle that slowed him down and hair that was thinning to a bald spot at the crown of his head. The fear that ruled Derrick's memories of him no longer affected him.

But Dempsey still had the knife-sharp ability to gut someone with his words.

He reminded himself he was bigger, stronger, and more dangerous than his father now. But it was up to him to control it. He could allow his father to force him back into the same pattern Dempsey had followed, or he could break the mold. He'd been working for seven years to break it.

"Your mother told me you're leaving today."

"Yeah. I thought I'd take a shower and get on the road."

His dad shoved into his space, his expression a warning that he was about to pound on someone. While Derrick was growing up it usually was him.

"I didn't raise you to be a coward."

Derrick laughed and gained some satisfaction at Dempsey's surprised reaction. "In the four years of being a SEAL, I saw and ran toward things that would have made you either puke your guts out or piss your pants. Calling me a coward isn't an insult, because I know it's not true, old man."

"You're running away from your family, and your responsibility to us."

"What responsibility would that be?"

"You owe us, Derrick."

"For what? For the letters you wrote while I was in the brig? No, because there weren't any. For the money you sent? No, there wasn't any. For the phone calls? Uh no, there weren't any. I don't owe you shit. I already paid for everything you ever gave me with blood, broken bones, and bruises. I don't owe you shit."

Dempsey's face flushed. "You owe us for having to live with the shame of you being in prison. It isn't only you who paid for it. All our neighbors know. And it's been an embarrassment to us for seven years."

"I was seventeen hundred miles away. Who, exactly, told them? Mom? Tina or Carter? Who spread the word? I'm betting it was you while you were drunk. So why is it my fault that everyone knows?" He started toward the door, but Dempsey grabbed his arm. Derrick met his hot gaze with one of his own.

He recognized the unreasonable rage in his father's face. Dempsey owned his anger, even enjoyed it. Berated people with it until he got his way.

"You need to stay and face everyone down."

Derrick took two slow steps back and jerked his arm free. With an effort, he breathed through the lava-hot reaction to having his father lay hands on him. "I can't take back what I did seven years ago, and I'm not sticking around here so you can punish me too."

He started past him again. The stinging slap to the back of his head drove him forward. He fisted his hand and rounded on Dempsey, caught himself, and breathed through the need to lash out. "Really? You're going to go down this road?"

Dempsey telegraphed the next blow, this time with his fist. Derrick dodged, the punch skimming past his jaw without making contact.

At the furious frustration in his father's expression, he braced himself to fight back. When Dempsey swung again, Derrick ducked, grabbed his father's arm, and let his momentum carry him forward. Dempsey tripped and almost went down, but regained his balance.

Dempsey gasped for air, the extra forty pounds slowing him down. "You walk away now, don't bother coming back."

Relief flooded him, and Derrick smiled. The weight threatening to flatten him lifted. "Thanks, I won't."

Dempsey charged him, and once again he grabbed his father's arm and pivoted. Now he used his strength to add to it. The older man hurtled past him and into the porch swing. The swing tipped back, and he tumbled over it and hit the porch railing, then crashed to the floor.

Without checking to see if his father was getting up, Derrick jerked open the door and strode into the house.

And nearly bumped into his mother. The anxiety and pain carved brackets around her mouth and glazed her eyes with tears.

"I'm sorry, Mom." He took the stairs two at a time and went straight to his room. Expecting his father to burst into the room and continue the fight, he threw his clothes, boots, and his ditty bag into his suitcase, zipped the bag, and hefted it down the stairs.

His mother hovered in the foyer, tearful and anxious. He could do it. He could walk away without a backward glance. But not from his mom. "Walk me to the car, Mom."

"You didn't even get dressed."

"I'm not giving him another shot at me. I don't want to have to beat him into the ground like he always did me, which means I need to leave the fuck now. Is he still out on the porch?"

"No, he staggered off the porch and went into the garage."

Jesus, was he getting a weapon to come back and have another go at him? "I need to go before he comes back out, Mom."

He preceded her to the car, giving her no chance to drag her feet. If Dempsey came after him again, he'd have to pound on him to stop him, and he'd end up back in jail.

He tossed his bag in the back seat. "Let me take you to Tina's for a while. Once I'm gone, he won't have anyone else to take things out on. I don't want to call back later and find out he's used you as a punching bag."

"He hasn't done that in a long time."

He didn't believe her for a second, but he couldn't force her to admit it. When he'd lived at home, he begged her for years to leave Dempsey. She wouldn't do it.

He learned a long time ago that a person had to be willing to change. After nearly thirty-two years of marriage, his mother was too afraid or unwilling.

"Come with me to Tina's. I'd like to say goodbye to her and the kids, and I need to shower and change clothes before I leave. I'll drop you back here on my way out of town." He wouldn't have thought about going to his sister's if it weren't to protect his mother.

She glanced over her shoulder toward the house. Sunlight struck the side of her face, highlighting every line and wrinkle. She was fifty and looked ten years older, thanks to the strain of living with Dempsey.

A rush of worry had him saying, "Come with me, Mom."

"I have to tell him where I'm going."

He looked away. She'd never leave the house if she went back in. "He's angry with me and out of control, and you'll be the only one here."

"I'll tell him I'm going to the store for some buttermilk for the cake I'm baking and I'll meet you at Tina's."

It was useless. He couldn't change this foot-thick wall of denial she'd built around herself. He hugged her and kissed the top of her head, breathing the homey fragrances of apple-scented shampoo and Ivory soap. She seemed so fragile pressed against his bulk, and a wave of protective anxiety hit him. He'd experienced the damage his father could do with a slap or a punch. "Stay away from him. He'll be primed for a fight."

"I will."

Though anxiety tightened like a fist in his stomach, he climbed into his Jeep and started the engine.

He wouldn't go to Tina's, because she didn't want him there because of her children. She looked at him like she did their father, as someone to fear. But he'd call her and tell her to somehow get their mother to her place until Dempsey cooled down.

He'd lost what little connection he'd had with everyone but his mom.

He might never be back.

An ache built in his throat and his vision blurred. Through the haze he saw his mom standing on the sidewalk as he got on the school bus. She'd always waved goodbye until he couldn't see her anymore.

She hadn't always been able to protect him from his father, but she'd tried to love him enough to make up for every hurt.

He blinked to clear his vision and pushed the button to roll down the window. "I love you, Mom."

She stood in the driveway and waved until he couldn't see her anymore.

CHAPTER 2

ELLA WIPED THE prep counter with a damp rag and set up the next round. It was hot as Hades behind the bar, but Larry wanted booze sold, and he'd do whatever it took to make sure it did. Turning down the air conditioning was one of his favorite tricks. The hotter the customers got, the more they drank. Good for him, bad for the bouncers, waitstaff and dancers.

Ella glanced up at the stage as Tasha spread her long legs on each side of the tall steel pole and hunched her way all the way down, her tiny thong leaving little to the imagination. That, too, would keep the men drinking.

She checked down the long the bar, making sure everyone's drinks were in good shape. For the most part the customers stayed at the tables or in chairs at the end of the stage, but just a few liked to sit at the bar and watch things through the mirrors behind her. Two waitresses brought trays to the bar and cleared them. Ella rang up the sales, stuffed the money in the drawer, then rushed to retrieve the waitresses' orders and send them back out on the floor.

Shit! She was the only bartender who'd shown up for work. And she didn't want Larry behind the bar with her. Every time he reached for a glass or bottle, he'd cop a feel or brush an arm against her breast. She'd rather work herself to the bone than put up with that shit. He'd been less than subtle with his overtures for weeks now.

She was a bum magnet. It didn't matter if the bum was the owner of a bar or a customer. She'd have to look for another job and get out from under this.

One of her regular customers raised a finger for a refill and she rushed to get the bottle of Jameson. She scooped three cubes of ice into a glass and poured scotch over it, whisked away the empty glass and placed the fresh one in front of him. He handed her ten dollars and she rang up the sale. He waved the change away, something he did on a regular basis.

"Thanks, Carl."

"You're earning your keep tonight, darlin'," Carl said.

She didn't argue that.

A new group of men walked into the club. All but one fanned out at the tables while the loner broke away and came to sit at the bar.

She waited for him to get settled on one of the barstools, then asked, "What can I get you?"

His blond hair caught the stage lights and his shoulders looked four feet wide. The strong planes of his face remained in shadow.

"A Bud."

She drew a brew for him, slapped a napkin on the bar and set the glass on it, slid a bowl of peanuts closer to him, and took his money.

Larry appeared to introduce the next dancer, but she rarely looked up to watch the performances. They brought in the customers and she sold the booze. That was her job.

At one time she'd been desperate and on the other side of the bar, and she wasn't ever going back. The girls made good money, but she didn't want Micah to ever find out she'd taken her clothes off to keep a roof over their heads and food on their table.

Her hands continued to work pouring, mixing, putting ice into glasses, though her thoughts moved in a different direction. Had Larry found out about that? Was that why he was pressuring her?

Like an ugly, twisted jack-in-the-box, Larry appeared at the countertop divider that accessed the back of the bar. In his early thirties, he was broad through the chest and shoulders, but his lifestyle was wrecking the muscular physique he had in the college football pictures she'd seen in his office. The man had a weakness for beer.

He flipped up the divider, shoved through, and lowered it back into place. "Why didn't you text me and tell me you were slammed?"

"I'm handling it. If you'll cash those tickets out, I'll finish up on this order."

His frown deepened into a scowl. His dark brown, deep-set eyes turned flat and unfriendly.

Screw him. She was done with being pawed and touched. She'd had enough.

In fact, ever since Micah's second birthday she'd decided life was too short to put up with any man. They just took up your time and gave nothing in return. Society had turned on a dime, and now men were the ball and chain they'd always accused women of being.

She fixed a Tom Collins, a Long Island Iced Tea, and a bourbon on the rocks and set the tray on the counter. Connie, one of the waitresses, swept it up and was gone. Carl needed another Scotch, then she studied the man next to him. The strobe light flipped on during this number, tracing his high, flat cheekbones and glinting off the crystal clarity of his blue eyes. He was damn handsome, and had that bad boy air about him she was drawn to. She stomped the momentary weakness like a bug. "Need a refill?"

"Yes, thanks."

She whisked his empty glass away and quickly replaced it with a full one, then took his money. She turned to find Larry blocking her way and handed him the cash. "The customer needs change."

She'd moved on to the next round of drinks when Larry's hand brushed her back as he passed her. Her skin crawled and she felt a little nauseous. If she filed a sexual harassment suit, she'd lose. The nature of the place where she was working and her history would count against her in court.

Larry laid the money on the counter and sauntered up to her.

"There's something I need to tell you, Larry." She grabbed his arm and dragged him away from the counter. "I've been trying to avoid telling you this because it's my own private business, but you need to know the truth."

His heavy brows met in a V over his nose. "What is it?"

"I'm a lesbian."

He laughed.

She kept her features blank and waited patiently for his amusement to peter out. When he finally stopped laughing, she gave him a flat, unfriendly look. "I'm serious, Larry."

"But you have a kid."

"Yeah, that happened when I was very young, before I realized what I need. I don't need a boyfriend, I don't need a husband. I don't want either. I need a wife. I want a wife." The more she said it, the more she believed it. Another woman around the house might actually be helpful. "Now, unless you can grow breasts and everything else that goes with them…I'm not interested."

Stella, another waitress, laid an empty tray on the side counter and waved an order. Ella moved past Larry to grab it and started mixing the drinks.

He spoke against her ear, "I could make you change your mind."

She struggled not to flinch away and shook her head. "That's not how it works, Larry. Could I convince you that you'd actually enjoy sucking a dick?" Saying the words made her cheeks burn.

He jerked back as if she'd slapped him.

"I didn't think so." She grabbed a cherry to garnish the cocktail she was making.

She looked up to find the blond guy listening to every word of their conversation. He grinned, dropped a tip in the jar and sauntered out.

After thirty minutes of grope-free work, Ella's guilt over the lie started to ease. If Larry continued to keep his distance, she might just be able to keep this job until she could find a better one. If he didn't fire her for being LGBTQ. Oh, he'd make up some kind of bullshit excuse, but he'd probably do it. She just couldn't win.

By the time Larry announced last call, her feet and back ached and a headache pounded at her temples. She'd taken zero breaks. Thank God tomorrow was her day off.

When the last customer walked out the door, the overhead lights came on and the cleaning crew started stacking the chairs atop the tables. Ella sat at the bar with Jasmine, one of the waitresses, and counted the money in the drawer and the tips in the tip jar. She studied the business card that had fallen out of the jar along with the cash. It was for a towing service. She absently stuck the business card in her jeans pocket to tape to the mirror behind the cash register. It might come in handy if one of their customers had car trouble.

She wrapped each bundle of cash with a rubber band and stuck the tally slip beneath it.

"You worked all night alone. I'm not sure any of the other bartenders could have managed. You deserve every tip in that jar," Jasmine said as she rose and threw a sweater around her shoulders.

Because Larry's bruised ego was more important to him than his business, he'd huffed off to his office for most of the night, leaving her to work alone.

"We all do our part, Jasmine." She dragged herself to her feet. "The men come in to watch the girls dance. I just sell the booze."

"I heard you came out to Larry. You're gay?"

News traveled fast. Her stomach fluttered with guilt. "Yeah." She slid the tally sheet toward Jasmine, she signed it, then Ella added her own signature.

Jasmine's young features took on a hard, world-weary look too old for her twenty years or so. "I'm not sure that will keep him off you, so watch your back."

Damn. Was it some kind of unspoken rule that every girl who worked for him had to sleep with him to keep her job? She needed to find another line of work, or at least a better place to do it in. She'd thought that's what she was doing when she accepted this job. "Thanks for the warning. I'll see you on Friday."

Jasmine gathered her purse. "Good night."

Ella lifted the drawer and carried it back to the office. Larry sat behind the desk and barely looked up when she set it down. She breathed a sigh of relief as she beat it back down the hallway to the bar and collected her purse and jacket.

Every muscle ached as she limped out of the building, pulling out her keys as she walked across the parking lot. As she approached her 2010 dark blue Malibu, she noticed the nose of the vehicle sat lower than the rear. When she got closer, she groaned. Her two front tires were flat. While she was using the light from her cell phone to check out the damage, several cars drove out of the lot. She braced an arm on the top of the car and rested her forehead against it.

Tires were at least a hundred apiece, if not more. She didn't have that kind of money.

But more importantly, she needed to get home to Micah. He'd be asleep, but Patsy, her overnight babysitter, would worry if she woke to find Ella wasn't home to fix Micah's breakfast and take him to school.

No buses ran this late. A taxi would cost a fortune. Maybe she could catch a ride with one of the other girls.

She rushed back inside the bar. With the lights on, the space looked tired. The walls were pockmarked where posters and shelving had once hung. The floors were shiny with water where they'd been mopped recently, so she walked gingerly over the slick surface and crossed to the hall leading to the dressing rooms behind the stage.

The cluttered dressing room stretched forlorn and empty. She took out her cell phone and stood looking at the screen. She hadn't known any of the girls long enough to exchange numbers.

"Trouble?" Larry asked from the door.

The hair stood up on the back of her neck. The bland, overly innocent look had her heart pounding in her temples and wrists. Had he punctured her tires to keep her here? Her throat went dry, and she tried to swallow. "I came back in to see if any of the girls were still here."

"I think they've all gone."

Beating back the breathless feelings of panic, she scanned the long narrow, space for a weapon. Hairbrushes, makeup and jewelry cluttered the counters. Skimpy costumes hung on the racks. Then she spotted a can of hair spray on the counter. She leaned back against the counter and slid a hand into her pocket for the business card, read the number, and dialed it with her thumb.

"Carpenter Towing."

"I'm at the Honey Pot strip club. My car has two flats, and I'm in a hurry to get home. I could use some help."

"I can be there in five minutes."

"Thanks. I'll be waiting outside, near the front of the building." She reached behind her, as though pushing away from the counter, gripped the can of hair spray, and put her finger on the valve. If Larry didn't try to harass her, she'd leave it on the bar. If he did, she'd spray the son of a bitch in the eyes.

She closed the call but hit the record button on the phone and put it in the front pocket of her purse.

"I can take you home," Larry said.

"No." Her stomach clenched. "Thanks anyway. I need to have the car to take my son to school in the morning." She fished in her bag for the car keys and gripped them between her fingers without removing her hand. She'd stab him with them if he tried something, then spray him in the face.

She forced herself to walk toward him as though she wasn't intimidated by his bulk standing in her way. Every muscle in her body tensed and her heart beat at the back of her throat.

"I could help you out if you'd let me. We could come to an agreement, Ella."

"An agreement about what?"

"I can pay for your car repairs."

Nausea forced her to take several deep breaths. Tears burned her eyes. "Out of the goodness of your heart? Will you let me take the cost out of my weekly pay?"

He smirked. "That isn't exactly what I had in mind."

"I'm not a whore. I don't turn tricks and never have."

"No money would change hands. It's just quid pro quo. I can make your life easier around here…if you'll cooperate."

Every tired inch of her ached, and his harassment seemed to sharpen the hurt. "You offered to buy me two new tires in exchange for sex. Two hundred bucks for pushing your dick inside me." Why couldn't even one guy surprise her by being more than she expected? She swallowed back more angry words. She couldn't risk inciting him to violence.

Her nausea rose. If she puked on him, would he leave her alone?

"It's just sex. You've done it before." After a pause he said. "If you want to continue working here, you need to give it up. Who knows, you might like it."

She'd rather die than let him touch her. She drew the keys free of her bag and gripped them in one hand while she held the hair spray can behind her. "I'm giving you my notice, then."

Larry's jaw worked. His features hardened when he saw how she held the keys. "You're making this harder than it has to be."

"It's against the law for you to sexually harass your employees. What makes you think I won't call someone about it?"

"You used to strip. You'd never win a lawsuit or anything else with your history."

"That was three years ago. I just danced and went home to my son. It was the only way I could keep a roof over our heads. I won't let you blackmail me into being your whore." It wasn't fucking happening. "I'm going home to my son."

She strode forward and tensed as she got close to him. When he stepped back, she breathed a short sigh of relief until he gripped her arm. Then she froze. "Don't." Her voice came out sharp with a blend of panic and rage.

His fingers dug in, and he grabbed the back of her head and attempted to force her close enough to kiss. She braced her clenched fist with the keys poking between her fingers against his chest to keep her distance and twisted her neck to try and dislodge his hand.

His fingers put enough pressure on the back of her neck to burn.

She squirted hair spray right into his eyes. The mist stung hers, too.

He yelled, released her, and dug at his eyes with both hands. She ran, her shoes squeaking as she dug in for traction. The bar floor was wet and slick as an ice rink, and she slipped and slid her way across it and past the men who were still working. They all looked up.

She hit the front door and ran out into the parking lot, still gripping the hair spray can. The loud rumble of a large truck came from the corner, and she turned to watch it pull into the parking lot. The wrecker's headlights spotlighted her, then stopped. She ran toward them.

CHAPTER 3

DERRICK SWUNG DOWN from the cab and sauntered over to the car while he waited for the owner to join him. He recognized the bartender from earlier in the evening and smiled.

He glanced at the can of hair spray she gripped in one hand while she clung to her purse with the other. "You have to hurry, okay?" She panted as she glanced back toward the bar.

He jumped back into the cab and pulled a flashlight out of the console. As soon as he squatted down and aimed it at the tires, he saw the punctures. Shit. Someone had done this on purpose.

"You have a run-in with one of the customers tonight?" he asked as she came to stand over him. He looked up and took in the long-limbed, slender shape of her, and the midnight dark cap of hair that hugged her head and feathered around her face. In the harsh glow of the headlights her skin looked sickly pale.

"No. You were here tonight," she said.

"Yeah for two beers." Did she think he was driving impaired? "I didn't come on the job until eleven, so the alcohol would be out of my system."

"You left your business card."

"Yeah. "I thought if someone had car trouble, whoever was working might call."

Her eyes narrowed and she gripped the hair spray can with her finger on the nozzle. "This isn't some double-teaming scam you and Larry have going, is it?"

"Larry?"

"My boss. The guy who couldn't keep his hands to himself." She glanced over her shoulder at the bar again.

"I'm not a part of any scam, lady. I just tow cars, fix flats, and do minor repairs."

She studied him for a long moment. Her breathing sounded uneven, and she was shaking.

Something bad had gone down, and the woman was close to a meltdown. He eyed the empty parking lot. He couldn't really leave her here alone. "You want to call someone else, I'll stay until they get here."

His offer seemed to calm her some. "I need to sit in your truck while you check out the tires."

"Are you cold? I have a jacket in the truck I can get for you."

"No." She searched his face. She rocked from foot to foot. "I just had a fight with my boss, and it got a little intense. I'm afraid he might come out here and start something."

He'd known while watching the little byplay between her and the guy earlier, what he'd been edging toward. He'd made his play and, from the look of things, tried to use force, and she'd gotten away.

The keys were in the ignition, and if she decided to take off in the wrecker... She'd never be able to handle the big truck. Besides, she was shivering, and anxiety dilated her pupils. "Go ahead and get in the wrecker."

She wasted no time rushing to the vehicle and opening the passenger door. Her long legs stretched easily up to the running board, and she heaved herself up into the cab.

He'd have to tow the car. If he couldn't patch them, would she have the money to purchase new ones? Probably not. Shit.

He went to the cab and tapped on the window. He heard a startled squeak from inside and she scooted up to look out before easing the window down.

She was spooked. Damnit. He didn't need this shit, didn't want it. Didn't want to be dragged into anything that put him on the cops' radar.

"I'm going to need your keys. I'll have to tow you into the shop to fix the tires."

"How much will that be?"

"It's a flat fee of a hundred dollars."

She bit her lip and her dark eyes looked a little glassy. "Okay." She rummaged in the bag and handed him the keys.

He angled the lift bed and hooked her Malibu up to the winch. A man came out of the bar and stalked toward him carrying a baseball bat.

Derrick recognized the guy who'd been harassing her earlier. When the man swung back and leveled a direct hit to the right rear quarter panel of the Malibu, Derrick leapt forward.

"Hey, you can't do that, man. I've been hired to tow this car. You damage it, I'll get blamed for it." He whipped out his cell phone and took a quick picture of the guy holding the bat. "One more swing and I'm calling the cops."

"That bitch sprayed hair spray into my eyes. She could have blinded me."

That told him a lot about what had gone down. Derrick had been angry like this before. Had he looked as demon-possessed as this dude?

Larry, that was the guy's name. "I was here earlier getting a beer, man. I saw her turn you down. You try to tap that when she already said no?"

Larry shot him a shifty, narrow-eyed look through swollen, red eyes. He hefted the bat and rested it on his shoulder. "She's a whore. She used to strip, and now she's acting all high and mighty."

Shit! His mind raced as he took in the bulk of the guy in front of him. No matter what she'd done for a living… She weighed maybe hundred and fifteen pounds, soaking wet. This guy would go two-fifty easy.

He flashed back to how he'd grabbed Marjorie too hard, shaken her, slapped her. He swallowed in an attempt to shake the nausea and focused on the guy in front of him.

"She wasn't acting high and mighty when she came out here and told me to tow the car. Shaky, pale, looking over her shoulder. Running off like she was scared. She brings charges, the cops will be asking me about that." He eyed the car. "You the one who punctured her tires?"

"No."

Derrick spotted the lie a mile off.

"You're gonna have to learn to lie better than that, man. Messed with her vehicle. Kept her here late after the other girls left. Cornered her somewhere private."

Three men exited the building and climbed into the cars.

"That your cleaning crew? Did they hear the scuffle? They see her run out of there the way I did?"

Larry's eyes shifted from the guys in their cars, then back to him. His jaw sagged a little, and the hands he'd wrapped around the bat tightened and released.

Derrick tensed and straightened to his full height and met the asshole's gaze full-on. If the guy swung at him, he'd take that bat away and feed it to him.

Larry broke eye contact and removed one hand from the bat to wipe it on his pants.

Slimy motherfucker. I'm not taking this shit.

"This whole thing looks premeditated to me, man. If I can put it together, I'm sure the cops will too."

Larry wiped an arm over his brow, missing the sweat trickling down his temples.

"How much to tow the car and fix the tires?"

"A hundred for the tow, one-fifty apiece for the tires. Then they'll have to be balanced and aligned, which will be another seventy."

"How much for you to keep your mouth shut?"

He'd go after the girl. Not a doubt in his mind.

"That depends on what you're going to do about her. You offer her a generous severance package to keep her mouth shut and move on, we're good. You try to cause her more trouble, I'll go to the cops myself."

Larry scowled. "Why? Do you know her?"

"No. Never met the lady before tonight and only talked to her long enough for her to ask me to tow the car. I heard what she said to you. Swinging like she does, I wouldn't have reason to ask her out. She's into girls." He shrugged one shoulder. "But I go along with this little venture and something happens to her, and the cops come calling, asking me about tonight, I'm singing like a canary."

He got in Larry's face and hardened his voice. "I'm not having trouble knock at my door over your shit, man."

"Okay, okay." Larry waved a hand and backed away. "I'll pay her tow and repair bill and add a little something for you, if you'll forget you ever saw me out here. And you'll delete the picture you took of me."

"Sure. I'll finish up here and write you a receipt. And I suggest cash. You won't want a paper trail. And because you're being so helpful, I'll see if I can knock out the bat damage on her quarter panel for free." He stepped to the drive that worked the winch and finished loading the car onto the bed. Once the bed was lowered and in place he turned back to Larry.

Larry balanced the bat against his thigh, withdrew a money clip from his front pocket, and peeled off several bills.

Derrick counted the cash. Fifteen hundred dollars. "I'm writing the receipt for just the tow and car repairs. Just a boss doing a good deed for a hardworking employee." He went to the driver's side of the wrecker and opened the door. The woman huddled on the floorboard of the cab. Her thin, oval face seemed honed down to nothing but angles, as though fear had sharpened the bones beneath the skin. Skin that looked creamy smooth and pale. He motioned with a palm straight down.

He pulled out a clipboard with a receipt pad attached, leapt down, and shut the door. He quickly wrote out a $512 receipt, signed it, and then extended it to Larry.

He raised his phone and pushed the button to bring up the photo, quickly sent a copy to himself, then raising the phone so Larry could see it, he pushed the button to delete the original.

He was tempted to caution Larry about doing this shit again, but it wouldn't do any good. If the woman in his cab grew a pair, she could take Larry to court.

He swung himself into the cab, saluted to Larry and pulled out of the parking lot. Half a block down from the club he said, "You can get up off the floor now."

She pushed free of the dash and settled into the seat. For several blocks she remained silent. "He hit my car with the bat."

"Yeah. I can knock out the dent while I'm changing the tires and balancing them for you. He gave me cash for the repairs."

"How did you manage that?"

"He set the whole thing up. I called him on it." He pulled to a stop at the red light and ran searching eyes over her. "He didn't hurt you, did he?"

"No." Though she denied it, she touched her arm as though she had some pain there. "He meant to. If he'd been able to get me down, he'd have done worse." Her voice shook, and she cleared her throat.

"The hair spray was a good weapon of opportunity. You did good."

"Thanks." She clamped her hands between her knees, but her knees bobbed like her feet rested on springs.

The light changed and he stepped on the gas. "How long you been working at the club?"

"About three weeks."

Shit, this was not his business. "If you want to call the cops, I'll testify to what I saw and the bribe he gave me to keep my mouth shut."

"Bribe?"

"Yeah. He gave me five hundred to pay for the tow, tires, and the alignment. And a thousand to keep my mouth shut about seeing you running out of the bar like it was about to blow up."

She gaped at him.

He shrugged. "It didn't take a mental giant to figure things out. He was all over you at the bar while you were working. And you were doing everything you could to avoid being touched. I can even guess how he set it up. He slips out while you're busy, punctures your tires, then waits for the girls to clear out. If you'd called someone to pick you up, he'd have tried something else another night."

"One of the girls warned me. And he followed me into the dancers' dressing room when I went back in to see if anyone was still there. I was going to ask for a ride home."

"He probably did the same thing to the woman who warned you."

She brushed a hand over her cap of short black hair, her throat working as she swallowed. "God."

"Do you want to go to the police with this?"

"I need to think about it." She fell silent, her face turned away to the passing street. She hugged herself.

He turned into the garage parking lot, hit the electronic door opener, and turned the wrecker to off-load her car, then exited the cab and moved to tilt the bed and turn on the winch to lower the car to the concrete floor over the rack.

He looked up as the woman swung down out of the cab and walked toward him into the light. Dressed in straight-legged jeans and a black turtleneck, she was slender and long-limbed. The slow, graceful way she walked reminded him of a dancer he once dated several years ago.

He'd seen women with dark hair, but none so dark it held a bluish sheen. Her large eyes, surrounded by lashes the same deep tone, had a golden, whiskey tint to them. Beneath a slender nose, the heavy pout of her lips drew his attention, and his rushing heartbeat picked up a notch. Damn, she was beautiful.

Pale pink traveled along her cheekbones and she looked away without making eye contact.

The very last thing she needed was him staring at her. "If you'll come into the office, I'll get the paperwork set up to do the repairs."

"Thanks."

Beneath the lights in the small office he got a good look at her injuries. "Your neck is red. You're going to have some bruises."

She touched the tender skin and flinched.

"You have a phone, I can take pictures of it for you."

She eyed him. "I'll get my neighbor to do it for me."

She didn't trust him enough to turn her back on him. He could understand that.

Once she'd signed the paperwork, he said, "If you have someone to pick you up, I'll get the repairs done and deliver the car to your house in the morning."

"I'll wait. I'll need it to take my son to school in the morning."

"Okay, but if I get called out to another tow, I'll have to go. That's what I get paid for around here. I'll hurry to get the flats switched out as fast as I can, and while I'm working you can take a seat in here and I'll close the door." He pointed to the leather bench seat against one wall opposite a long row of filing cabinets. And a desk. "The hydraulic wrench is loud as hell."

He closed the door behind him, slipped on noise-muffling headphones, and went to work. The whole time he was positioning the car onto the rack, removing the lug nuts and changing out the tires, his thoughts dwelled on her.

How did someone as beautiful as she was end up at a strip club? And was her suspicious, hard edge a new thing, or one she'd developed over several years? He'd bet it followed the birth of her kid. And why was he thinking about her like this, when he wouldn't have a chance in a million with her?

It wasn't like he'd even want one. He was carrying too much baggage already, and she'd just be one more complication.

Besides, she was a lesbian. He had to keep reminding himself of that.

He took a picture of the dent in her damaged quarter panel before he beat it out with a rubber hammer and put on the last tire.

Would she decide to go to the police over Larry, or would she just move on like so many others probably had before her? She was stuck in the same boat as he. Their pasts made it impossible to rock it. It made everything they said suspect.

He'd ended up having to quit more jobs than he'd held in the last seven months because his bosses had either thought they could work him like a slave at slave wages and he couldn't say anything about it, or they expected him to do something illegal without a qualm.

If she'd really stripped for a living, she was trying to pull herself up by her bootstraps and move into a different line of work, just like he was.

He'd toed the line the whole seven months since his release, leaving behind the people who tried to take advantage of him, and finally landed this gig. He worked alone and was his own boss at night, and it suited him just fine. He was better alone than with people.

His work phone rang and he tugged it off his belt and answered the call. He'd get this last wheel back in place and have her come back for the wheel alignment tomorrow morning.

CHAPTER 4

THE BANG, CLANG, and ear-shattering rev of the hydraulic wrench rattled and screamed through the door as though the barrier wasn't there. Ella wondered how he stood it.

The muscular width of his shoulders and the air of pent-up energy had made her wary. She'd been able to fight off Larry because she'd been warned. This guy could pin her like a moth to a board without breaking a sweat.

Yet he'd been decent so far. And he'd played Larry like a guitar. Which told her he had some street smarts.

But guys rarely did anything for free.

She recognized the look in his eye when she got out of the wrecker and came into the garage. It was the look of interest she'd read in every male face since she'd turned fourteen and started to develop breasts. Would he come into the office and demand his payment for saving her?

She got the hair spray can out of her purse.

By high school the boys were all over her. She'd managed to keep them at arm's length until she met Trae. He had such dreams, and she'd believed in him. All that promise lost. But she'd gotten the most precious thing in her life from him—her boy, Micah.

Her thoughts were ripped back to the present as the office door opened and she jerked in reaction.

"I've been called out on another tow, but I've got the tires changed out. Do you want to wait while I tow the other car in, or would you like to drive it home and come back in the morning for the front-end alignment?"

"It won't be dangerous to drive without the alignment?"

"No. It may list to one side or the other, but that's all. If you don't align the wheels, your tires will wear unevenly and you'll be tugging at the wheel to keep it straight."

She drew a relieved breath. "I'll drive it home and bring it back."

"Okay. I won't be here, but I'll leave a note for the other guys that you'll be back and the alignment is already paid for."

"Thanks."

He went to the cash register and made change. He extended some money to her.

"What is that?" she asked.

"The change from the thousand dollars. I took twelve dollars out of it for the tax on the services."

She focused on his strong, masculine features. The brown scruff that darkened his jaw gave his clean-cut features a hint of bad boy she found appealing. His hair was cut military short, his brows matched its golden hue. His pale blue eyes, surrounded by light brown lashes, maintained their focus on her in a way that sent heat climbing into her cheeks.

"You more than earned the money for saving me from being beaten with a baseball bat. And for playing Larry to get the money for my repairs."

"You'll be looking for a job, you'll need the money, and you deserve it for the three weeks of shit you put up with. Unless you're going to turn him into the police."

Ella was silent for a moment, distracted by the hint of the South she heard in his accent. "I haven't made up my mind yet. I have a history...nothing criminal, but it would come out. I have to think of my son."

Derrick was silent for a moment. "Larry's done this before. I'm no detective, but this was premeditated. He'll continue to do it until someone draws a line in the sand. If it can't be you, I understand."

"I need to think about it."

He nodded and extended the money to her again.

It would pay for groceries, other bills, or a large chunk of the rent.

"Put it in an envelope. The only proof you have that you got it from Larry is that his fingerprints will be on the money." She swallowed. "I need twenty-four hours to think things through and contact some of the other girls. Especially the ones I worked with last night."

"Okay." He reached in the desk for a business envelope, put the cash in it and handed it over to her.

"How do you know I'll contact you again?" she asked.

"If you don't, I'll know you decided not to go through with prosecuting him. Or you and the other girls could sue instead."

She bit her lip, her thoughts snagging on that idea. "I'll have to think about that, too. I want you to keep this until I make a decision." She placed the envelope on the counter. "I don't even know your name."

"Derrick Armstrong." He extended his hand, then jerked it back with a quick "sorry," rubbed it on his work pants, then extended it again.

His hand was hard with calluses, and his fingers wrapped around hers with easy pressure.

"I'm Ella Bailey."

He got another business card off the desk and wrote something on it. Then held it out. "If Larry—that is his name, isn't it?"

"Yeah."

"If he tries to make trouble for you, my cell phone number's on the back. I'll pay him a visit and remind him of our agreement."

"Agreement?" Suspicion reared its head like a lion scenting prey.

"I told him if I heard anything happened to you after tonight, I'd go to the cops and tell them everything he and I discussed. He may be contacting you with the promise of a severance package."

"Oh my God!" She laughed. Where had this guy come from?

He flashed her a smile that arrowed deep into the intimate areas of her body and stole her breath.

He held out her keys. "I'll lower the rack so you can back your car out."

She gripped the keys in one hand and the card in the other as they walked into the work bay. "Why would you help me?"

A flicker of emotion crossed his face, a hint of sadness darkening it. "I have a mom and a sister. There's nothing I can do to look out for them, but I can warn this fucker off if he tries to make trouble for you."

"You're not responsible for Larry's actions."

"No, but if I stood back and allowed him to get away with it, I'd be complicit."

She had a feeling there was more to it than that. She tucked the business card in her jeans pocket. "Thanks."

"You're not worried that I'll try and stiff you?" He held up the envelope.

"If you were going to do that, you'd never have mentioned the money."

He nodded and lowered the car.

Ella breathed a sigh and grinned at him when the vehicle settled on the new tires just the way it should. "Thanks."

He raised one shoulder in a shrug. "I just did my job."

"We both know that isn't the whole truth."

She slipped inside the car and started it. He pulled the wrecker out of the way and she backed out. The automatic door closed to the garage. He tooted the wrecker's horn and, with a wave, pulled out ahead of her.

She released a breath with a whiff of regret. He seemed like a nice guy. But they all did when they were trying to get something from you. She should have taken the money and run.

Exhaustion lay on her like a heavy blanket as she drove toward her apartment. She usually arrived home by two-fifteen and it was now closer to four in the morning.

The apartment parking lot was still, and a chill hung in the air. She shivered as she keyed herself into the lobby, then took the elevator to the second floor.

A lamp cast a dim glow over the sparsely furnished living room-kitchen combination. She scanned the room. It was neat as a seven-year-old could make it. Micah's precious video games were carefully stored in baskets in the wooden shelving unit beneath the television. They'd gotten the games and the television from a local pawnshop, and the rest of his clutter was contained in the one bedroom, his room. She was so blessed her son actually took care of his things, but sad knowing it was because he knew there was little money for anything else.

The couch let out into a bed, but her back ached, and her feet burned from standing on them. She left her purse on the coffee table, kicked off her shoes, and stretched out on the couch fully dressed. She'd be getting back up in two and a half hours to fix Micah's breakfast and take him to school, so there wasn't much point in getting undressed.

As soon as she closed her eyes Derrick Armstrong's face popped into her head. Why had he gone out of his way to help her? And would he really hold on to the nine hundred and seven dollars? Somehow, she thought he might.

THE SOUND OF the key in the door woke her, and, with a groan, she curled on her side as everything that had happened the night before rose up to slap her. She'd quit her job. What the hell was she going to do?

Micah burst into the apartment like he'd been shot out of a cannon. "Mom!" He came to a stop so suddenly the area rug bunched. "What are you doing sleeping on the couch? Why didn't you sleep in my bed?"

His incredible pale green eyes, so much like his father's, were so expressive she had to smile. Even at seven he worried about her. They worried about each other. The unfairness of it squeezed her heart.

He should be worry-free, fearless, oblivious to problems like a million other kids. But they'd both learned life for a million other kids didn't include eviction notices and ramen noodles for breakfast when there wasn't any other food. They were alone.

He was her only constant. She'd worked fifteen jobs in the past seven years to keep a roof over their heads and food on the table.

"I got in a little later than I expected, so I just rested here." She pushed up off the couch, stiff from lying in one position too long. "I'll fix breakfast, while you go get dressed."

"French toast?"

His hopeful expression tugged at her heart. It was hard to tell him no. She limited his sugar intake as much as possible, for both his teacher's sake and hers.

"It's Friday, so I guess it will be okay." She pointed a finger at him. "If you're even tempted to hop around like a Mexican jumping bean at school, though, don't do it. You know how much your teacher dislikes it."

"What's a Mexican jumping bean?"

"I'll get some to show you. We'll make it a science lesson." Although she'd be grossed out about the larva inside the beans. Just the thought had her skin crawling. Micah, in typical boy fashion, would think they were cool. She needed to encourage those natural expressions of masculinity.

"Get dressed, wash your face, and brush your hair. I'll get the French toast started."

Micah ran into his room.

She shook her head. He never walked anywhere if he could help it. He'd probably be on the track team in high school.

She turned her attention to preparing Micah's breakfast. She broke eggs into a bowl, added milk, vanilla, and cinnamon, and whipped them while the cast iron skillet heated and the pat of butter she tossed in melted.

The bread, a little stale, soaked the egg up, and it sizzled when she placed two slices in the skillet and let them fry.

What was she going to do about a job? And why couldn't she find a place to work that didn't involve some guy hassling her? Or worse.

Just the thought of Larry last night made her shudder. She flipped the toast.

If being a receptionist paid enough for her to make her bills, she'd do it, but she depended on her tips to augment what she made. She'd tried working two jobs to make enough money, but never got to see Micah. And she'd ended up paying most of what she made to babysitters.

Micah needed her. They needed each other. It was a constant balance to fill his emotional needs along with taking care of food and shelter.

She could apply for unemployment. Would Larry kick up a fuss about it? Possibly not, considering the circumstances. She'd do that today.

She flipped the French toast onto the plate and placed it on the table, poured the remaining egg mixture into the skillet, scrambled it, and put it on a plate for herself.

The thousand dollars—well, the nine hundred and seven dollars—Derrick Armstrong had would almost cover her rent. But it wasn't really her money. It was his for saving her.

But she'd be leaving the next girl who took her place to walk into the same sickening situation.

She needed to check her phone and see if it had recorded any of her encounter with Larry. She hadn't been ready to listen to it last night. And since it was buried in the front pocket of her purse, it probably didn't pick up anything anyway.

Micah ran into the kitchen, his midnight dark hair slicked down with water. He tossed his backpack into one of the barstools and hiked himself up on another. He'd hit a growth spurt and his jeans were a little short. Plus, his tennis shoes were worn and probably wouldn't last much longer.

Damn!

She poured him some milk and got the syrup out of the cabinet. When he reached for it, she held it away from him.

"Just a reminder, a little syrup goes a long way."

"I know. My French toast doesn't need to swim in syrup to be good."

He repeated what she'd said a hundred times.

"But I still like it to." He pulled the top to open the valve on the bottle, flipped it upside down and gave it a squeeze.

Ella fought the urge to grab it and breathed a sigh of relief when Micah put a reasonable amount of syrup on the toast, then set the bottle down.

She bent and brushed the top of his head with a kiss and squeezed his shoulder. "Good job."

The cinnamon gave the eggs an odd flavor, but worry knotted her stomach and she couldn't handle anything heavier right now. She went into the bathroom to wash her face and brush her teeth while he finished eating.

She glanced at the microwave clock on the way back into the kitchen to fix his lunch. "You have fifteen minutes to finish eating."

"What did you and Patsy do last night?" She added an apple and a box of raisins to his lunch box. A precut bag of seven cheese cubes she'd prepared two nights ago, and four carrot sticks because she hoped he was eating the vegetables as well as he did the fruit.

"We watched zombies."

You're fucking kidding me. She stared at him.

He shoveled in a bite of French toast and snorted as he laughed around it, flashing chewed-up egg. "Gotcha!" He giggled. "Your face is funny, mommy. Patsy let me watch *Star Wars* after I finished my homework, then we crashed."

She narrowed her eyes at him but smiled. She laid out two slices of bread, folded sliced turkey on one, garnished it with a lettuce leaf and placed the top slice on, then cut the sandwich into triangles and put it in a square plastic container.

"How come you were late getting home?" he asked.

She focused on what she was doing, because Micah was good at reading her expression and picking up on tension. God, she needed to find another job, fast, so she wouldn't have to tell him she'd lost the one she'd just gotten. "How do you know I was late getting home?"

"You slept in your clothes. You never sleep in your clothes."

He was way too smart for a seven-year-old. "I had a flat tire and had to call someone to fix it for me."

"The tire's okay now, though, isn't it?" Just like that, a tiny bit of stress filtered into his tone and expression.

She closed the lunch box and turned to face him. "Yes. Our chariot is in good shape."

His grin held relief. He chased the last piece of his toast around the plate with a fork, sopping up every drop of syrup possible, then popped it in his mouth.

"You need to wash the syrup off your face and brush your teeth." She wiped away a drop of syrup glistening on his chin with her thumb.

One day, when he was a teenager, she'd miss getting to tell him what to do, but sometimes, like now, when lack of sleep was making her a little pissy, and worry over the lost job weighed on her, she wished he'd do the things they did every single morning on his own without being told.

"Do you think sharks have stuff stuck between their teeth after they eat seals and fish?"

"They probably do, and I bet their teacher thinks it's just as gross as Ms. Lamm and I do. Go brush, French Toast Breath."

"Sharks don't swim in schools, Mom." He darted off his chair, back to the bathroom.

He always surprised her at how quick he was to pick up on things like her reference to school. He was so smart—sometimes too smart.

She took a deep breath. She'd drive him to school, swing by the garage, and let them do the front-end alignment on her car, come home to get online and file for unemployment, then crash to get some sleep. Later in the day she'd call the bar and leave her number with one of the girls along with a message asking Jasmine to call her.

Micah raced out of the bathroom and grabbed his backpack. She gripped his chin to check his face for food and, seeing none, bent to brush his forehead with her lips. "Beautiful."

"Moo-oomm!"

She couldn't help the grin that popped out. "I was talking about how clean your face is, not how cute you are. Let's go."

CHAPTER 5

DERRICK FLIPPED DOWN the front of the welding mask, turned on the welding gun, and focused on running a straight weld along the edge where the two steel plates met. He dragged the stick along, directing the gun with a combination of feel and sight. The electricity ran through the stick, melting the metal within a protective gas. Once he reached the end of the weld, he backed off the edge of the plate, turned off the gun, and shoved up the mask.

He hit the slag with a hammer and broke the outer shell away from the weld, then took a wire brush to it. Berk Straus, his instructor, came over to check out his work.

"Nice weld, Derrick. You have a feel for this work."

"Thanks." It was the one thing he'd done in prison that was productive and helpful.

"We'll be working on more complex projects next."

He shot up a thumb. "I'm ready." He wrote some notes in his work journal.

His training as a SEAL had helped him through this. Without it, and the therapy he received while in prison, he wouldn't have kept his life together. As soon as he walked out of jail he'd have fallen back into the same patterns that had cost him so much.

He didn't deserve this second chance. There was nothing he could ever do to make up for the mistakes he made. But he was trying.

When he looked back at that time, he didn't recognize the man he'd been. He'd allowed his rage to consume him. In therapy, he finally recognized he'd done so because he learned the behavior from his father from infancy.

Class ended, and he left the building. He approached his car and paused as one of the school security guards circled it. *What the fuck?*

He had to keep his cool. He could not have any trouble here. He had too much money invested in these classes to blow things now, and it had taken too many steps for him to even be accepted into the program because of his background.

As soon as he moved close enough to speak to the guard without shouting, he asked, "Is there a problem?"

"Is this your vehicle, sir?"

"Yes, it is." There were times he really missed his 2011 Jeep, like now. If he hadn't needed to eat…

The body of the 2008 Camry looked like it had been wrecked several times—which it had—but the engine purred like a kitten.

"Are you a student here?"

"Yes, I am." Derrick shifted the notebook to his left hand, pulled his wallet out of his back pocket, and produced his student ID card.

"I just wanted to be certain it isn't an abandoned vehicle."

"I have the student parking pass hanging on the rearview mirror."

"So I see." The guy still looked doubtful.

"I live in a rough area of town, so I don't want my ride to look too good. It's camouflaged to keep it from being stolen."

The cop handed him back his student I.D. with a half smile.

"That's the best excuse I've ever heard for keeping a rattletrap going, What classes are you taking?"

"I'm taking two welding classes."

"Maybe you can practice on the car." The guard shot him a grin.

Was he trying to be funny?

"Maybe, after I move to a safer neighborhood. I work the night shift in a garage towing wrecks. That's where I picked up this car." He took a business card out of his wallet and handed it to the cop. "In case you ever need an abandoned car towed."

The guard raised the card. "I'll keep you in mind."

"Thanks. You could do me a favor and tell the other security guys about my ride so they don't get the same idea."

"Will do."

Derrick unlocked the car and got behind the wheel. When he started the car, the guy grinned and shook his head, as though he couldn't believe the thing actually ran.

Derrick threw up a hand as he pulled out and drew a deep breath. He needed to complete the mission, just as he did while in the teams. He had to get through his classes so he could move on with his life. But always having to be Mr. Nice guy when someone was being an asshole was tough.

Seven years ago he'd have given the guard shit and would probably have ended up being hauled in by the cops. So he *was* better. But there were still times when the rage bubbled up beneath the surface—

He wouldn't think about it. Wouldn't allow it to undo what he was building.

Maybe he really could have a life. Meet a woman, have a relationship, whatever that meant. He hadn't had sex with anyone but his hand in nearly seven years.

He needed to have sex, wanted to have sex. But the thought of having sex terrified him. What if he started to obsess about the woman like he'd done with Marjorie? What if those feelings of jealousy and anger took over and he lost control and hurt her?

Those worries kept him from bridging the distance he kept between himself and all women. He hid behind the professional front he kept in place while he worked.

But, Jesus, he wanted more than just work and school in his life. There were times when the walls of his apartment closed in on him, and it took everything he had not to do something crazy.

The girls dancing at the club yesterday hadn't even moved

him. Which was weird. Wasn't it? After seven years, he should have had a raging hard-on for one of them, but he'd been too focused on the bartender to notice the dancers. Even in the dim lighting of the dive, he'd been fascinated by the way Ella moved and that dark cap of hair that hugged her head and feathered around her face.

He couldn't get her out of his mind. Her hair with the deep blue tint. Her eyes, such an odd chestnut brown. Her figure, ballerina-thin and graceful.

He grew so hard it was almost painful.

Ella Bailey. Ella sounded like someone sweet and innocent. Someone who should be living a protected life in a suburb somewhere.

Instead she had a sharp distrust of men, probably learned while stripping, and now thanks to this experience with Fucker Larry.

If that wasn't a big enough deterrent, she was a lesbian. He hadn't a hope in hell of dating her or going to bed with her.

Why was he lusting after the unattainable?

Maybe because it was safer than fulfilling his need with a woman he might actually have a chance to care about.

He'd finally gotten his head on straight, and he was afraid to introduce any element into his life that might mess with that.

He found himself turning the car into a familiar neighborhood and parked across the street from the house. It hadn't changed much. Colorful cushions made the chairs on the front porch more inviting. The lawn looked freshly mowed. Orange and red flowers created a border along the edge of the porch. That had to be Zoe's touch. Hawk wasn't a flower kind of guy. None of them were.

Those dabs of bright color and comfort made the place look more like a home. He heard they had a baby, a son. He'd be almost six now. Hawk would be a commander by now, and he deserved it. He'd been a great SEAL.

Hawk tried to help him, but he'd been too crazy to realize it. And even after all he'd done to hurt Zoe, Brett, and Marjorie, the men hadn't reported a lot of his actions that day, for the good of the team, so he'd only gotten seven years instead of the twenty or more he'd deserved.

His throat ached with emotion, and tears stung his eyes. He never cried. Men didn't cry. But goddamn, his need to choked him. He wiped his eyes with the heel of his palm.

A dark blazer turned into the drive. Dressed in desert BDUs, Hawk exited the vehicle and strode up the short sidewalk to the front door. Derrick's heart hammered in his throat.

He reached for the door handle. He hesitated. It might not be a good idea to confront him at his front door. Hawk would pound him into the ground.

He couldn't speak to him here at home, and he couldn't go on base. Maybe he could contact him and set up a meeting on neutral ground. If he still had the same number after seven years.

He pulled out his cell phone and dialed the number from memory. Remembering the number after so long proved he was clinging to this like a burr. It rang three times, four.

"Hello."

It took him two seconds maybe three to answer. "Hawk, this is Armstrong."

"What do you want, Derrick?"

The aggression in Hawk's voice gave him pause.

"I want to meet with the team."

"Not a good idea." That tone said adamantly NO!

"It isn't what you think, Hawk. I just want to tell everyone how sorry I am for everything I did."

"You're just asking for trouble, Derrick. And I'm not going to encourage my guys to meet with you, then have one of them arrested for assault because he lost it."

He'd been beaten before. Besides they wouldn't kill him. "I need to do this. I'm trying to move on with my life, but I can't. Not completely. Not until I talk to the guys.

"I've spent seven years trying to untangle what was going on in my head those last several months in Iraq, and then when I got home. I know I should have gotten more than seven years for what I did. I know you and the guys protected me from some of it. I need to say my piece, then I'll be gone from your lives and you'll never hear from me again."

The sound of Hawk breathing was all he heard for long, tense moments. "Some of them have moved on to other teams. Okay, I'll reach out to them, but I can't promise anything. If they don't want to see you, that's the end of it."

"Okay." The wave of emotion overpowered him, and he rested his forehead against the arm he placed across the steering wheel while tears streamed down his face. Taking a deep breath, he swallowed and managed to steady his voice to say, "Thanks, Hawk."

Silence stretched across the line, and he closed the phone.

He started the car and pulled out. He had to go home and sleep for a while. But first he needed to run and release some of the pent-up emotion.

CHAPTER 6

A PICNIC TABLE at one of the area parks seemed a good, neutral place to meet. It was almost certain none of the other employees would see them here.

In the harsh sunlight, Jasmine's bright auburn hair, pulled back in a ponytail, was shot through with threads of copper. Her dark green eyes were wary as she cupped a water bottle in her hands.

"I've quit tending bar at the Honey Pot," Ella said, "and I want to thank you for the warning. You saved me from being raped last night."

Jasmine focused on the water bottle as though it were the only object in the universe.

"How long have you been at the Honey Pot?"

"A year."

Every one of the girls had a story about what had led them to the strip club. She had one too when she stripped. *Desperation.* She wouldn't sit in judgement of any of them. There was no shame in trying to survive.

"I went out to drive home and my car had two flat tires. I went back in to see if any of you were still there, and Larry cornered me in the dressing room."

Jasmine didn't look surprised. "How did you get away?"

"I sprayed hair spray in his eyes and ran like hell."

"Good for you!"

She spoke with such feeling, Ella flinched inside.

"Did he do the same thing to you?"

Jasmine's features crimped in pain, and a glassy sheen of tears filled her eyes. "Yeah."

"Why didn't you report him, Jasmine?"

"I have a solicitation charge on my record. They'd say I was lying."

"Not if he's done this to the other women too."

"What difference does it make? We can't prove it."

The hopelessness in Jasmine's expression, her tone, had quick tears stinging Ella's eyes. "If all of you come forward together, it wouldn't be so easily swept under the rug."

Jasmine stared at her hard. "Why don't you report him to the cops if you think it's so easy?"

Ella placed her cell phone in the center of the table and pushed the play button. Her own voice sounded muffled, but the words were clear enough as they came through the phone's speaker. "Out of the goodness of your heart? Will you let me take the cost out of my weekly pay?"

"That isn't exactly what I had in mind." Larry's slimy smugness slicked his words.

She heard the stress in her voice. "I'm not a whore. I don't turn tricks and never have."

"No money would change hands. It's just quid pro quo. I can make your life easier around here if you'll cooperate."

"You offered to buy me two new tires in exchange for sex. Two hundred bucks for pushing your dick inside me."

"It's just sex. You've done it before." After a pause he said, "If you want to continue working here, you need to give it up. Who knows, you might like it."

Bastard. "I'm giving you my notice, then."

"I'm sorry you feel that way. You're making this harder than it has to be." His intent was clear in his tone.

"It's against the law for you to sexually harass your employees. What makes you think I won't call someone about it?"

"You used to strip. You'd never win a lawsuit or anything else with your history."

"That was three years ago. I just danced and went home to my son. It was the only way I could keep a roof over our heads. I won't let you blackmail me into being your whore. I'm going home to my son." Her footsteps were barely discernable.

"Don't." Her voice sounded raw with fear. "Let me go."

His yell was loud enough for anyone to understand what had happened.

"You have him recorded. You have proof." The hope in Jasmine's face was almost painful to witness.

"If the powers that be will allow it as evidence. With all the girls he's raped coming forward, we'd have him by the balls, Jasmine. We could file a lawsuit against him on top of criminal charges. We could ruin him financially."

"And then what would we do? We'd be fucked again by the system. We'd have no jobs."

"Which is more important to you? Getting justice or holding onto a job with him just waiting in the wings to hurt you again?" She paused and tried to formulate the question burning inside her in such a way it didn't sound accusatory. "How could you stay afterward?"

"All these club owners know each other. He put the word out that I was trouble. That I solicited customers after hours. You see, he wants us all to himself. Like a harem."

Fuck!

"So, he still…hits on you even after…?"

"Yeah. We're just meat." The bitterness in the woman's voice went deep.

"No you're not! None of us are."

There were freckles across her nose Ella hadn't noticed before. It made her appear younger than her twenty-one years.

Tears sheened her eyes again. "Our names would be in the paper. I don't want my family knowing, Ella."

"They're not allowed to put sexual assault victim's names in the paper, Jasmine."

"It happens, though. We'd all be put on trial because we stayed after he...did what he did."

She couldn't say the word. After coming so close, Ella understood. Once she said the word it would be even more real.

Without Jasmine and the other girls' support, the cops might not believe her either. Word would get out, and no one would hire her. Bartending and dancing were all she knew how to do. Her stomach pitched, and she pressed a hand against it. They'd think it was a scam. Everyone was out to scam everybody else.

She sucked in a deep breath. "If we don't do something, and he rapes another woman, it will be both our faults. I want to send the audio files to the local television stations and identify him as the voice, but I don't want to come out and accuse him without backup."

Jasmine's brows went up. "That sounds like a good idea. You know how quick the press is to jump on stuff like this. They'll start investigating, and they might find other women even before us who'll come forward. Then you can come forward."

Ella couldn't imagine being trapped in a situation like this woman. She was both terrified of losing her job and traumatized by what had happened at work. "What will you do if he tries something again?"

Jasmine fell silent for a long moment, rocking back and forth. Ella thought it an unconscious movement that probably soothed her. "I don't know."

"How many of the other women is he doing this to?"

"At least four of the dancers and one of the waitresses that I know of."

Jesus!

Jasmine stood abruptly. "I have to go."

"Okay." Ella rose. "Band together, Jasmine. Protect each other. If there's always more than one of you together, he won't have the opportunity to get you alone and force you into anything."

She nodded, though Ella doubted she even heard her. She was too deep in her thoughts, and the pain had overridden everything else.

Her head came up, and she focused on Ella. "When will you send it?"

"As soon as I get home."

"Good. What will you do now?"

"Look for a job and file for unemployment." If only there was more that she could do to help Jasmine and the others. "Take care of yourself, Jasmine."

"I will."

She breathed in the warm air scented with freshly cut grass and absently traced around one of the heavy rivets holding the tabletop in place. How could she out Larry and not herself?

She could go to the library and send the audio file from there. If she could figure out how to do it with her cheap phone. She looked up the directions and read them several times.

Would any of this make any difference?

In times like these, she longed for someone to talk to.

Patsy would be all for her walking into the police station and reporting Larry. She'd take the moral high ground and have to pay the price for it. There was always a price. Jasmine knew that, and she did too.

That's why the bad guys with money always came out ahead. They had the resources to go the distance while the little guys like her starved. She raked her fingers through her hair, giving it a frustrated tug

She left the picnic table and stalked across the grass to the car.

She checked the time, because it always seemed to pass twice as fast when she wasn't at work. She'd pick Micah up at school and use the library computer while he searched for books to check out.

Fifteen minutes later she sat in the car in front of the school and waited for Micah. In the meantime she used her phone to look for the email addresses of some of the department heads at the police department and found nothing. There were phone numbers aplenty, but no email addresses.

Shit!

Could she call from a phone there at the library and play the tape for a detective without identifying herself? But they probably wouldn't take it seriously if she didn't identify herself and file charges.

God, she was such a coward. But everything in her life had to revolve around Micah. She had to provide for him. He *had* to come first. Being able to find another job was the most important thing for both of them. And she needed one now, before he found out she'd quit this one, because he'd be so worried.

The anxiety she'd tried unsuccessfully to ignore came roaring back to life. Why couldn't things stay stable for just a little while?

She rubbed at her eyes. She had yet to take the nap she promised herself. And it didn't look like she was going to. The bell rang inside the school but she could hear it from the car.

Children exited the building to stand in bus lines while teachers and aides kept the excited crowd under control. A group of boys Micah's age and size exited through the front door with two more teachers.

She scanned the group. Another group of five older students came out and ran down the flat concrete incline that served as a wheelchair ramp. Behind them was Micah, scanning the street, his backpack hitched over one shoulder. He smiled when he saw the car and loped forward.

A protective rush of love rocketed through her. She would do whatever it took to nurture that smile and make him feel safe.

She could put the audio file on a flash drive and mail it to the police with a note explaining what the other women were going through and hope police would look into it. Then she could send it to one of the television stations. She could post it to YouTube, but no one would find it there.

Micah opened the door and tossed his backpack into the floorboard before getting in.

"How was your day?" she asked as she did every day.

"Bryan Scott wants me to come to his birthday party at Chuck E. Cheese's on Saturday." He unzipped and fished inside his backpack for the invitation and handed it to her.

The fact that he actually remembered the invitation meant he really wanted to go to the party. She opened the card he handed her. Saturday at one. She'd be free, since she didn't have a job any longer. "I guess we need to get a gift. We'll do it right now so we'll be ready."

While they were shopping, she'd pick up a flash drive and a padded envelope. She was going to tear down Larry's house of horrors by shining a light on it.

CHAPTER 7

DERRICK STUDIED THE wrecked cars stacked like Lincoln logs. One car was crushed beneath the weight of a Dodge Charger. Another smaller car had been flipped on its side. Had anyone been killed? He scanned the neighborhood. Neighbors stood on their doorsteps watching him.

The driver of the Charger had left with only minor injuries, and his car sustained the least damage. How the hell had that happened? The vehicle's nose was hooked on the car lying on its side, and its bumper almost dragged the ground.

Derrick maneuvered the wrecker into position and lowered the bed to create an angled ramp. He hooked the winch cable to the rear axle of the Charger and, using the winch and hydraulic lift, he dragged it free and up on the bed.

He eyed the other crumpled vehicles. If he could get another one loaded, he'd only have to make one more trip.

His personal phone rang, and he paused to take it out. He rarely got calls. On occasion his mother would call. The number was a local cell number. He hit the screen and answered.

"Is this Derrick?"

Her voice was as familiar as his own. He'd thought about it enough. She sounded as suspicious as he remembered. His heart drummed against his ribs and he got an immediate hard-on.

"Yeah, this is Derrick."

"This is Ella Bailey."

"Hello." He walked to the cab, got in, and shut the door to block the noise of the street traffic.

"I'm calling to let you know—I won't be going in to talk to the police about Larry. I tried to convince one of the girls to go in with me, but she's so traumatized she refused. But I've sent the police and one of the television stations some information I hope they'll follow up on."

"That's good. Has he contacted you?"

"No. And I hope he doesn't. I don't want to have anything else to do with him."

He could understand that. "That's probably smart."

"I just wanted to thank you for having my back last night."

The phrase she used triggered a memory of asking Brett if he had his six. Would Brett have kept his mouth shut? Had he ever regained his memory of that night? He'd never come forward to report what he remembered, so possibly not.

I'd still be in prison if he had.

"Hello?"

"Sorry, I'm at a wreck site. When would you like to meet me at the garage so I can give you the money?"

"You need to keep it."

He could certainly use a thousand dollars, but she had the same air of desperation he'd felt his first few months of freedom. And she had a kid. "I wouldn't feel right about it. I conned him out of it because he's a certified asshole and he deserved it. He was also easy pickings." He didn't feel a damn bit guilty about doing it, either.

She laughed and his flagging erection went stone hard again. He tugged at his pants where they pinched him.

He continued. "You're the one who had to put up with him, so you pretty much earned it."

"We could split it."

If he asked her to meet somewhere besides the garage, it might spook her. "I work nights. I'm taking welding classes in the mornings from seven until three. I can meet you somewhere after that, before I go back to my apartment and crash."

"That can't give you much time to sleep."

"I crash around five and sleep until ten, grab some grub, then go into work. I'm able to catch catnaps in between tows most nights, then I catch up on Fridays and Sundays."

"I have to pick up my son at three from school, so we could meet after that."

She'd want it to be somewhere public. "Pick a pizza place and I'll meet you. He'll probably want a snack after school. I know I will."

She laughed again. "You're right, he probably will." After an extended pause, she said, "Meet us at the Chuck E. Cheese at four fifteen, the one at Sports Arena Boulevard."

"Will do."

"Thanks. See you later."

She was gone so quickly he had no time to say anything else.

He'd like to know what made her so skittish. It was probably more than what almost happened at the strip joint. He'd bet money on it.

She'd probably run up against a guy like him. Or like he used to be. He wasn't the same guy. At least he prayed he wasn't.

Whatever caused her wariness was none of his business.

She was just a momentary fantasy. He'd been alone too long He'd hire a hooker to get this out of his system, but his money was already spoken for.

And once he handed over the cash Larry gave him.... he'd never see her again. He rubbed at his temples, more bothered by that than he wanted to admit. He shoved open the door and went back to work.

ELLA STARED AT her cell phone screen. Why was she so touchy about this? She could have waited to call him in the morning, but he might have been asleep by then. Now she knew he wouldn't have been because he was learning to weld.

She couldn't even have a phone conversation without freaking out.

It was nearly one o'clock in the morning, and she was just as restless as she was at ten, eleven... She'd tried relaxation techniques and a warm bath. They hadn't helped. She was saving the only alcohol she had around the house, a bottle of wine collecting dust in the cabinet over the refrigerator, for when she got desperate.

She'd spent two hours online filling out job applications, hoping something plum would fall into her lap. It wasn't going to happen, but she could dream.

Something was wrong when your dreams were centered around simply making enough money to pay the rent and feed your seven-year-old. Those weren't dreams, those were necessities. And when you were so busy with the necessities, there was no time for real dreams....

She'd given up on hers when she followed Trae to LA so he could pursue his. She'd been a stupid kid of seventeen, in love for the first time. Trae was going to make it big, and they were going to be set. Then she was going to work on hers. Four months later he was gone and she was alone in a city that had little pity for young, stupid, grieving girls. She shuddered at some of the memories and cradled her head in her hands.

Why was she thinking about this?

Because Derrick Armstrong was pursuing a dream. He was going to school, taking welding classes. He was trying to make a better life for himself. She'd missed her opportunity for that. She had no money to pursue anything because it was eaten up every month just trying to stay safe and fed.

If she got unemployment benefits, could she make it until she could find a better job? And what could she do to supplement it by working for someone willing to pay her under the table? Not what she'd want to do.

Could Patsy keep Micah extra hours so she could work a day job? And who was she going to get to pick Micah up and bring him home?

She looked around at their barren apartment. The places they lived always looked like just a place to rest their heads. All but Micah's room. He had his superhero posters and action figures all over the place. She'd do whatever she had to do to make sure he had what he needed.

She had to do something to make it easier to provide for Micah. God, she didn't want to go back to stripping.

She could clean houses on the side if she could get a clientele built up. She dragged her sticker-covered laptop...bought secondhand from a neighbor who needed the cash to move...onto her lap and borrowed the next-door neighbor's internet once more to search for any job that didn't involve strip clubs.

She typed in dance and exercise and found openings for yoga instructors and ballroom dancing.

Along the edge of the webpage an advertisement for modeling caught her eye, and she opened the link. Two hundred and fifty dollars an hour to have her picture taken for a magazine! No way. It had to be a scam.

But the more she read, the more she was torn between hope and disbelief. When something sounded too good to be true, it usually was. But it wouldn't hurt to look into it. Would she have to have what the stars called headshots?

And they had an office just downtown. She went to the Better Business Bureau and looked up the company. No complaints were listed for them. She looked for litigation against them. Nothing.

She'd drop Micah off at school and go down and check them out. Exhaustion overwhelmed her, and she closed the laptop. She needed to get some sleep, or the modeling agency would take one look at the dark rings under her eyes and send her right back out the door.

SHE WOKE WHEN her alarm went off at six-thirty and rushed Micah through his normal slow-as-possible morning routine.

Why did boys move at light speed when they were playing, but poked along like they had rocks in their pockets when adults had something to accomplish?

She dropped him off at seven-forty, right on time, then battled morning traffic to the downtown area, where she parked in a multi-level parking structure and walked the four blocks to the office building housing the modeling agency.

She tucked a stray tuft of hair behind her ear and tugged open the door. The address guide next to the elevators directed her to the fourth floor.

The doors slid opened to soft music and a colorful arrangement of overstuffed, comfortable-looking chairs circling a coffee table the size of a car. Offices with large glass partitions framed in steel opened the space to lots of light. A man and two women sat at desks behind panes of glass. The man was on the phone, and the woman had two women sitting in front of her desk, their body language all business.

A woman, mid-thirties and a little plump, rose from behind her desk. "May I help you?" She brushed back a strand of silver blond hair. Her makeup was flawless.

This was a mistake. Ella knew how she looked. She was skinny and lanky, with short hair that was always mussed and her eyes were too big for her face. She was no model. The ad had said normal people. "I read an article that you were looking for models for a magazine shoot. I'd like to fill out an application."

"We're looking for regular people, not professionals."

Ella laughed. "Regular is me. I'm a bartender, not a model."

The woman's brows rose. "I'll get you the paperwork to fill out. Then I'll have Mr. Morgan come out and speak to you." She extended a clipboard with a form attached and a pen clipped to the top.

Ella took it. "Thanks." She wandered away and eased into one of the very comfortable seats. Balancing the board on her thighs, she began to fill out her personal information, though with every answer she again debated whether she should make a run for the elevator.

The phone beeped, and the receptionist picked up the receiver and spoke to someone for a moment, then hung up.

She got to the area for work history pretty quickly and hesitated there. This was a bad idea. And she certainly wasn't going to put Larry down as her current employer…and the other jobs she'd worked weren't much better. She wrote down her last two bartending jobs. Though they were at lower-class bars, her bosses had been decent guys. The stripping she left off completely.

Two long-legged blondes, stunning, poised, dressed like fashion plates, walked down the hall as though they owned the world and got on the elevator.

Shit. She really was in the wrong place. She rose, took two long strides to the receptionist's desk, and laid the clip board on the corner.

A man came out of an office at the end of the hall, his long legs eating up the distance in a loose, rolling gate.

She gathered her small purse.

"You haven't signed or dated the application," the receptionist pointed out.

"I think I made a mistake coming here. I'm sorry I wasted your time."

"I don't think you've made a mistake at all. Please stay long enough to speak with Mr. Morgan."

The man reached them. "Is this the young lady you were telling me about, Angela?"

"Yes, Mr. Morgan."

He was easily six four or five, broad in the shoulders and narrow at the hips. His dark hair curled atop his head, around his ears, and at the nape of his neck. Fine lines bracketed his mouth and fanned out from his deep-set, hazel eyes as though he'd spent a lot of time out in the sun without sunglasses. The heavy masculinity of his face was emphasized by thick brows and dark scruff intermingled with silver.

"Davis Morgan," he extended his hand.

Ella studied his weathered face a moment before offering hers in return. "Ella Bailey."

"Come back and talk to me for a few minutes. I'd like to take some quick shots of you."

"I don't think I'm model material, Mr. Morgan."

He studied her a moment, his gaze speculative. "I bet you are, and I know the camera is going to love you."

Ella glanced at the receptionist, then back at him.

"Give it a try," the receptionist urged. "What have you got to lose?"

That's what she was wondering.

Davis motioned for her to precede him down the hall. With him at her back, her heart hammered in her throat and her breathing was shaky. She paused by the open office door.

"I promise it's completely painless, and if you don't like the photos, I'll delete them."

She should have done more research into the company. She should have looked up the owner and all their photographers. She walked into the office and went directly to one of the photographs on the wall. The actress looked into the camera, a lush, furry top pulled up to cover her breasts, leaving her shoulders bare. She'd seen that shot at the grocery store four months ago on a national magazine. The only way he could have blown it up like this was if he'd taken it himself.

Some of her anxiety eased. What was she being so damn skittish about? This guy was a professional, she could see that. And this office wasn't some backroom porn set.

She drew a deep, cleansing breath and turned to face him. "Spectacular shot."

"Thanks."

"What do you do for a living?" he asked. He crossed the room and reached for a camera on a glass shelf behind his desk.

"I tend bar."

"Where?"

She'd be honest with him. It might help her land a gig. "Nowhere right now. I lost my job a couple of days ago. I saw the advertisements about models on the net and thought…maybe I could do it."

"But you almost left."

"I'm not blond, tall, and drop-dead gorgeous."

"You're not blond and tall, but I'd argue the latter." He shoved a battery into the camera, checked something else, then took the lens cap off "Go ahead and look around the room." She heard the click of the camera as she went to the shelves to look at the cameras there.

"How long have you been doing this?" she asked.

"Twenty years."

She turned to look at him, and he took her picture. She looked down, embarrassed. "I haven't had my picture taken since my last driver's license photo."

"A lot of people have a phobia about having their picture taken."

She must be one of them. She felt naked every time he pushed the button. "Why do you think that is?"

"I think they're afraid the camera might pick up more about them than they want people to know."

That could be true. Could he see her desperation for a job? "I don't have to take my clothes off for this gig, do I?"

He lowered the camera. "No. You'll be wearing the clothing we choose for you."

"Good." Some of her tension drained away and she finally relaxed enough to smile.

He raised the camera again and caught the shot.

"What would the hours be?"

"That would be determined by the shooting location The beach, the mountains, the desert, inside a car, inside a building."

"I have a son. He's seven. I'd have to know ahead of time so I could make arrangements for him." Patsy could pick him up after school.

"Is it just the two of you?"

"Yes." Me and him against the world. She studied Morgan's face for any hint of subterfuge. She couldn't be too careful.

He snapped her picture. "You don't look old enough to have a seven-year-old."

"I was young."

"Have you trained as a dancer?"

"When I was younger and through high school." She should tell him about the stripping. If they found out later it could cost her the job. If she told him, it could cost her the job now.

"You still walk and stand like a dancer. What made you give it up?"

"I had my son, and my priority was him. It still is."

"That's understandable."

"Do you dance for pleasure?"

"Sometimes." Rarely. After stripping, the pleasure had gone out of it for her.

"Walking the runway is like a dance. You dance up the runway then back down."

"I didn't realize I was applying for runway work."

"We don't really specialize in that, though I have photographed the shows for publications. But if you get an agent, you could do that. You have the build for it."

An agent?

He kept up the conversational style of the meeting, pumping her for information about herself. Some questions she could be honest about and others she deflected.

Eager to end the interview, she dropped into one of the chairs in front of his desk. Morgan extracted the digital card from the camera and placed it on the desk. He took a seat behind it, slid the laptop on the desk close to her, pushed the card into the drive and hit a few keys.

He picked up the computer and came around the desk to sit down beside her. "Let's look at these together."

Her stomach cramped and her nerves revved up again. She clamped her hands between her knees.

The first shot was her in profile. She was surprised by the clarity of the image. Her normally sharp-edged cheekbones only looked like cheekbones. She was looking up and her eyelashes looked longer somehow.

"You're looking at it with a critical eye of someone who looks in the mirror every day. I'm looking at it as a marketable image I can shop around and sell to a magazine or corporation. But with a little more makeup this could be a cosmetic ad. We do quite a few of those, and the models they choose get free samples. And are paid very well."

"We also take photos that can be used to illustrate magazine articles. If it's for a nursing home, you'd be visiting your grandmother, smiling down at her with sincere affection." He hit the key to progress the photos to the one where she was smiling. "Or a restaurant ad, where you're enjoying a meal. Just another customer visiting the location. But even in those, they want attractive people, because attractive people sell their product."

"So, I'd be doing mostly this kind of thing?"

"Yes, unless you want to do more commercial work. You have an Audrey Hepburn look and poise about you, so I know they'd be very interested in you. But you'd have to invest in some headshots."

Would any of the men who'd seen her strip recognize her in any of those photos? The thought grabbed her by the throat.

How many would be looking at ads in magazines? That thought almost made her smile. She couldn't picture the kind of clientele she'd served or danced for cracking a newspaper, let alone a magazine. Maybe *Sports Illustrated* or *Popular Mechanics*, but nothing like he was talking about.

She looked up into his face. "Why are you giving me the full court press?"

"Because you have the look. My receptionist recognized it. She's been at this for a while, not as long as I have, but long enough. She texted me as soon as you sat down to fill out the application."

Ella pushed free of the chair and went to the window to look out. He seemed straightforward, professional. "Okay. I'll give it a try. When and where?"

"Tomorrow. Here. Nine a.m. We'll be doing some preliminary shots before we change location to a restaurant in Old Town."

She nodded and picked up the small purse she'd left lying on the edge of his desk.

"There's just one other thing."

She looked up.

"It's none of my business, but who left those bruises on you?"

She fought the urge to touch her neck, but her cheeks burned. "My ex-boss. That's why I no longer work for him. He made a pass, and I dealt with it, but it cost me my job."

Davis's jaw tensed. "I hope you're pressing charges. I can guarantee no one will be harassing you here."

"I appreciate that." She met his eyes with a short nod so he'd know she meant it. "Thanks."

"I'll see you tomorrow at nine."

His voice followed her down the hall. "Sign the paperwork before you leave."

"I will." She pivoted and took two steps backward. "Thanks."

Angela, the receptionist, smiled as she extended the form. "I think you'll like working here. Mr. Morgan is very talented."

Yes, he was.

She made it back to the car before a fresh wave of anxiety hit and she leaned back against the quarter panel. That was way too easy. She wasn't used to easy. Something would happen to spoil it. Something always did.

CHAPTER 8

DERRICK SCANNED THE parking lot in search of Ella's car. When he didn't see it, he decided to park and wait inside the restaurant. The place wasn't packed with kids or parents…yet. That would happen closer to dinnertime. She'd probably be in a rush.

He ran his palm over his hair. He needed to let it grow out. He was no longer in the military, no longer had to follow regs. Though a lot of the guys in the teams had let their hair grow, he'd kept his short since blond hair didn't really blend in in most of places they'd been deployed. But he couldn't seem to break the habits he'd acquired while training while a SEAL or in the brig.

With his work and school schedule, it was just easier to get it buzzed than deal with it. At least it wasn't so short it looked like he didn't have any hair.

A mother and two children came in, and she hustled them to a booth.

Did the people working here think it odd he was sitting here alone in a place for families and kids? Would they think he was some kind of—

Ella walked in, a boy at her side, and whatever he'd been thinking ground to a halt. He stood as they walked toward him.

"Hello, Derrick," Ella greeted him. "This is Micah. Micah this is Mr. Armstrong."

The kid had the look of his mother stamped on his features, his hair, his build, but his eyes were a pale, startling shade of green.

"Hey, Micah."

He extended his hand for a shake, and though the kid took it, he eyed him with the same suspicion Ella had the night he towed her car. What had they both been through to put that look in their eyes?

"I haven't ordered since I don't know what you like," Derrick said as the two sat down. He removed an envelope from his jacket pocket and slid it across the table to her.

Ella eyed the envelope, then stuffed it in her jacket pocket.

"A large should do for the three of us," Ella said. "I'll order for us. What do you like?"

He'd eat almost anything, but why ruin a perfectly good pie with some of this shit? "Anything but anchovies or pineapple."

"You're safe. Micah and I wouldn't touch either of those. Drinks?"

"A Coke."

"Want a salad?" she asked.

"No. Pizza will do."

She shot up a thumb and sauntered over the counter to order their pizza.

Derrick dragged his attention away from Ella, though the desire was strong to follow her progress all the way across the room. He focused on Micah instead. "How was school?"

Micah slouch in his chair and raised one shoulder in a shrug. "Okay."

He remembered being as withdrawn and edgy around strange adults as Micah seemed to be. The fear that something he or someone else said would set his dad off had been behind his wariness. He dreaded the inevitable embarrassment the old man would cause him.

Micah's seemed rooted in distrust instead. "What's your favorite subject in school?"

"Science."

"My favorite was math, but I liked science too. My mom and I built a volcano out of a tin can, some cardboard, napkins, and wheat paste. I painted it and put plastic trees and moss bushes at the base. Scattered some dinosaurs here and there. We made it erupt using vinegar and baking soda with a little food coloring in it to make it red. I kept it in my room for months." Until his father had destroyed it in a rage.

"My mom helps me with school stuff sometimes, too."

"I thought she might."

Micah nodded though he continued to look at the nearest arcade game as though he might disappear into the screen with the space invaders who bobbed across it. "I'll get pizza twice this week. Bryan Scott's birthday party is here on Saturday, and I'm going. We already bought a gift."

"That's good?"

"Yeah." He looked up. "Why are we here now?"

"Your mom left something at the garage the other night when I fixed her flat tires. I'm just here to return it to her."

The tension in Micah's features relaxed a little. "You didn't want to keep it?"

"It wasn't mine to keep."

That earned him a smile. "Thanks."

He was no hero, but to have the kid look at him as though he'd surprised him sealed the deal for him. He'd done the right thing.

Derrick extended his fist and Micah bumped it with his.

Ella sauntered up to the table. "Pizza and drinks will be up in just a few minutes." She held up a card. "I've got a time card so you can practice some of the games. Want to go try a few?"

"Yeah." Micah shot out of the booth. Card in hand, he ran to the space invader machine he'd been eyeing earlier and popped in the card.

"How was school?" she asked, while sliding the envelope he'd given her back to him, a little thinner than it had been.

Derrick chuckled. "I just asked Micah about that." He laid a hand on the envelope but didn't pick it up. "Are you sure?"

"Yeah. I'm sure." She ran her fingers through her hair, fluffing it up. "I know how Micah answered you." She shrugged in a perfect imitation of him and said, "Fine."

"Yeah he did."

"It's a boy thing, isn't it? It's like pulling teeth to get him to tell me things."

"It is. If you don't say too much, Mom can't harp on all the stuff you're not telling her."

"I figured as much. Last year he couldn't wait to tell me about his day and show me all his papers. This year he's a vault, and if I didn't clean his backpack out, I'd never know what he was learning at school."

Derrick's gaze swung back to Micah. Was he being bullied? With his slight, wiry build, he'd be a perfect target. "Do you check in with his teacher?"

"Yeah."

"He come home with any bruises or anything?"

"No."

"Then he may just be going through a phase and exercising his independence muscles." He grinned. "And going through the typical my-head's-so-full-of-boy-stuff-there's-no-room-for-remembering-anything-else phase."

She smiled, her whiskey-colored eyes homed in on him. "How could you know that? Do you have children?"

"No. Never been married. But I was once a boy, and I was a handful."

"In what way?"

"I liked to fight. That was my go-to solution for everything."

"And now?"

"No. Not anymore. I got a lot of my aggression out through football in high school and college. But not all of it. Lost my football scholarship because of a bar fight, but I was able to finish school, then went into the Navy."

"How long were you in the Navy?"

"Six years." If he told her the whole story she'd get up and walk away. She wouldn't want him anywhere near her kid.

"And now?"

"I work at the garage towing cars all night. You'd be surprised how many wrecks happen at three in the morning. And I take welding classes so I can hopefully move on to something more constructive."

"That's good."

He nodded. "How's the job hunt going?"

"I applied for a job today. They want me to come in at nine in the morning."

"What kind of job is it?"

"Modeling."

Derrick's stomach clenched. "What kind of modeling?"

"It's to illustrate magazine articles. Did you know they use models to do that? Like if a hospital wants to put a face to their facility, they'll hire models to be patients and doctors and pose them."

"You're kidding."

"No."

"Sounds like an easy gig." The knots in his belly eased some.

"Yeah. It's just part-time to bring in money while I look for something steady. This won't be an every day thing."

He spoke his thoughts aloud. "It might turn into more, Ella. You never know."

She shook her head. "Not unless I invest in head shots and shop myself around to different agencies. I'm not interested in that. I need to be here for Micah."

His taut muscles relaxed. He didn't want to look too closely at why it meant so much to him that she wasn't looking at the modeling thing as a springboard to more. She was certainly gorgeous enough to be successful with it.

He was a dick. She was trying to support her kid.

He was just feeling protective of her. Or was it territorial, like before?

And he'd never wanted a woman so much in his life.

He ignored the voice in his head telling him it might have something to do with the seven years he'd been without one.

But there was one big barrier standing in the way of his asking her out. "I heard what you said to Larry that night. Are you really a lesbian, or was that just an attempt to keep him from jumping you?".

She traced a pattern on the table with her fingertip. "No, I'm not gay, but I don't need a man. I don't have time for a man." Her expression was less than open.

"What about one who can cook, keep your car running, and take care of plumbing issues and other things around the house?"

Her lips twitched, and he smiled. He could carve away at her resistance as long as she didn't freeze him out.

Her attention shifted to Micah when he changed games to one with a steering wheel. "I do two of those myself, and my building has a super who takes care of the rest."

"Yeah, but what if you didn't have to wait for things to be repaired? It would make your life easier."

"To have a maid there to meet me at the door after work with a drink and my slippers would be nice, too, but I'm not in the market for that either."

He'd known it was going to be a hard sell, but he wouldn't give up so easily. What did he have to lose? "Just have to do it all yourself, huh?"

"I've learned you can't really depend on anyone else."

"That's true a lot of the time, but I came through for you before. I just want to get to know you. If you decide you're not interested after dinner or a movie I'll back away. Micah can come too, if you like."

She remained silent for a beat. "I'll think about it."

At least she wasn't shutting him down. But that could be because of the money. He'd take what he could get.

A waiter came to the table bringing with him their pizza and the scent of garlic, oregano, and Italian sausage.

"I'll go get Micah."

MICAH'S FIXED CONCENTRATION made Ella smile. He was the

same at home on his video games. "Pizza's up," she announced.

"I'll be there as soon as I finish this game, Mom."

She watched his skill as he guided a speeding vehicle through a narrow opening between two cars and shot ahead of them. She was half impressed, half terrified by the move.

"Don't get too lost in the game, Micah. Your pizza's getting cold." Which he wouldn't care about. He'd eat pizza if it was stone cold and hard as a brick.

"I'll be there as soon as my time on this game runs out."

"Okay."

She turned to wend her way back through the game machines and back to the table, taking the time to study Derrick.

He had shaved. She noticed it first thing. With his scruff gone, he looked younger, and his pale blue eyes appeared even bluer with the help of a button-up shirt the same color.

She'd bet, because he was making moves to get her to go out with him, he'd dressed and cleaned up to meet them. His muscular biceps bulged against the fabric of his short sleeves as he reached for napkins and placed them next to each paper plate. His broad shoulders strained against the fabric, and she could see the delineation of the muscle between his shoulder and neck. He lifted weights. He'd have to, to get that kind definition and be strong enough to lift the heavy tires and other things his job demanded.

He looked up as she approached, and she admitted that he wasn't hard on the eyes. He had lean, chiseled cheekbones, a wide forehead and a strong jaw, but his mouth was his most expressive feature. When he smiled it softened the angles and projected enough sex appeal to melt metal.

The flutter of attraction she felt upon seeing him again beat against her resistance like hummingbird wings. It wasn't fullfledged yet. Her instinct to look before she leaped kept it at bay, but the urge to shut the feeling down was strangely delayed.

She'd been so excited about the job, and she actually shared it with him because she'd thought he'd be excited for her. And he was, cautiously so. Just as she'd been at first.

They looked at things similarly. He was just as cynical as she.

And wary that people might be out to screw him. What had happened in his life that caused that attitude? She'd never know unless she gave him a chance and got to know him.

But did she want to?

She spent some time last night thinking about him.

He had looked out for her that first night. Would he be so quick to do it if he was a bad guy?

Probably not.

He'd have been even quicker to pocket the money he sort of extorted from Larry instead of giving it to her. It was $978 now because of the thirty bucks she'd paid for the pizza and drinks. Her cut had been $464, enough to pay more than a third of their rent.

"Micah's on the race car game and said he'll be here as soon as he finishes his last lap. Do you think games like that will make him more likely to be a daredevil behind the wheel when he gets old enough to drive?"

"Probably, but you have nine years to drum caution into his head."

"You could have just lied and told me no." She pulled off a slice of pizza so he'd go ahead and dig in.

He shot her a wry smile. "Sorry. But this way you'll get a jump on things, and maybe he'll drive like my grandma instead of Kyle Busch."

"Please, God!" She bit into her pizza, which was loaded with a variety of meats and vegetables.

Derrick laughed. "He seems a cautious kid. He may stay that way all through school."

For a minute they concentrated on their pizza.

There was a difference between responsible and cautious. It was a fine line, but she'd begun to worry that maybe Micah was overly cautious. Did it drain the spontaneity out of his life? He seemed to spend too much time worrying about things. They both did.

"Are you going to go back to tending bar, or look for something different?"

She cleared her throat, then sipped her coke. "I'll take what I can get. I've submitted my application for several different types of jobs, plus I applied for unemployment."

"That and the modeling gig should tide you over until you find something."

She hoped. "What kind of welding are you learning to do?"

"A variety of different techniques. Right now, I'm working on MIG welding."

"And that is?"

"To put it in layman's terms, an electrode sparks within a gas to melt the metal and fuse it together."

Micah wiggled into the booth next to her and reached for a slice of pizza. Ella grabbed his arm before his hand could touch the food, pulling out a miniscule bottle of germicide. "How many grubby hands have been on the joysticks or steering wheels of the games you've been playing?"

"At least a gazillion. They're the funnest games."

She laughed and squirted a generous drop of the liquid in his palm, and while he was rubbing his hands together she put a slice of pizza on his plate, handing him a napkin to dry his hands on and waiting until he'd balled it up and put it on the table. Then she handed him another to wipe his mouth while he ate.

"Will you play a game with me after we eat?" Micah asked.

She was surprised to find he was talking to Derrick instead of her.

Derrick wiped his mouth. "Sure. I'm a little rusty, but I'll give it a shot."

"Cool!" He crammed a huge bite of pizza into his mouth and chewed, then washed it down with Coke. "You won't let me win like Mom does."

Ella bit her lip to keep from smiling. "I don't let you win. I just suck at games."

When Micah rolled his eyes, she bumped him with her elbow. He flashed her a pizza-smeared grin.

Derrick shot her a raised brow. "If you win, you have to win fair and square."

"Good." Micah took another big bite.

ELLA LEANED AGAINST the side of one of the games while she watched Derrick and Micah go head-to-head with miniature bowling and soccer.

When they turned their attention to another racing game the two of them could play together, their body language changed to a focused competitiveness.

The clashing and screeching of the cars on the screen modeled an aggression she wasn't used to. Her thoughts jumped back to Derrick's comments about his go-to solution for everything as a boy.

Had his six years in the Navy changed that behavior? Wasn't a normal enlistment four years? Had he been injured before he finished out his second enlistment? And what had he done afterwards?

Was she interested enough to give him a shot at a date?

God, how long had it been since she'd been on a date? At least a year. The kind of guys she met at strip clubs weren't exactly dating material.

But Derrick had been at the club. He didn't look the type, but then neither did old Carl. And come to think of it, neither of them had paid much attention to the girls. They just sipped their drinks and left.

There were cheaper places to get a beer. Why had he been there?

Micah gave a whoop of victory and danced back and forth behind the machine, wiggling his narrow butt. Derrick's deep, masculine laughter struck a chord inside her, and a rush of desire triggered a tingling heat in areas she'd ignored for far too long.

Going out with him would not be a good idea.

Micah bounced over to her. "I won, Mom."

"I'd have never guessed. It's customary for the winner to shake hands with the opposition."

Derrick grinned as Micah strutted over and shook his hand.

"We'll do this again sometime soon. My treat."

"Awesome."

Micah's enthusiasm worried her. She needed to know more about Derrick Armstrong before allowing him into their lives.

THEY LEFT THE restaurant together and Derrick walked them to the car. Micah jumped into the back seat and strapped in. Ella handed him the leftover pizza box and shut the door.

"Thanks for sharing the money with us." Her expression was once again distant, and he could sense she was going to cut things off.

"You're welcome."

"What were you doing at the club that day?"

He hadn't thought about how she'd feel about him coming to the club. "Not what you think. One or two days a week, I hit a bar or restaurant and leave business cards for the tow company."

"Does your boss know you do that?"

"No, but I get bored sitting at the garage waiting for a call, so I try to drum up business."

"You should tell him. Maybe he'll give you a raise."

"I doubt it, but I'll think about it." He stepped closer and inhaled the soft floral scent of her shampoo. "How about Sunday for that dinner date?"

"I may be working by then."

"You have my number, so you can call me if you are. And if you're not...maybe we can share a meal and get to know each other a little better."

He ran his fingertips down the back of her arms because he couldn't not touch her. "I get that you and Micah are a unit, but it doesn't mean you can't share your world with someone else. I got along with him today. I'm certain it can continue."

Since becoming an adult, he'd never hurt a kid in his life. Never would. He'd come close in Iraq...once. And it had scared the shit out of him. He'd been on the receiving end of his dad's open palm and his fists too often to allow himself to go that far. He didn't need to hurt someone a quarter or less than his size to feel in control of the situation. Not then and not now.

But he had done just that with Marjorie. He flinched away from the thought.

Could Ella read what he was thinking or feeling?

"Where would we go?"

"What do you like to eat other than pizza?"

"Mexican or Chinese."

He could afford to feed her, but would she want to get into his vehicle to get there? It might be time to fix the rattletrap up. "I could bring takeout over to your place. Mine isn't in a very safe neighborhood, and I wouldn't want you to drive there alone."

"Isn't it just as dangerous for you?"

"The lady I rent from is well-known and liked in the neighborhood. Even the neighborhood thugs don't want to cost her the rent I pay. Plus. I mow her grass and do odd jobs for her. And I help them with car issues when they're having trouble. That keeps them from messing with me." And it earned him a little extra money on the side. He could probably sweet-talk his landlady into fixing some Mexican food for him to take over to Ella's.

His lie of omission was going to catch up with him soon. He needed to tell her. But not yet. If he told her now, she wouldn't even give him a chance, and he desperately wanted a chance.

But putting pressure on her wouldn't help. He stepped back out of her space. "Will you call me tomorrow and let me know how the job went? You can tell me then if you want to get together."

"Okay."

"See that car over there?" He pointed toward his vehicle.

"Yeah."

"That's my work in progress. It was a wreck I bought from the tow yard, and I'm fixing it up a little at a time. I don't know how you feel about being seen in a junker, but it won't look like that in a few more weeks."

"If you're trying to convince me you're as handy as pockets on a shirt, you've already succeeded. And I don't care what kind of car you drive, Derrick. I'm not that kind of girl."

He smiled. "I didn't think you were, but I want something better for you to ride in."

Her expression softened. "Dinner on Sunday would be nice. Micah loves tacos. And be prepared. He usually eats three. How's five-thirty or six?"

"Five-thirty sounds good."

"I'll text you my address."

"Great." He couldn't help but grin like a fool.

"We'll see you on Sunday." She walked around the car.

He knocked on the passenger window and threw up a hand to Micah.

The kid returned the gesture.

There was a spring in his step that hadn't been there in a long time as he walked to his car.

CHAPTER 9

S INCE WHEN HAD anyone ever smiled this much while they were eating? The steak in front of her was stone cold, and the baked potato was beginning to look a little dry around the edges. Or was it her imagination? The guy sitting across from her was attractive, but she'd never seen a guy fuss so much with his hair or shirt cuffs in her life.

The wine glass half-filled could ease the pain—if she was allowed to sip it. Which she wasn't, unless it was to catch a picture of her about to take a sip.

She'd never worn this much makeup or owned anything like the dress she was wearing. The black fabric had tawny copper overtones, as though an artist had dry-brushed metallic paint over the darker color. It did wonderful things for her skin. It was gorgeous and expensive, and she'd been terrified she might spill the wine and ruin it. Not so much now, since her nerves had decided there was no emergency and were taking a nap out of boredom.

Every detail of her appearance had been checked over and over again. They even gave her a manicure and painted her nails with clear polish so they'd look nice against the crystal glass and the red wine.

Davis stalked from table to table, taking shots of some of the other models, but seeming to gravitate back to their table more and more.

She placed an elbow on the table and leaned toward her partner for this picture. "Shouldn't some of the food we've supposedly been eager to eat be gone from our plates by now? It would sell more food if we made it look like it was good enough to eat."

He stretched an arm out and pinched the stem of his wine glass as Davis circled back to their table. "They'll get to it soon enough. They take hundreds of photos, then chose the best ten or so for the client."

"Pick up your wine glass and hold it up as though you're looking through it before taking a drink," Davis instructed.

While she did, he took pictures of her profile.

"Hold that pose while I circle you."

She held the pose, concentrating on the wine, which happened to be a pretty good vintage. Much better than the swill they served at the strip clubs.

"Wet your lips."

She did, and looked up at the camera. Davis took the shot. He grinned behind the camera. The first expression she'd seen since the shooting began.

She dropped her eyes back to the glass.

"You can put it down now."

The added lights they put up here and there beat down on them, and sweat trickled down her side. She hoped it wouldn't ruin the dress.

The session went on for nearly an hour more. Food off their plate. Dessert reduced to crumbs and a trickle of chocolate. Coffee. Which smelled so delicious, she cradled the cup in her palm and took a sip. Davis was there to snap the picture.

She was exhausted by the time he ended the shoot and she headed upstairs to the dressing room.

"Ella!" Davis caught her before she could leave. "Fantastic work today."

She shrugged. "Thanks, but all I did was stare at the wine and drink a little coffee."

He laughed, showing off attractive creases in his cheeks and making the fine lines at the corners of his eyes deepen. She felt a trickle of quick interest, but he was her boss, and getting involved with someone she worked for was a hard and fast no-no. It could end up costing her a paycheck.

"You really haven't ever done this before."

"No. It's a little weird."

He laughed again. "You'll get a check in the mail in about five days. Two-fifty an hour. You worked three hours."

Seven hundred and fifty dollars for pretending to eat. After taxes she'd get a little more than two-thirds. They'd be able to make their rent.

"Thanks. Really."

"I'll definitely be calling you back for the next campaign. Expect a call in three or four days."

"I appreciate it."

She took the elevator upstairs to the storage room they'd blocked off for the women's dressing room. The space was small, stuffy, and packed with seven women. Tall, short, chunky, skinny... Brunette, redhead, blonde. They were definitely a cross section of the population.

She stripped down to her panties and bra and sighed with relief while she put on her jeans, T-shirt and sneakers. She hung the dress on the padded hanger and put it inside the bag it came in, then the shoes. Though Gregory hadn't taken pictures of her feet, she supposed they were to give the model the illusion of reality.

The dress and shoes had probably cost the seven hundred fifty dollars they would pay her. She found the idea a little surreal.

A woman with a clipboard accepted the bag, checked it and had her initial the form. She put another form in front of her. "You've signed your contract with the Morgan and Tolliver Agency, haven't you?"

"Yes."

"Good." She withdrew the sheet and smiled. "Thanks."

Driving back to the apartment, she thought about calling Derrick and telling him about the photo shoot. But he'd be in class.

She'd have to wait until she picked up Micah.

It had been a while since she'd had someone to share things with.

The thought triggered a case of jitters. She was only sharing because he'd asked her to call him and tell him about it.

This was just going to be a casual thing. Their schedules were too much of a barrier to seeing each other much. It probably wouldn't go anywhere.

But she kept seeing his expression when she said he could come over on Sunday with dinner. And, damnit, that remark about his car... He was a hunk. Gorgeous. Tall. Had a smile and a laugh that did it for her. Had a work ethic that outdid her own.

Why the hell was he alone?

Well, he was working a full-time job, going to school, and living on five hours of sleep a day. That might be the problem.

But he hadn't always been doing those things, otherwise he'd be living in a better neighborhood.

She wanted to know more about him. Wanted to know she could trust him.

DERRICK PAUSED JUST outside the classroom building to answer his phone. "Hey, Derrick." Roger Carpenter's voice was distinctive. He had a Texas twang thick as mud. Derrick often went a month or more without seeing his boss since he was usually gone by the time Derrick showed up for the night shift. And he liked it that way.

It wasn't that he didn't like the guy. He'd given him a job when other employers wouldn't, so he owed him. Which made him nervous. When you owed someone, they eventually expected payback.

"Can you come in for a few minutes today? I want to talk to you about a project I'd like you to do for me. It'll mean extra money for you."

He could always use extra cash. "Sure. What time?"

"How about now?"

"I'll be there in twenty minutes."

"Okay."

When he arrived the garage was packed, the bays populated with vehicles in one state of mechanical repair or another. The crash and rev of machinery inside the space was nearly deafening, but he still would have known where he was with his eyes shut and no noise, just from the familiar smell of oil and rubber.

He spotted Roger in bay five and wove his way through the activity to him. Roger's hair was practically shaved on the sides, but the top lay in heavy waves. A square-jawed face and heavy brow gave him an aggressive look.

Roger nodded toward the far door as soon as Derrick joined him. "Come with me. We'll go into the office where we can actually hear each other."

They wove their way to the reception space where customers usually went to pay their bill or wait while their car was repaired. Ella sat in there on the bench seat while he worked on her tires. Behind the desk a secretary typed away on the keyboard. He'd only met her once, but still nodded as they went by. In the middle of a long row of filing cabinets, Roger pushed open a door that led into his private office cabinets.

Derrick followed him into the space. A leather sofa sat against the wall just inside the door, a coffee table in front of it. Roger strode across to the desk opposite and picked up a stack of papers. "How are the welding classes coming?"

"Good."

"I have a project for you, if you think you can do it."

"Okay."

He handed Derrick the papers. "I'm a partner in a business across town, and we need a gantry crane we can move easily from one location to another. Capacity two tons. I have all the materials to build it, but the guy who said he'd do it is laid up now with an arm injury after a fall. So I thought if you're up for it, I'd get you to do it."

Derrick sat down in one of the chairs and looked over the

design. It seemed a straight-up welding job. "Have you already had the pieces machine cut?"

"Yeah. We're using steel tubing to keep the weight down, but you'll have to wield the two pieces together to form the beam, then flange the sides and the base."

"The design is interesting. You'll be able to break it down and move it from site to site easily. I can do it with the right equipment."

"That's the idea." Roger picked up a notepad and pen and laid it on the edge of the desk. "Make a list and I'll get the equipment."

Derrick bent over the pad and jotted down the list. "Why didn't you just order one?"

"It was one of those deals where you have this guy saying, 'oh, I can do that for you for a lot less,' then he gets hurt. Now I have money invested in the materials and no one to finish the job."

"I can finish it for you."

"Great! Will five hundred be enough for the labor?"

"Yeah." Actually, it was very generous. He handed Roger the list. He'd need an extra pair of hands once he got the beam welded, but there were a couple of guys in the neighborhood who'd do it for a few bucks.

"Nights still working for you?"

"Yeah."

Roger grinned. "You're a man of few words, Derrick. I have another garage where you can work on the crane." He ripped off a sheet from the note pad. "This is the address. When can you start?"

"I don't have classes on Friday. I can work on it then, and on Saturday after I get through with my night shift. I should be able to knock out the lion's share of the work in those two days."

"Good. I'll have the materials ready and waiting for you."

"Okay." Derrick rose to leave.

Roger pulled a set of keys from his pocket and worked one loose. "You'll need this to get into the building." He held the key out. "If you have any problems, let me know."

"Will do. Thanks for the extra work. Now I can get the junker a paint job."

Roger shook his head. "I thought you were crazy when you bought that thing, but you have the touch. You could have your own garage like this one day."

"I'm not interested in the day-to-day hassle of running the show. I got enough of that when I worked for my dad. But I like building things."

"Don't stretch yourself too thin."

"I won't."

"I'll come out and check on the work on Saturday evening."

"Okay."

His phone rang as he exited the garage, and he pulled it free of his back pocket. "Hello."

After a beat Ella's voice asked, "How are you?"

"I'm good." He caught himself grinning like a fool again. She'd actually called. "How did it go?"

"It was really weird. We sat inside a restaurant empty except for waitstaff and pretended to eat while a photographer took a gazillion pictures."

He laughed. "Easier than mixing drinks, huh?"

"It was that. But we didn't get to drink the wine, which would have made it better, because it was a pretty good wine. But the pay made it worth it."

"So, are you going to do it again?" He opened the car door and slid behind the wheel, then shut the door to reduce the sound of the machinery from the garage and the passing traffic.

"Yeah. The photographer said they'd probably call me to do another one in four or five days."

"Whatever brings in the money. I got another temporary side job, too. My boss had hired someone to build a gantry crane but the guy got hurt and can't finish the job. He's hired me to weld the crossbar and put the thing together."

"What exactly is a gantry crane?"

"It's a structure with a crossbar at the top and sides strong enough to hold a great deal of weight. You usually hook a machine with a pully onto the crossbar that will raise the weight of, say, an engine out of a car."

"Oh. That sounds like something useful."

He laughed. "And there's no reason at all you should be interested in any of this."

"Will you still have time to come over and bring a meal on Sunday?"

"Yes. Sunday is my day off. We could take Micah to the zoo. Or do the Ferris wheel and all the stuff at Balboa Park."

"He's been there before. Trust me, he'd rather throw down a challenge for you to play a video game. He's obsessed with his games."

"It's been a while since I played. He beat me pretty easily at Chuck E. Cheese."

The last time he'd played a video game had been something to do with war, since that was all they thought about back then. Seven years since he played a video game. But then the arcade games were close enough. He needed to make a bucket list of the things he hadn't done in what seemed a lifetime and do them.

That thought led to others, and he found himself saying, "Let me come over for a few minutes, Ella. I can't stay long. I need to sleep, but I want to see you."

She was silent a moment. "Why me, Derrick?"

He closed his eyes, and she was just there in his head. "I could say look in the mirror, but it's more than that. I think we've both had a rough time of it, and you need someone as badly as I do." He opened his eyes and stared at the glaring sunshine beating down on the windshields in the parking lot and was suddenly sick of the sight of cars, trucks, all sorts of vehicles. He'd had a steady diet of little else for months. "I can be a friend if it's what you need. We can take it slow."

Her silence stretched. "I hope you're a patient man."

"I can be patient." He'd been out of prison for seven months and he hadn't been with a woman yet. That was patience. And fear. But his fear was starting to diminish under the flooding influx of his need.

His phone signaled a text. And he looked down at the screen

for a moment It was her address.

"I'll be there in a few minutes," he said.

"Okay."

CHAPTER 10

WHY WAS SHE so nervous about having a guy over to her apartment? She'd had a few over for dinner, but never anything else. Besides, she wouldn't make love with a man in the apartment while her son slept a doorway away from her sofa bed.

And she'd never even come close to living with a man, especially after Trae.

The place, though a little barren, was clean, even Micah's room. And though they didn't have much furniture, they had a television and a DVD player, and Micah had his games.

She fixed a peanut butter and jelly sandwich for Micah because he was always hungry when he first got home, and he practically inhaled it while he did his homework at the small kitchen table in front of the window.

When the intercom buzzed, her heart gave an uncomfortably hard thump and started pounding. When she heard Derrick's, "It's me," on the intercom, she pushed the button to release the lock downstairs.

"Who is it, Mom?" Micah asked.

"It's Derrick."

Micah eyed her for a moment. "Is he your boyfriend now?" he asked.

She studied his expression. If Micah didn't like him, he'd be out of here in five minutes. "No, not yet. To be boyfriend and girlfriend, you have to figure out if you like the same things, and if we like each other. He's a stranger, so I'll have to decide if I like him enough to continue to see him."

"He seems okay. I think he likes you."

"Why do you say that?"

"He looks at you like he's trying hard not to stare. So he's trying hard to be polite, like you taught me."

She fought hard not to smile.

"And he sucks at games, but not as bad as you."

"He and I both work a lot. He may not have much time to practice."

A knock came on the door and she strode over to open it. "Come in."

Derrick looked tired, but he smiled.

She'd been nervous about him being here and hadn't realized it had probably been seventeen hours since he'd slept. She didn't know how he managed with the schedule he worked. "Come in and have a seat. Would you like some coffee?"

"Sure." He raised a hand to Micah.

"Hey. Play a video game with me?" he asked.

"Micah, Mr. Armstrong has worked all night and been to school like you this morning and afternoon. He's tired."

"He can call me Derrick, if it's okay with you." He looked at her.

That he asked her permission told her he recognized the boundaries. "Yes, that's okay."

"You're doing your homework, aren't you, Micah?"

"Yeah."

"After your homework is done, I'll give you some play time on one game before I leave."

Micah grinned and raised a fist in the air. "Yes."

"He'll have to show me how it works. I haven't played video games in years."

"You'll do fine. You did okay at the arcade."

"I think Micah might be a video game shark."

She laughed. "He may be. I can't beat him either."

"I like to hear you laugh. I don't think you do it as often as you should."

Derrick's eyes shone a crystal-clear blue, and their depths held something that made her breathing hitch and triggered a tingling heat, intimate, tempting.

"I wanted to see you," he murmured, close to her ear.

Heat rose in her cheeks. "Have a seat at the bar and I'll fix you some coffee and something to eat." She got out bread and cheese. "Will grilled cheese be okay?"

"Sure. My mom used to fix me grilled cheese sandwiches when I was sick. I haven't had one in a long time."

She tried to keep her attention on the simple task at hand, but was aware of his eyes following her every movement. "Why not? They're probably on every restaurant menu."

He seemed to give the question some thought. "Most men are meat-eaters. When we go out to eat, we order meat of some kind. No soup or salad for us. Unless it's a side dish."

"What about chili?" she asked.

"Chili's a totally different subject. It's meat with a few beans, so it passes the man test."

She glanced over to find him smiling. "So, you cook?"

"And grill. Every man needs to know how to take care of himself."

She flipped the grilled sandwiches onto a plate and expertly sliced them in half diagonally. She slid the plate in front of him "Cream or sugar for the coffee?"

"Black is fine."

She poured him a cup and set it beside his plate. Though she rarely drank coffee during the day, she poured one, added cream, then hiked a hip up on the barstool next to him. "Have you lived in San Diego long?"

"On and off for nearly fifteen years. And you?"

"Almost seven years. I came out to Los Angeles with Micah's father. He was a musician trying to break into the business as a songwriter and musician. He sold one song to a guy signed by Capitol records and we were hopeful it would go somewhere. He died before he got a single royalty check." She sipped the coffee. "I couldn't stay in Los Angeles without him."

"I'm sorry."

"Me too. I went home for about a month, for the funeral, and tried to make sense of things. It didn't help, so I moved here to San Diego."

"Mom, I'm done with my homework." Micah shoved in between them with his school paper.

"I'll check it in a minute. Derrick and I are talking. What have I told you about interrupting adults?"

Micah's cheeks reddened. "Unless it's a emergency, say 'scuse me, then ask my question."

"Is that what you did?"

Micah hung his head. "No."

She cupped his chin and brought his face up so his eyes had to meet hers. She loved him so much, and she hated having to discipline him. It hurt her almost much as it did him. "You'll do it next time, won't you?"

"Yes, I promise."

"Pinky swear." She extended her hand, her little finger crooked.

He looped his finger through hers, his smile peeking out. "Pinky swear."

"You can play *Incredibles* while Derrick and I talk."

"Okay."

She watched Micah set up the game, then sit cross-legged in front of the television and began to play.

"He's a good kid. And you're patient with him. That's good."

"There's been times it's been hard. My family was upset that I was pregnant when I returned to Utah. My father is a bishop in the Mormon church there, and he pressured me pretty hard to give Micah up for adoption." They'd more than pressured. And the response of other church members had added enough stress and heartache that she left without looking back.

"I wouldn't do it. My mom sends birthday and Christmas cards with gift cards in them for those two occasions. In return, I send her pictures of Micah."

"What about his father's people?"

"They threatened to take him from me. Even hired a lawyer." She'd always wondered if her father had something to do with that. "Social services came around and insisted on drug testing me, though I'd never had a history. Never have had one. They could see I was struggling financially, but Micah was well cared for, and I was offering him a stable environment, working two jobs to do it. Once they established that I was clean, they actually helped me. They enrolled us in some programs that helped me pay for his diapers and formula. The judge ruled in my favor, and Trae's family dropped the case."

"Have you gone back to visit?"

"No. I'll never go back." She was too afraid the whole thing with Trae's family would start again. It wouldn't be what was best for Micah, because then being raised in the church would take priority over everything else.

"Do you still have to worry about social services?"

"The social worker who checked on Micah came around for a while, but that stopped by the time he turned two."

"Good."

Derrick placed a hand over hers. For a long moment she was aware of the size of his hand cradling hers, the warmth of his touch, the comfort it offered. But she was also wondering how that large hand would feel sliding down the curve of her back to cup her ass and pull her in tight. It had been a long time since she felt those things. Heat flooded her face again.

"Would you like some more coffee?"

"No, but water would be good."

She slid off the barstool and scooped up his plate, cup and saucer like the professional waitress/bartender she was. She put the dishes in the sink and filled two glasses with ice, then water.

"I don't get along with my father, so I don't go home anymore either. I Skype with my sister and mother on holidays like Mother's Day and Christmas, that kind of thing. I talk to my brother now and then, too. He's getting married in June."

"Are you going to the wedding?"

"I haven't decided yet."

"You're from the South."

He smiled for the first time since arriving. "Yeah. Baton Rouge, Louisiana. I guess my accent gave it away."

"It's very slight, and only when you say certain words. I've never been to Louisiana. What's it like?"

"Baton Rouge isn't as large as San Diego, but it has all the same things...malls, museums, the zoo, good restaurants. Great food. I went to LSU there. And Baton Rouge Theatre puts on some good shows.

"It's wonderful in spring and summer, with everything in bloom. There are plantation houses you can tour. We have willow oaks, weeping willows, and magnolia trees. Casinos. And the city sits right on the Mississippi River."

He obviously loved his hometown.

"I'm sold. Let's go."

He laughed. "I guess I did kind of..." Whatever he was going to say was swallowed up by the sadness she read in his expression.

She jumped in to redirect his attention. "It sounds wonderful. If you love it so much, why are you here instead of there?"

"Because Baton Rouge isn't big enough for both me and my dad. He won't keep his distance, and the two of us can't be in the same space without something bad happening. That's why I'm on the ropes about the wedding."

"I'm sorry."

"I've made my peace with it, Ella. I'm trying to build a life here."

With his attention focused on her as he said it, a flutter built in her belly.

"I need to go, but I owe Micah some playtime. I won't be able to stay for a whole game, though."

"You don't have to play him if you're strapped for time."

"I have time for half a game, and I wouldn't want to disappoint him." Derrick slid off the barstool. "How 'bout some game time, Micah?"

Micah's face lit up. "Awesome!" He dragged the basket of games over and pulled each one out to explain what the game was about so they could decide which to play.

As she watched the two together, regret hit her. Micah was hungry for male attention. But she'd been wary of bringing anyone into his life, worried it might leave him heartbroken if things didn't work out.

When Micah popped in the game and handed Derrick a control, Ella went back into the kitchen to load the dishes. Before she finished the two were already moaning and yelling at the screen. Guys were the same the world over. Even the little ones.

While they played, she perched on one of the barstools and watched over their heads. Derrick had some issues with getting his guy moving, but once he figured out how, his experience playing football gave him an advantage. But not much of one, since Micah had played the game so often with one of the older boys from upstairs.

Their linemen took position on the forty-yard line. The ball snapped, the quarterback dropped back and threw a pass down-field to his wide receiver. The receiver spun and cut between two men like hot butter, but one of Derrick's tackles hit him on the ten and brought him down.

It started all over again, the two of them alternating between grinning like fools and grumbling and shouting. Micah's team got the touchdown and the field goal.

It was easy not to think about what-ifs when she was with Derrick, because he was so different from Trae. He exhibited no artistic temperament, but there was a loneliness and a hunger in the way he looked at her that gripped her down low.

After watching them for nearly twenty-five minutes, she slipped away to use the bathroom.

When she returned, they had paused the game and Derrick was explaining a play he'd made after the kickoff return. He got to his feet. "I have to go, kiddo. I have to get some sleep before I go to work later."

"I know. Mom does that, too." He looked downcast.

"I'll be back on Sunday, and I'll be here long enough for a full game, Okay?"

Micah brightened. "Okay."

Derrick patted his shoulder and got to his feet.

"Why don't you call upstairs to Shanna's and see if Tim can come down and finish the game?" Ella suggested.

"Cool," Micah wasted no time grabbing her cell phone.

Ella walked Derrick to the door. He caught her hand and tugged her outside the apartment. "What time would you like me to come over?"

"If you're going to be playing at least one game with Micah, you'd better come about three."

He grinned. "I'll be here. Thanks for the snack." He bent and brushed his lips against her cheek.

She moved into him because she needed to be held, had needed to be held for days, weeks, months. She rested her head against his chest and listened to the steady beat of his heart. His arms came around her, and though he held himself a little apart, she felt the muscular strength of his body, a body honed from hard work and lifting weights.

"I've been working, I smell like motor oil and God knows what else."

"You smell like work, sweat, and soap." And him. He felt strong and warm, and he held her like he was afraid of breaking her. He cupped the back of her head and his fingers stroked her hair.

The stiffness went out of his posture, but other things began to stir against her belly. When she raised her face to look up at him, his pale eyes darkened with need and his mouth covered hers with eager heat.

Her pulse skyrocketed. His tongue found hers, and a tingling heat took root between her thighs. It intensified as Derrick's hand crept down and he anchored her against him more tightly.

He raised his head, his cheeks flushed and his breathing a little ragged. "I need you to remind me how slow we need to take things."

"I just wanted to know what it would feel like for you to hold me. It's been a long time for me."

"For me, too." He swallowed and drew her in close again. "I'd better go. I'll see you on Sunday." He caught her lips again in another heart-rocking, libido-firing kiss.

"Three o'clock."

He caught her face in both his hands and kissed her again. "I'll bring Mexican like we planned."

His eagerness had her smiling. "Sounds good."

He looked back one last time before getting on the elevator. "I'll call you."

"Okay."

DERRICK'S HEART RACED like a car with a stuck gas pedal. By the time he climbed into his car, reality was knocking on his conscience, and guilt lay on his chest with the weight of an anvil.

He had to tell her. And if he didn't tell her, he needed to break it off before they got involved.

If social services came around and found out she was dating a convict, it could cause her and Micah trouble and she would never forgive him. But she'd said they didn't come around anymore And they wouldn't, because he intended to be a model boyfriend. If she'd let him be.

He'd paid his debt to society for what he did, but in reality it would never be done. Society would never forgive him, any more than his teammates would.

And though he'd thought again and again about Marjorie, he hadn't had the nerve to find her and attempt to ask her forgiveness. Would it help her to hear his apology, or would it just bring back the bad memories and cause her more pain?

He had hurt her more than once. Left bruises on her arms. Had slapped her. Every time he thought about it, he cringed away from the memories and the feelings he experienced during those moments.

He'd been a different person then, needing to dominate and control because it had eased his feelings of panic and desperation. He'd never believed he deserved to be loved. He'd never believed anyone truly did love him. Even his mother. Otherwise, why would she let Dempsey hurt him, Tina, and Carter? Why couldn't she have put their safety ahead of his father and herself?

But Marjorie had loved him. She'd given him everything she could, and he'd hurt her, emotionally, physically. He'd been as bad as Dempsey. He'd been worse than Dempsey, because the PTSD had fired his paranoia, and his days without sleep made him dangerously delusional.

He needed to talk to his counselor.

He hadn't told her about Ella. She'd said he needed to concentrate on getting his feet under him for a full year before attempting a relationship. But the loneliness was driving him crazy. He'd been alone for seven years. Filled his own needs and run himself into exhaustion to curb them. He rested his head on the steering wheel.

Ella had held him. Let him hold her. He'd felt comforted and needed. Wanted.

Her lips were soft and giving. She'd tasted faintly of coffee and her.

He couldn't give up Ella when it had only just begun. He couldn't.

CHAPTER 11

E LLA SHOVED HER key in the mailbox and opened it. She'd put it off for as long as possible. Bills were due, and she didn't know if she had the money to pay them. She hadn't received her last week's pay from the bar and probably wouldn't. So much for her much-fantasized severance package.

She couldn't go by and demand it. There was no way she could bear being near Larry, and she certainly wasn't about to give him another shot at her.

As she got on the elevator, she flipped through the envelopes. She paused at the plain white envelope with her address on it. It was probably junk mail, but just in case... She ripped it open, took out the letter and unfolded it.

A check lay in the folds. She stared at the amount. Her pulse skyrocketed, and she swore, bundling the mail against her as the elevator door opened and she stalked down the hall to her apartment.

She propped the check against one of Micah's game controls and reread the letter.

If she kept the check, it would mean she condoned what Larry had attempted to do. If she kept it, it would mean she'd keep her mouth shut about what he tried to do to her, and what she knew he was doing to the other women working for him.

It was enough to pay six months' rent, or four months' rent

and all their other bills.

She read through the letter one more time. "Misunderstanding, my ass." Her stomach twisted every time she relived those few minutes when she felt trapped inside that cluttered dressing room. The sour smell of Larry's aftershave, and his horrible, blank look as he said, "It's just sex."

It wasn't.

It wasn't fair that she and Micah had to struggle because of him. But it wasn't right that he used the need for a shelter and food to molest and demean the women who worked for him, either.

She'd sent the flash drive and a letter to the police, giving them Larry's name and telling them what he was doing. But she hadn't walked in and filed a complaint.

Because she was afraid for Micah. The other parents at his school, the teachers, would think she was a whore. She knew how it worked. Everyone needed someone to demean and sit in judgement on to make themselves feel better. It helped them overlook their own missteps. The children would pick up on it from the adults and torment Micah.

And how would he feel, knowing his mother had taken off her clothes and danced for men? They had needed the money to live. She'd tried waiting tables at restaurants, washing dishes, holding down two jobs, and cleaning other people's apartments. It had barely been enough.

She'd been good at dancing. At using her body to seduce and offer them the illusion of desire through her art. And the tips she earned had been enough to tide them over and give them an emergency cushion.

But she'd felt sick inside. By simulating an act of love, she'd cheapened it and cheapened herself. And eventually she felt numb. That numbness frightened her more than anything she had faced before or since.

It had driven her to learn how to tend bar and move on from dancing.

How would Derrick feel about her if he found out? How

would Davis Morgan feel about one of his models being a stripper? Would she lose the job?

Had he ever been strapped for cash, living out of a car with a three-month-old baby? She'd done what she had to do. The tears came quick and hot.

She scrubbed at her cheeks with the cuff of her long-sleeved pullover, got up, and dragged the computer out from under the couch to search the web for jobs. She put in her application for a receptionist at a law firm that paid twenty-four thousand a year. If she did that job and was able to do the photo gig on the weekends...

After half an hour longer of searching, she rubbed her aching temples and went to make a cup of tea. Her cell phone rang and she answered.

"Are you available tomorrow at nine?" It was Angela at the photo studio.

"For how long? I'd have to leave to pick up my son before three."

"You should be done before then. If not, you can leave and pick him up and return to the shoot."

"Okay."

"Glad you can make it."

"Thanks for encouraging me to stick it out."

"You're welcome. I know you're between jobs. Any luck yet?"

"I've put in several applications all over town. I'm hopeful."

"I'll keep my fingers crossed."

"Thanks."

With the next photo gig lined up, her attention shifted back to Larry's check. She couldn't afford to do the noble thing and send the check back or tear it up. And he certainly couldn't expect to buy her silence.

If Larry's escapades came to light and the police came around to ask questions, she'd tell them exactly what he'd attempted to do to her, and what Jasmine told her he'd done, though that would be hearsay.

If only the women would bond together and go to the police.

The inactivity was driving her crazy. She went into the kitchen, got out a cake mix, and turned on the oven. Using eggs and oil she turned the cake mix into a crust for cookie bars, popped the pan into the oven, and set the timer. Then she blended cream cheese, powdered sugar, an egg, lemon juice, and vanilla. The timer went off, and she poured the sugar mixture over the crust.

A knock at the door had her rushing to slide the baking dish back into the oven.

She opened the door to Patsy and smiled.

"Cookie bars will be out of the oven in fifteen minutes."

"I think I smelled them baking through the wall." Though Patsy was in her late sixties and white streaked her temples, her trim figure would put a lot of younger women to shame. No one would ever guess she had a sweet tooth.

Ella laughed and urged her into the kitchen. She got out a mug to make Patsy tea.

Patsy hiked herself up on one of the barstools "So, did you tell Micah about losing your job?"

"No. I'll tell him this afternoon when we get back from picking him up, and now I can also tell him I have money coming in with the photo stuff. They called me again to come in tomorrow."

"That's great!"

"I got something in the mail today, too." She set the steaming mug down in front of Patsy, moved around the island to get the check and letter off the coffee table and handed it to her.

She got her own tea out of the microwave and took a seat on the stool next to Patsy.

"This is hush money."

"Yeah."

Patsy eyed her.

"I intend to spend every dime of it on rent, and if the cops come around, I'll spill my guts. I'm not making that asshole any promises."

"Good. You can look at this as hazard pay for the month you wasted at the bar."

"Exactly. And I filed for unemployment, too. Let him pay

while I look around for something better." Two something betters, if she intended to make their bills. It was unbelievable that, just to keep a roof over their heads and the lights on, it cost two thousand dollars a month. And she couldn't qualify for food stamps because her bills were three hundred higher than the minimum allowance for a family of two.

The photography thing seemed too much of a pipe dream to depend on for any length of time. It wasn't steady.

Patsy placed the letter and check together on the bar. The timer went off on the oven. Ella hopped down off the stool, turned off the timer and grabbed a potholder, setting the glass baking dish on a trivet to cool a few minutes.

"It still turns my stomach to have to accept the money," she admitted. "If I could have talked Jasmine into going with me to the police, or even talked to the others…I tried to call a couple of the dancers, but they never returned my calls."

"You can't help people who won't help themselves, Ella."

"I can't sit in judgement on them, either. I've walked in their shoes. When Micah was a baby, we lived in my car for three weeks until I found work and a place to live.

"I washed dishes in a Chinese restaurant with him strapped to my chest in a sling until I could find someone to watch him for me while I worked that job and another to make my rent and feed us."

"You couldn't go home?" Patsy asked.

"No. Trae's parents would have swooped in and taken Micah away from me. It's different there, Patsy. The church has tremendous influence. I'd have been looked on as less-than by my family, other church members, and the law. And my parents had already tried to force me to give him up for adoption."

"You never told me that."

"It was before he was born."

"You're a good mother, Ella. You always put him first."

"That's what a mother does. My mother put us first, while my father put the church above everything." It hadn't been about God, it had been about the church. Shouldn't she have come first?

The hurt was still there.

"And what about this guy who came over?"

Too surprised to cover her response, she eyed Patsy.

"Micah mentioned him when he came over to get the spelling book he left at my apartment yesterday."

"I'm still on the fence about Derrick. He saved me that night. I hid in the cab of the wrecker while he dealt with Larry." She told her the whole story about the repair money and the extra thousand.

Patsy's cynical expression was similar to her own, as was her comment, "This guy seems too good to be true."

"He was that night. And he seemed good with Micah at Chuck E. Cheese and here the other day."

"But?"

"I'm taking it slow." Was that what she called leaning into him and practically begging to be kissed? She still couldn't believe she'd done it. "He's coming over Sunday for a little while.

"Why don't you send Micah over to my house after you eat so you can have some alone time with this guy—if you feel comfortable enough with him."

That was the problem. When she was with him, she wanted to do exactly what she'd done last night, lean into him and be held. Wanted the response she'd gotten in return. She'd seen interest in his face that night in the garage, and she'd seen his desire yesterday. It had been so long since she'd been touched, wanted, or simply held.

It was better just to continue on the way they were and not take a chance. But there was something about Derrick...

She looked up to find Patsy watching her. "Why don't you come over and meet him on Sunday? He'll be here about three. He promised to play a video game with Micah before we eat."

"He isn't using Micah to get to you, is he?"

She'd given that a lot of thought. "I don't think so. Micah is the one who approaches him. He needs male attention. And Derrick is all male. About six two, pale blue eyes, strong jaw, muscular. He was in the Navy for a while." She explained about the welding classes.

"When does he have time to date?"

"Exactly."

"You couldn't just find some guy who works nine to five, huh?" Patsy teased.

"It seems easy and rich aren't in my dating vocabulary."

"Rich isn't all it's cracked up to be. My ex-husband had money, and the girlfriends to go along with it."

"I'm sorry, Patsy."

Patsy shrugged one shoulder. "I got a good settlement in the divorce, and he got one of the bimbos he was dating. She took him for everything he was worth and left him to file bankruptcy. What goes around comes around."

Patsy didn't sound bitter, only satisfied. Then hesitated briefly before she said, "Charlie wants me to marry him."

"Wow!" It took a moment for Ella to filter through her pleased surprise. The two had standing dates, and Ella knew he spent the night several times a week. "Congratulations."

"I wanted us to just live together. Who the hell cares if we live in sin at our age? But he wants to make it official."

Ella grinned at her tone. "So what are you going to do?"

"I'm going to marry him, Ella. He loves me, and he's rock-solid in more ways than our sex life."

Ella snickered at the pun.

Patsy's smile held an extra gleam of happiness. "I have to admit he's grown on me."

Her attempts to make light of her feelings only made them that more apparent.

Charlie had his own home, and of course she'd be moving out to live with him. The repercussions for her and Micah clattered through her thoughts. She'd be losing a neighbor, and a friend, and Micah would be losing a woman he looked on as a surrogate grandmother. Not losing, but the change in proximity and situation would be an adjustment.

She hugged Patsy and tried to kick her more selfish worries to the curb. Patsy cared about them both, and she deserved to be happy. Ella needed to show her support. "I'm happy for you. Let's celebrate with some of these cookie bars." She hopped down from her stool to slice the bars and dish them up.

She slid a plate across the bar to her. "So, when's the wedding?"

"We're just doing a very small ceremony at the courthouse. I'd like you and Micah to be there with my girls and their families."

"We'd love to be."

"I'll let you know when we've made the arrangements. This doesn't change how I feel about you and Micah, Ella. You'll always be welcome at Charlie's house, just like you are at my apartment."

"I appreciate that."

Patsy should settle happily into life with a husband. She and Charlie were both retired, and they'd probably travel and do other things together. Ella turned aside to get her own cookie bar and freshen both their teas. By the time she'd dealt with those simple, distracting things, she had her emotions under control and was able to smile normally.

"I'll pack up some of these for you to take home and share with Charlie."

"They're a temptation. Have you ever thought about working at a bakery?"

"No. But I'll look into that, too. I'm open to new things. The bartending thing doesn't seem to be working out."

They talked more about the wedding, and for a time Ella was able to engage in Patsy's excitement.

It was after Patsy left with cookies in a container that the full weight of the change coming hit her. Patsy was her entire—and only—support system.

What was she going to do?

CHAPTER 12

E LLA CONCENTRATED ON pouring the potting soil into three clay pots, then started the process of potting the flat of petunias one of the garden center workers brought her. A khaki-colored work apron protected her jeans and top while a pair of garden gloves covered her hands.

"I never thought potting petunias was sexy until now," the owner of the landscaping business said to Davis as he took the picture.

"Sexy can sell your product, Mr. Newman."

Newman was late thirties, stocky, with well-worn features battered from either a boxing career or some other earlier misadventure.

Ella ignored his comments and continued to ease in one of the tender plants while Davis took one shot after another.

"All the guys who see the ad will come here looking for her."

"And all their wives will come in looking for the plants she's potting," Davis said, his hazel eyes intent on her face for a moment from above the camera instead of through the lens. "We're through here, Ella. I'd like you to move on to the outdoor area."

She finished potting the last petunia, pulled off the gloves, and left them lying on the table to stroll through the aisles displaying gas grills, insect repellents, and lawn furniture, to the automatic doors leading to an outdoor area. Ella recognized Shelly from the last shoot and approached her.

"You'll be helping a customer out here find what he needs. Why don't you wander around until Mr. Morgan finishes inside? You may find something interesting to include in the shoot."

While Ella wandered the rows and rows of plants, a woman stopped beside her, her buggy heaped with peat moss and two big bags of top soil. "I'm looking for tulips and hyacinths."

"Those are perennials. Do you see where the big fountain has been set up over there?" Ella pointed to a tall display of blooming flowers in large pots. "The tables behind that display hold tulips, hyacinths, daffodils, irises, crocuses and primroses. Those are all bulb plants and will propagate and come up every year."

"Thank you."

"I wasn't aware you actually know something about gardening." Davis spoke from behind her.

She turned to face him. "My mother's a gardener." Or at least she was the last time she'd seen her. "She has flower beds all around their house. There's always something blooming spring and summer."

"Do they live here?" he asked.

"No. Salt Lake City, Utah."

"You could probably snag a job here if you wanted one," he said.

"I don't think I want all the men who see the ad looking for me here."

Davis shook his head. "I'm sorry about Mr. Stanley, the owner."

She shrugged. "As a bartender, you learn to let sexist comments roll off you. You seemed to handle him pretty well."

"I get more practice than I want to admit. Before we set up, I want to see if you can come out for coffee after the shoot. I have someone I want you to meet who'll be joining me. She's a fashion designer, and I think she'd be interested in using you for a marketing campaign."

Ella bit her lip. Was she interested in walking a runway? She'd done worse things to bring in money. She glanced at her watch. "I have to be at the school to pick up Micah before three."

"We need to get back to work if you're going to have time, then."

As she followed Davis to the restaurant where they were meeting the designer, she asked herself if she was doing the right thing. She was opening the door to a world she knew nothing about. Not really *opening* it, but cracking it open.

The spark of attraction she felt toward Davis when he shot her those smiles was just transference because he was subsidizing her income. She had a good thing going here...if she kept her distance.

And there was Derrick. The need in his eyes, the hope, tugged at her in a way Davis's smiles didn't.

She pulled in the parking lot and got out of the car, and Davis waited outside the front door of the shop until she joined him. He opened the door, and she slipped inside ahead of him. Light from the large windows at the front of the shop reflected off the cream-colored walls, and a large mural stretched behind the serving space and seemed to bring some of the landscaping from outside into the room.

"What would you like Ella?" Davis asked.

"A caramel latte, thanks."

"You can go over to that table against the wall and join Brigitte while I wait for our order." He motioned toward a dark-haired woman sitting alone, drinking a cup of tea. "Go ahead and introduce yourself. I texted her you'd be coming with me."

The walk over gave Ella a few seconds to study the woman. Thirty, maybe a little older, slender, gorgeous, and she studied Ella in much the way Ella was eyeing her. Was she a model?

Ella stopped behind one of the chairs at the table. "Hi, Ella Bailey."

"Hello. Brigitte Simpson. You're as gorgeous as Davis says you are."

Ella flinched from the compliment and looked away.

"With the right makeup and a little styling gel, I can turn you into a modeling sensation."

"Why would you want to do that?" she asked, seriously confused. Why anyone would want to be in the limelight with every aspect of their lives put under a microscope was beyond her.

Brigitte seemed taken aback for a moment. "Because you can help me sell my latest fashion collection, and you can make a lot of money when you become the latest hot model in the fashion world."

Dear God. "I just want to make enough money to pay my bills and keep my son safe and happy."

Brigitte flipped that comment away with a hand and a smile. "We all have to make sacrifices to get what we want."

She was used to sacrifice. It was trust she had an issue with. This woman would use her to get what she needed, just like everyone else. How deep in the muck would she leave her afterwards?

But she couldn't do it unless Ella allowed her to. She'd listen to their proposition and see where this went.

Davis joined them, set the latte in front of her, and pulled his chair out. "Have a seat, Ella."

She pulled the chair out, sat down and pulled a to-go cup he set in front of her closer. She sipped the drink and found it delicious. "Thanks."

His attention shifted from Ella to Brigitte, as though sensing the tension between them. "So."

Ella bit her lip to keep from smiling. She turned her attention back to Brigitte. "I'm not a professional model. Since I've been looking in the mirror at the same face and body for the last twenty-five years, I'm not all that impressed with my looks, either. I trained as a dancer, and looks don't really play into that. You become a character and use your body to project emotion and tell the story. I can do that if that's what you need, but I'm not interested in walking a runway. I thought this was simply a marketing campaign you wanted, just photos."

Brigitte leaned forward and rested her arms on the table. "Once the photos and commercials come out, Ella, people will want to see you on the runway, too."

"Commercials?" She shot Davis a glance. "You didn't say anything about commercials. And runway work takes you all over the globe. I have a seven-year-old who needs me. I'm not leaving him to globe-trot."

Brigitte repositioned her cup and saucer. "There aren't any grandparents who'd like to have him for a weekend? No father in the picture?"

"No. His father died before he was born." Neither of these people needed to know anything about her family situation. "And there's no close family. Micah and I are alone."

"I'm sorry."

She was surprised by the woman's sympathy and glanced away.

Davis leaned back in his chair and rested his cup on his thigh. "She's a natural in front of the camera, Brigitte. And she has that long, lean line that will set off your designs and sell them. A little mystique about the woman wearing them will build interest. And she has a moderate speaking voice that will sound good on tape. When you have a show on the weekend, she could take Micah with her to walk the runway."

"Are you her agent now?" Brigitte asked.

Agent? Am I supposed to have an agent now? Not happening.

"No, but I know her situation, and I'm the one who'll be looking through the lens when we do the magazine spreads, and Silas will work with me on the commercials."

"I'm not used to bending over backwards to ensure an employee isn't inconvenienced, Davis."

Ella ignored the small twinge of disappointment and focused on the larger sweep of relief that followed. She looked at her watch. She had to leave if she wanted to make it in time to pick up Micah and go on to the job interview. "You don't have to bend over backwards for me, Ms. Simpson. You have to do what's best for your company, and I understand that. Just like I have to do what's best for my son. He has to come first."

She rose. "Thanks for the latte, Davis. Thank you for thinking of me for this." She extended her hand to Brigitte. "It was interesting meeting you. Good luck with your new clothing line."

Brigitte's brows rose. "You're leaving?"

"Yes. I have to pick up Micah, and I have another job interview at four."

"Another design company?"

Ella laughed. "No. A bakery. I'm going from bartending to becoming a pastry chef if I get the job."

As she pulled out into traffic, she decided if the money had even been close to what Davis paid her, it would have been great, but the disruptions of their life would have been a hassle. And what about the cost of travel? Would she have been responsible for all that?

Micah would have gotten a kick out of traveling some. They'd gone to Disneyland once when he was younger, and he loved it. He'd only asked "are we there yet" a hundred times along the way.

She'd find a safe, dependable nine-to-five job, and she and Micah would be fine.

CHAPTER 13

THIS WAS CRAZY. He'd never been nervous around women before. And he had opportunities to talk to women at the brig, but they'd been guards, not girlfriends.

He didn't know how to romance a woman. He'd thought he might have forgotten how to kiss one until they shared that heated lip-lock last time.

This had to get easier.

The scent of spices and tomato made his stomach growl. He'd slept through breakfast, and he hadn't had time to eat a snack after mowing Mama's lawn. Hopefully Ella and Micah hadn't eaten either. As soon as he tapped on their apartment door, it opened and Micah stood there.

"Hey," he offered his hand for a fist bump.

"Hey." Derrick returned the gesture. "Are you hungry?"

"Yeah."

"It's a constant condition," Ella teased as she joined them at the door. "Come on in." She tilted her head. "That isn't a restaurant bag."

She'd trimmed her hair, and it framed her face like the spiky petals of some exotic flower. Her gold-hued eyes look just as exotic. Every time he saw her, he experienced the same one-two punch, first to his heart, then lower.

"Why have takeout when you can have the real deal?" he said.

"My landlady cooked the meal while I mowed her little patch of grass and edged the sidewalk. I did help a little. I stuffed the tacos and wrapped them. Even if they don't look restaurant-perfect, they'll taste like spicy ambrosia. There's dirty rice to go with the tacos and sopapillas with honey for dessert."

Though it was early, they dished up the food while it was hot.

After the first bite, Ella made a sound somewhere between a hum and a groan that went straight to his groin.

She chewed, then swallowed. "This is great. Your landlady can really cook."

"Yeah, she can. When I do extra work around her house, she cooks for me."

"She sounds sweet."

He laughed. "Sweet isn't exactly how I'd describe Mama Fernandez. She's tough. She raised five children alone, then raised two of her grandchildren. She's no-nonsense, but loving with it. She treats me like I'm one of her kids."

He'd been straight with Mama about his prison record, and she hadn't batted an eyelash. Would Ella be as understanding?

Probably not. She didn't know him well enough yet. And she had Micah to consider.

"I'd like to meet her," Ella commented. "We have a neighbor who sort of took us under her wing, too. But Patsy will be getting married in a few weeks and moving." Her eyes strayed to Micah.

The kid hadn't said much since they filled their plates. His mouth curved down in an unhappy pout and, though he'd said he was hungry, and while he was fiddling with his food, he wasn't eating much.

"I know how awful it is to miss people when they move away, Micah." The crushing desolation of having his team wrenched away had nearly crippled him. And knowing it was his own fault... "When I was in the Navy, I had good buddies transfer in, and we'd get to hang out, then they'd deploy...that means they'd go to another country...or transfer to another duty station. And because I was working all the time and deploying a lot, I didn't get to see them, even when they were stateside.

"But Patsy will still be close by, where you can go see her or even call her on the phone. I couldn't do that because my buddies were in places where they didn't have a phone, or they weren't allowed to contact anyone."

He turned to find Ella watching him. "Where will she be moving?"

"Coronado."

"That's about thirty minutes away, Micah. No distance at all. And the phone's only a few feet away."

"When Mom goes back to work, I won't have anyone to stay with." There were equal parts worry and sadness in his tone.

"You know your mom isn't going to leave you here to hang out alone. She always does right by you, doesn't she?"

"Yeah."

"So what are you worrying about?"

A rueful grin spread across his face. "Can I have another taco?"

"Sure."

The phone rang and Ella answered it. She pressed a hand over the receiver of her cellphone. "Patsy says that after you finish eating, she'd like you to come over for a little while. She's rented a movie and has a surprise for you."

"I was going to play a video game with Derrick."

"We can do that later. You can't pass up a movie and a surprise." Besides, while Micah was busy, a little alone time with Ella sounded like a fantastic idea.

Micah grinned. "Tell her I'm almost finished and I'll be over in a minute."

Micah's appetite rebounded and, two tacos later, he wiggled out of his chair. "May I be excused?"

His manners were a credit to Ella's influence.

"You want to take some sopapillas to share with her?" Derrick asked.

"She likes cookies," Ella said, the inflection of her voice more than a hint.

"Sure."

Ella rose, "I'll get something to put them in."

After Micah left the apartment seemed too quiet, and Derrick scrambled for something to say but Ella beat him to it.

"Thanks for what you said to Micah. I've tried to comfort him, and I've told him the same things, but sometimes just having some backup helps."

"Glad to provide backup. How did your photo session go Friday?"

"It went well. And I had two job interviews afterward. One was a bust, but I'm hopeful about the other."

"That's good. What kind of interview?"

"A bakery."

He grinned. "You bake?"

She actually blushed. "It was Patsy's idea. And yes, I bake. I used to do birthday cakes to make extra money."

"What are you embarrassed about? It's an art form."

"I don't know. It just seems weird. After being a bartender for so long, it just seems…"

"Like switching from rocky road ice cream to vanilla."

She laughed. "Yeah."

"I'm sure you'll be able to deal with people jonesing to feed their sweet tooth just as easily as you did unreasonable drunks."

"When you put it that way, I'm looking forward to it."

"You could do Patsy's wedding cake," he suggested.

"Yeah, I could. I'll have to ask her about that."

"When's the wedding?"

"Three weeks. They're trying to get all their children and grandchildren together for a meet and greet before they tie the knot. All of Patsy's kids have met him, and all his have met her, but they haven't really met each other."

"Sounds like the thing to do. What about you and Micah?"

"We're invited to the wedding. Not the meet and greet. I think they're both expecting some emotional family stuff." She rose to clear the table.

Derrick grabbed a couple of the plates and his water glass.

"How did your welding project go?" she asked.

"I finished up earlier today. Roger, my boss, will want to try it out to see if there are any adjustments that need to be made, but I think it's good to go."

"How can you go for days without sleep, Derrick?" She started rinsing the dishes and putting them in the dishwasher.

"I catnap at work on the office couch between tow jobs. And this Friday and Saturday thing was a one-time deal. I slept for a solid seven before I mowed the lawn today, so I'm good." He leaned back against the kitchen counter.

She shook her head. "I don't know how you do it." Her amber bright eyes held a hint of concern.

"I look at it as a mission I have to accomplish."

"Your stint in the Navy seems to have stuck with you."

His stomach knotted. "Yeah, it did."

"Why didn't you stay in?" She leaned back against the counter next to him.

His mouth dried and his breathing grew unsteady. He'd known she'd ask eventually. "I was in the Navy for six years. Four of them, I was a Navy SEAL, and I did five deployments during that time. With everything I did and saw during those deployments, added to the emotional baggage of a really shitty childhood, I developed severe PTSD."

He wasn't making excuses for what he'd done by acknowledging the factors that helped trigger some of his actions. It had taken him years to accept that. But he still felt guilty, and unworthy of forgiveness.

Ella turned and put her arms around him. For a moment he clung to her until the spike of emotion eased back. "I was a different man back then. You wouldn't have liked that man. I didn't like him much either."

She rested her hands on his chest and smoothed the collar on his knit pullover. "I like the one you are right now just fine."

He might have been able to tell her the whole story, but the trust he read in her face stole the words. He couldn't take the chance. Not yet.

"You can tell me when you're ready, Derrick."

She was too much of a temptation, and he refused to make a move when her sympathy might urge her down a path she'd later regret. "How about a drive to the beach while the game shark is hanging with Patsy?"

She smiled. "Thanks, I'd love to. I'll text Patsy and tell her we're going."

THE WIND OFF the ocean was brisk, and Ella was glad she'd brought along a jacket. In his short-sleeved shirt and khakis, Derrick seemed comfortable enough. His bare feet were wide, and looked as strong as the rest of him. His shoes dangled from his fingertips as they trudged through the powdery sand to the water-slicked stretch packed down from the tide, where they strolled toward the Hotel del Coronado.

"How long have you lifted weights?" she asked.

"Since middle school. I run five miles three times a week, too."

"I don't run five miles a year, but I still do my dance exercises three or four times a week, just to keep limber."

"Why haven't you pursued your dancing again?"

She was silent for a long moment. Would he think less of her if he knew she'd danced next to nude for money? "There's never been enough money or enough time. I'd have to train again, and you have to be obsessed with it above and beyond everything else to be good. I can't do that to Micah."

"We could go dancing some night. I have two left feet, but I'm willing to give it a shot."

"You played football. I bet you have fancy footwork and some moves."

He laughed. "I haven't played in a long time. I think my moves may be pretty rusty. I did date a dancer once, when I was a newbie on the teams, many years ago."

"Really?"

"A ballet dancer. She was a member of the California Ballet."

"And?"

"She was into SEALs and I was into pretty girls. We didn't have anything else in common, so it was a very short-lived relationship. I was a bit of an arrogant shit back then."

She laughed at his self-deprecation. He grinned back at her.

"You were young, in a profession that was dangerous and heroic, and a hunk."

He grinned again. "I'm a shadow of my former self."

"Do you think you're as driven now as you were then?"

"Yes. But I try to direct my drive toward something more creative now. That's one of the things we have in common. We both want to work toward something better." He bent to kiss the tip of her nose. "You look cold."

He threw an arm around her shoulders, cuddled her against his side to share his warmth and turned back toward the car.

She looped an arm around his waist and leaned closer, feeling fragile against his larger bulk. The clean scent of soap and him wafted to her, and his scruff emphasized the structure of his jawline. A heated wave of need washed through her, making her stumble, and the careful pressure of his hand increased, steadying her.

To cover for her clumsiness she said, "You know that severance package you mentioned to me that first night?"

"Yeah."

"It arrived in the mail yesterday."

"No shit?"

His surprise had her smiling. "A check for five thousand dollars."

"Is that enough for the harassment ol' Larry heaped on you?"

Her shudder had nothing to do with the breeze coming off the ocean. "No. But it will pay my rent for a few months until I find another job."

"Good."

"Your ride is looking better," she commented when they reached the car.

"I sprayed the primer a couple of days ago. Any suggestions

for what color I should paint her?"

"Her?"

"All cars and ships are female."

She studied the vehicle. He was ruggedly handsome, but for all that, he wasn't flashy. Wanted no part of flashy. Why was that?

"What about metallic gray? Not mist, but the kind of gray you find in shadows. It'll look like a muscle car."

"Not red?"

"If it was going to be my car, I'd go for red. But it's going to be yours, and the interior is already black."

He raised a brow.

"What were you going with?"

"I thought I'd make the body silver and the top black."

Maybe she'd been wrong.

She just couldn't get a handle on him. He was educated, smart, physically fit, a vet. The PTSD he'd mentioned had derailed his life and caused him to start over. but there had to be more to the story. A divorce, an accident. Something worse? She hoped not.

She could tell he was into her from the way he rested his hand against the small of her back when they walked together, and from the way his attention settled on her with that heated look of intent interest. But he was taking his time about making any moves.

"Will you show me where you live? I want to meet your land-lady."

He hesitated for a moment. "Okay." He opened the car door for her. She was beginning to enjoy that.

CHAPTER 14

"**H**OW ABOUT SOME hot chocolate or a cup of coffee before we head to my place? Neither of us ate any dessert."

"Okay."

He took her to Clayton's Coffee Shop on Orange Avenue. It was like walking back in time to the fifties, with the red Naugahyde booths and the chrome-edged, horseshoe-shaped counter surrounded by barstools. Glass-domed cake stands sat on the counter at intervals, and the small Seeburg Juke boxes offered song selections from a different era. Too bad they didn't work

After a short wait for a seat, they bellied up to the counter and ordered hot chocolate, the good stuff made with cocoa and real milk with whipped cream dolloped on top.

"Derrick Armstrong?"

The voice sounded familiar. He swallowed the spoonful of whipped cream he'd just spooned into his mouth and turned to look over his shoulder. Shock galvanized his heart until it was hammering in his throat and his face felt stiff. He found himself on his feet without even thinking about it. "Captain Jackson, sir."

"It's Admiral Jackson now."

He couldn't have known with him dressed in his civvies. "Admiral, sir." The habits of those seven years before prison were impossible to break.

"I heard you were back."

From who? The words were there on the tip of his tongue, but then he remembered speaking with Hawk. "For the past seven months."

"What are you doing now?"

The Admiral's amiable tone threw him. "I'm driving a wrecker and taking welding classes. I want to do commercial welding."

"Sounds like a challenging field. I'm glad to see you're putting some of your training to good use."

"That's the plan, sir."

"I'd like to speak to you outside for a moment." He turned toward Ella. "You okay with that, miss?"

Her curious gaze traveled from him to Jackson and back again. "Sure."

Derrick's stomach knotted. To refuse to accompany him outside would be a shit-bird move. He had to go. But with every step he braced himself harder. He couldn't allow Jackson to push him over the edge, and he'd try. It would suit the Admiral just fine to see the police drag him back to jail.

"Does she know?" Jackson asked.

Damn him. He just had to hit him right where he didn't want to go. "Some of it. Not everything. Not yet."

"You'd be doing her a favor if you walk away from her before she gets to know you too well."

The blow hurt, and he swallowed against his rising temper. After everything that happened, even prison, opening himself to change had shaved away some of the calluses his father's abuse had formed. But prison life had given him more. It would take more than that to get him angry enough to fight. "I'm not the man I was seven years ago. I've been in counseling, and worked hard to change."

"You're still a convict and a liability."

"I'm trying not to be one, Admiral Jackson. I'm learning a new skill, I work every day, and I'm trying to rebuild my life. You may not feel I deserve it, but the law says I paid my dues and I deserve at least to live."

"You'll fuck up her life by tying yourself to her, or anyone else. Your conviction will not only be a stain on your life, it will spread to hers."

The words dug a hole right through him. "I paid my debt, and I deserve to have someone in my life."

"Does she know you beat women?"

He flinched from the accusation. "You don't know anything about what I was going through back then. All you wanted was a machine to carry out the missions. And for a while I was one. I was a good SEAL until I couldn't be one any longer. Until the missions became my nightmares." He saw he'd hit a mark with his honesty. "I was a liability because I had PTSD, and Hawk tried to help me. But we're told to suck it up, follow orders, complete the mission. No matter what it costs us."

Jackson leaned forward, his face so close the man's breath fanned his face. "Stay away from Coronado. If any of my guys run into you and decide to go postal, it will be your fault, not theirs "

Jackson shoved past him and stalked down the street.

The urge to go after him was so strong it left Derrick shaking. He leaned back against the building and took deep breaths to ease the tightness in his chest, his throat. The blend of pain and rage knotted inside him so tightly it nearly doubled him over.

He had to pull it together. He had to face Ella. He sucked in one breath, then another.

His military record would never change. His conviction would stand for the rest of his life. Wasn't that punishment enough?

He couldn't go on alone. It had been nearly a decade since he'd felt a woman's touch. Been kissed, been caressed. He looked at Ella and he saw all of it was possible.

What would be the point of going on if he didn't believe he could build a life? Hope of doing so was all he had.

He walked back into the coffee shop. Ella looked over her shoulder and glanced toward the door.

"Are you all right?" she asked.

"Yeah." He forced himself to sit on the stool and drink his now-cold hot chocolate. The whipped cream had melted, but he spooned it off the top and ate it.

He took out his wallet, removed some bills, and tossed them on the counter. "Finished?"

"Yes."

"I'll take you to Mama Fernandez's and show you my apartment."

"Okay." She slid off the stool.

He placed a hand against the small of her back to urge her out of the restaurant.

"Who was that man, Derrick?"

"He was my Captain seven years ago."

"What did he say to you?"

What every man in his team was going to say. That he was a traitor to them, a waste. That he should have died like Brett almost did. Not a one of them would wish him well. "When I left the teams, it wasn't under the best of circumstances. He just cleared the air."

"It was seven years ago. Isn't there a statute of limitations for how long someone can hold a mistake against you?"

"In a perfect world there would be, Ella, but we don't live in a perfect world." He stopped next to the car. "In a perfect world, my father wouldn't have beaten me every chance he got and turned me into an angry asshole just like him."

"You're not an angry asshole, Derrick."

"I was, Ella. Sometimes I still am. I fight it every day. Otherwise I'd end up right back where I was seven years ago. Blinded by rage to everything but what *I* needed." He thumped his chest at the word I. "I had to control my world, no matter the cost, even if I hurt people to do it. And I did hurt people."

"But you got help. You had to get help to be so very different now."

"Yeah, I got help." Because he had no choice. And now he couldn't do without it. "But it doesn't change the things I did. And the guys in my team depended on me, trusted me. I betrayed them."

"What did you do, Derrick?"

He leaned back against the car and for a moment tracked the

other vehicles as they drove by. He was about to lose her before he ever had a chance with her.

"We'd done five deployments with only short spaces between. I saw things I hope never to see again. Did things I'm not ashamed of, but I'd give anything to forget. And it all caught up with me.

"I was having physical issues. My blood pressure was through the roof, and the meds they had me on weren't working. I had insomnia and couldn't sleep much more than ten minutes at a time. Who could, with assholes outside the camp shooting RPGs over the fence in the middle of the night, every night? But that wasn't what was keeping me up.

"I had dreams about some of the shit that went down. Stuff I couldn't talk about with anyone outside the team. And we didn't talk. We just locked it up and left it to sort itself out. But that didn't exactly work when it was rolling around in my brain every time I closed my eyes."

"We were sent home when Hawk, my CO, and Brett, one of my teammates, were hurt during a mission." *Because of me. Because of me.* "I thought everything that went down could be left in Iraq, but it wasn't. I still had insomnia, and I still had the nightmares, the night sweats, and I couldn't pull it together at home any better than I had in Iraq." The guilt over what he'd done had eaten at him like acid. "I was irritable, angry, paranoid, and I became dangerous.

"I thought my teammates were turning on me, talking to my CO about me. I thought I was going to lose my position on the team. I lost my girlfriend, I had a meltdown, and I ended up getting arrested. And I was dishonorably discharged."

"What did the Admiral say to you, Derrick?"

Surprised by the question, he focused on her face. She looked pale, but calm. "He told me to stay away from Coronado. He didn't want me running into any of my teammates and causing an issue."

"Admiral Jackson is full of shit."

A single bark of laughter escaped him.

"Why is what he says important to you?"

"It isn't, Ella. He didn't say anything I haven't said to myself. I did my job and gave them everything I had. Then when I started having issues, I was supposed to be tough. All that shit was supposed to roll off of me. But it didn't."

"Because you're not Superman. You're human. I can't imagine what you may have seen or done, but everyone has their breaking point. Even Admiral Jackson."

She was being understanding, but if she knew the whole story…

He opened the car door for her and waited for her to get in. "We'll go by my apartment and see if Mama Fernandez is home."

CHAPTER 15

T HE SMALL SPANISH-STYLE cottage baked beneath the glaring
afternoon sun on a small lot with no trees. The wire fence
surrounding the property had seen better days, but the cream-
colored stucco covering the exterior of the house had been
patched, and the steps had received a fresh coat of gray paint
recently, as had the porch.

Ella admired a trellis heavy with purple clematis at one corner
of the porch, and the flowers were alive with bees popping in and
out, their happy hum audible from the sidewalk.

"Mama's car isn't here. She must have gone to visit one of her
grandkids or gone shopping."

"It looks like you do more than mow the grass, Derrick."

"I help out when repairs need to be made."

With a hand resting against her waist, Derrick guided her
across the driveway to the one-car detached garage. Stairs ran up
one side of the structure to a door. "I'm lucky she let me have the
apartment. This was the fifteenth place I tried."

She remembered the same struggles finding an apartment she
could afford.

He flipped back the screen door, unlocked the wooden door
and opened it. He stood back for her to enter.

"I don't know how you accomplish everything you do."

"My job is more flexible than most. I worked on the junker at night in between wrecker calls. It barely ran at first."

"It runs fine now." She couldn't help herself. He was working so hard to get back on his feet. And she'd been there herself. Alone. Broke. There was more he wasn't telling her.

"I've been overhauling everything, one system at a time, for the past four months. Next paycheck I'll have enough to paint it."

"And it almost looks like a regular car now." Ignoring the sofa bed, except to notice it was made with military precision, she scanned the one-room apartment. The small kitchenette opposite the door had cream cabinets over the ugliest orange countertops she'd ever seen, but there were no dirty dishes piled up, and the room smelled faintly of a pine-scented cleaner.

She admired the woven rug on the floor.

"That was here when I got here. It's probably worth more than anything else in the room."

"It's a work of art. And it matches the countertops."

He laughed. "Mama said her grandson Julio lived here while he finished school. Now he's married and they have their own place."

She sat down on the foot of the bed and was surprised at the firmness of the mattress. "I sleep on a sofa bed, too. Micah has the bedroom. It's easier to keep the clutter down to a minimum."

Derrick took a seat in one of the chairs and leaned forward to brace his elbows on his knees. "It's a boy thing. Be grateful he's a city dweller. You won't have to worry about opening a drawer and having a snake or salamander pop out."

The thought triggered a smile. "I have four brothers, two older and two younger. They all did things like that. Is that how you were as a boy, bringing home salamanders and making volcanos with your mom?"

"Yeah. When I wasn't playing sports or getting up to stuff I shouldn't have." He looped his hands together. "Later... I loved skydiving. Loved leaping into space, then freefalling. When you're up there, everything on the ground seems unimportant."

"Except that the ground is rising up to meet you."

He grinned. "That's what the chute is for."

He was a physical man, but he wasn't being physical with her. The careful way he touched her, as though he thought over each move before making it, made her wonder and want to ask. But would he tell her? "Where are your weights?

"They're downstairs in the garage."

She patted the bed next to her. "Come sit with me, Derrick."

His expression turned serious. "I didn't bring you here to rush things."

"I know." But she needed to feel his hands on her. To know he wanted her as much as she thought he did. They both needed someone to hold on to. She needed him. Because despite everything he'd told her, she trusted him not to hurt her. "I don't invite men to my apartment and sleep with them with Micah in the other room. We've been there nearly two years, and it's been a long time for me. I want you to touch me. I want to touch you."

As though a leash had been released, he was out of the chair in one swift, smooth move. He tugged the knit shirt over his head, laying the broad, muscular width of his chest bare before he ever reached her.

And she caught her breath. He was all lean muscle and smooth skin, his body sculpted by hard work and lifting weights. Dear God, he was magnificent. He dropped the shirt on the corner of the bed.

He cupped her face, and his mouth captured hers with such focused, hungry need it stole her breath. Hot arousal shimmed through her to settle in the heart of her sex. She'd known this was going to happen, and despite the secrets, the uncertainty, still hoped it would. She groaned and looped her arms around his neck.

He cupped her ass, lifting her with ease. Her legs went around his waist, and he rested a knee on the bed and brought them to the middle of the mattress. When his body covered hers, they were center to center.

Ella ran her hands down his chest to the button on his khakis while he was busy getting the buttons on her blouse unfastened. His lips settled on her neck, her collarbone, then her breast, the warm, wet heat seeping through the thin lace of her bra. He eased the strap down, baring the nipple to the suction of his mouth, and her hips rose against him in a quest to be filled as her core ached and throbbed with need.

When he pressed a long, slow, lingering row of kisses down the center of her stomach to the top of her jeans, she groaned aloud and clutched at him.

Derrick drew back, unfastened her jeans and peeled them and her panties away, his mouth following the path of the fabric as he kissed the inside of thighs and his tongue tasted her.

"Tell me you have a condom," she gasped as he tugged her jeans free of her feet.

His cheeks were flushed and his eyes had never looked bluer.

"Emergency stash." He jerked his wallet out of his back pocket and flipped it open, dug into it and pulled one free. He tossed his wallet on a chair and shucked the rest of his clothes while she did the same.

He was so aroused. She tore the condom package open and slipped it over him. As she cupped him in her hand, he grew larger, tighter.

"I'll make it up to you later, but I have to be inside you right now, Ella."

Make up for what? Her body hummed with need. She ran her hands over his chest, his back, his hips, a fierce need to touch, to hold on, tumbling through her.

He said her name like a prayer as he thrust deep. The climax hit her, and she rode the pleasure even as he started to move. The sweet, sharp heat began to build again, her body gripping and releasing him. At the first throb of Derrick's release, another wave of sensation ripped through her, and she gripped his ass, holding him still as he pulsed inside her.

HE FELT HOLLOWED out, as though seven years of need had poured out of him in minutes. Every muscle felt warm and pliant.

And the way Ella caressed the back of his neck was close to heaven. But he was too heavy for her. He reluctantly rolled onto his back.

Small-boned and reed-thin, she looked fragile when dressed, but undressed he recognized the muscle tone she worked so diligently to maintain. Her breasts were firm and high, more generous than he was expecting on a frame so trim. Her pale pink nipples beckoned him. He wanted to taste them again, nuzzle them and just lie there for a year or more. Her large, black-lashed eyes settled on his face, tawny bright.

"You may be the most gorgeous woman I've ever seen."

"Don't say that." She touched his lips.

"Why not?"

"It's embarrassing."

Surprised, he propped himself up on an elbow.

She raised a hand to touch his shoulder, and her fingers traced the muscle there. God, it felt so freaking fantastic to be touched.

"I met with a woman who wanted me to do a marketing campaign for her new clothing line. She said with a little makeup and some hair gel she could make me the next hot modeling sensation."

She certainly had what it took to carve out a career with her looks. And so unaware of it. "You may want to be a little wary of people promising you the moon, Ella. They usually have an ulterior motive."

She laughed. "I know. And there are thousands of beautiful women out there who want the brass ring and the craziness that goes with it. I'd have to travel all over the country, maybe overseas, too. I won't leave Micah, and I couldn't expect to drag him around with me. And worse, I'd be in the public eye."

He paused to think about her flying off to leave him behind and felt immediate stirrings of uneasiness. They hadn't known each other long, but he already felt a connection to her and her son.

"It would be a good way to thumb your nose at all the people who've left you behind." Like her family. "And all the people like

Larry, who've tried to take advantage of you." The kind of money she could make could change her life and Micah's. He couldn't compete with that.

"I want stability, not craziness."

He couldn't offer her that any more than the people who were promising her the moon. He never knew when something might happen to turn everything to shit for him. And shit had a way of spreading.

But he was trying. Surely that had to count for something.

"I used to strip for a living, Derrick. Every man who saw me on the stage would be crawling out of the woodwork to out me and tear me down. I couldn't handle it."

He met her anxious gaze with a level one. "We all do what we have to do to survive, Ella. I'm going to say this…not to brush your concerns off as if they're not important, or to piss you off, but because I'm a man and I can offer you a male perspective."

"Yes."

"The majority of them weren't looking at your face. Chances are they won't remember you."

She laughed. "God, I hope not."

"Everyone has a past. Like you said to me, there should be a statute of limitations for the length of time you pay for it. You can't let this one thing hold you back." He needed to believe in that himself. He climbed out of bed to go deal with the condom.

When he came back out of the bathroom, she'd borrowed his shirt to cover up, and now in front of his bookcase was studying the titles.

"Julio left most of those, though I've read almost all of them. And the engineering and welding texts are mine."

"What was your degree in college?" she asked over her shoulder. He placed a condom on the end table, then stretched back out on the bed. He adjusted the pillows behind him and tugged the sheet over his lap, covering one hip and thigh.

The flare of heated interest he saw in her eyes had him hard as a rock again. "Applied mathematics."

"You could apply for any number of jobs in a wide range of

fields with that."

With his record, even if he got his master's or doctorate, he'd never be allowed to work on government projects. And who would trust him to work on anything to do with public safety?

He'd never survive being indoors all day long, not after being in prison. "Being trapped inside an office all day isn't for me, Ella. I got the math degree because I found numbers easy to understand. There's a certain consistency with them, and I was interested in their application to so many different things, but I need to be outdoors doing something. That's why I took the wrecker job and am learning to weld. I may go into underwater welding, too, since I'm scuba certified." He'd been quick to get that done as soon as he hit San Diego.

She wandered back to the bed, drawing his eyes to the way the hem of his shirt brushed the tops of her well-toned thighs. Jesus, how he wanted her! He'd already hardened again to full readiness.

Why was she here in this bed with him? Why wasn't she out with some other guy who could give her more?

"I haven't been with anyone in a long time."

"Why?"

"I've been busy making changes in my life, taking inventory. When you're in the SEALs, you expect everyone to make all the sacrifices because you're driven by your job, and you kind of expect everyone to understand that and accept it. It's easy to be selfish. I've been a selfish shit in the past, and I didn't think it was fair to bring anyone into my life until I could give as much as I would take."

Ella sauntered back to the bed and braced a knee on the foot of the bed to crawl up and stretch out beside him.

She rested her head on the pillow beside his. He turned to look into her face. She ran her fingers over his cheek and jaw.

"We'll have to leave soon. I can't leave Micah for long. Patsy may have plans." She wiggled close and rested her head on his shoulder.

She ran her palm over his chest, pausing to toy with each nipple. She nibbled his earlobe, and his erection swelled to the point it was almost painful.

He turned to tuck her beneath him. "I promise to be quick but thorough."

Ella grinned. "I've noticed how thorough you are. You're great with details."

He laughed.

Then he took his time kissing her, building the heat with the pressure of their lips, the advance and retreat of their tongues. The steady rising heat of his need blended with hers as he caressed her breasts and teased her by running his fingertips around in circles over the flat plane of her stomach. He found her with his fingers, tempting her with his touch, until her legs parted wide and he delved into the moist heat with one finger, then two.

She was so tight and wet, for a moment he had to fight back his own release. He found the rhythm that triggered her response and more, the spot that had her writhing. He kissed her, matching the movement of his tongue to the friction of his fingers. Her hands gripped his shoulders as though she might fall, and then she did. Her breathing came in raged gasps, the contractions of her release making her hips piston, and her body trembled. He waited for it to pass before he eased his fingers away.

She rose up, pushed him back to straddle him. "Condom," she reminded him and he gestured to the end table where he'd placed it.

She tore open the package and sheathed him, leaning over him to place an open-mouthed kiss in the center of his chest, then glued her mouth to his at the same time she sank over him, burying him deep into the warmth of her body.

He hummed at the pleasure of it, so aroused he knew he wouldn't last long this time either.

Her breath blew warm against his throat as she traced his ear with her tongue. He shivered in response. He cupped her breasts as she straightened and started a steady, quick rhythm that drove him to the brink.

Her breathing went ragged and her rhythm choppy, so he echoed her downward thrusts with more force, deepening their connection, his own release building to the point it was the only thing he could think about. When she said his name, her voice wispy and breathless, it threw him over the edge.

When his vision cleared, her smile hit him like a punch.

"You are not a selfish shit. I think I could get spoiled to this."

He laughed. "Me too." He sat up to hold her close while she slid her arms around him and rested her cheek against his.

Sometimes you just had to accept what was offered without question. He was okay with that. For now.

CHAPTER 16

MICAH LAY IN sprawled abandon, taking up the entire twin bed. His Wolverine sleep pants were getting snug and a little short, so she needed to buy him some new ones. And his dark hair, the color of hers, feathered across his forehead and needed to be trimmed over his ears and along the neckline. She'd take care of that tomorrow after dinner.

Ella eased the bunched blanket at the foot of the bed over him and removed the crumpled comic book he'd been reading when he drifted off. He'd been thrilled when Derrick stayed to play a video game with him before going to work. The revving of the motorcycle engines would have gotten on her nerves if their male banter hadn't been so funny. She decided guys were born with a talent for creative insults.

She set Micah's book bag in the chair at his small desk so he wouldn't trip over it if he got up in the night to pee, turned off the light, and eased out of the room.

With the closing of the door, her thoughts leaped back to the afternoon in Derrick's apartment. He'd been an attentive lover, generous and careful. She'd felt energized and relaxed at the same time afterwards.

Those feelings still lingered, but after he left, the questions she wanted to ask him still lingered. The pain she read on Derrick's face as he told her about his past triggered an ache in her chest.

His history of PTSD seemed a distant thing. He seemed focused, driven, and well-adjusted now. Whatever he wasn't telling her didn't involve drugs, she'd bet money on that. He took good care of his body, she hadn't seen him drink anything but iced tea and hot chocolate, and he didn't have the look of a drinker. So booze wasn't involved either.

She could speculate all night and allow her concerns to ruin the afterglow, or she could wait for him to tell her everything when he was ready.

Her cell phone rang, leaned forward to pick up the phone, and, recognizing Davis's number, touched the icon to answer the call.

Davis didn't beat around the bush. "Brigitte wants you to do some test shots for the clothing line. Are you up for it?"

Ella hesitated. "She understands I have to arrange my schedule to accommodate Micah?"

"Yes."

"I really believed she wouldn't want me because of that. And...well, the fact that I don't have a clue what I'm doing."

Davis chuckled. "You're a natural, Ella. And it could mean a contract. You're one of three she's chosen from a range of models."

So there was still a possibility she'd be passed over. Why wasn't she bothered by that? She wasn't exactly striking gold with her job search. She still hadn't heard from the bakery. "When do you need me?"

"Tomorrow morning, as soon as you can drop your son at school and get here."

"Davis, I want you to be straight with me. Is she as hot stuff as she thinks she is?"

His masculine laughter was a rumble. "Haven't you googled her?"

"No."

"Do it. I'll see you in the morning."

He was gone before she had time to say anything. Why did he do that?

She got out her computer and went online. When she typed in Brigitte Simpson, a number of articles popped up. She opened the first one and began to read. Brigitte had been a model from the time she was a baby, nearly twenty-five years, building a reputation. And obviously banking every dime. Then, at age thirty, she brokered a deal with one of the big fashion houses to handle her designs, and had released a collection every year since. Two collections, actually. Every year. One for the rich, and one for the masses. She was starting to expand, and had opened two exclusive boutiques as a showcase for her designs, one in Los Angeles and one in New York.

She was a self-made woman, had paid her dues, and was living her dream now. Or so one article said.

Ella leaned back and shut the computer. Evidently, this fashion stuff was a big deal, even if she had no interest in it herself.

She kept telling herself that, but even she liked pretty things. She wanted to look nice for Derrick. And she had a thing about comfortable shoes.

Ella cupped her hands over her face, mortified by her behavior. Brigitte was someone she could learn from. And she'd practically blown her off without a thought. But then, as usual, even with the five thousand dollars Larry had paid her, she'd been worried about keeping a roof over their heads and providing for Micah.

But Brigitte was still interested in having her do the campaign. The other two models were probably pros, but she could still learn from the experience. And she'd be paid.

A FEW MINUTES before eleven, Derrick unlocked the side door and sauntered into the garage. He set the takeout bag on the counter to eat later. The quick nap he'd caught before coming in had been just what he needed.

It had been a good day. No, it had been a freaking fantastic day. Sharing a meal with Micah and Ella, making love with her, playing the video game with Micah... He had felt like part of something. The two of them had taken him in. Like Mama Fernandez.

Now if he could just keep from doing anything to screw it up. Like hiding his criminal record.

Then he heard sound from inside the office. The door had been locked, though the lights remained on as always. Roger, the only person allowed in the inner office, would be home sleeping. If someone had broken in to steal something... Derrick would be blamed and lose his job.

No, he wouldn't, because he'd fucking tear their heads off.

He reached for the office door knob and twisted it slowly. It was always kept locked, but this time it wasn't. He shoved it open with enough force it bounced off the wall.

Roger started and jerked away from the filing cabinet he was searching. "Jesus, Derrick. You scared the shit out of me."

"I thought someone might have gotten in and was rifling through, looking for cash or something."

"And you were going to take them on bare-handed?"

He shrugged. "I had the element of surprise."

"Good point." Roger gave a chuckle and moved back to the filing cabinet. "I appreciate your willingness to defend my property."

He nodded. "Have you had an opportunity to check out the crane?"

"Yes, this afternoon. You did a good job. And the motorized pulley works perfectly."

"Good." He pulled out his keys and removed the garage key Roger had given him, crossing the carpeted space to hand it to him.

"Thanks."

Derrick's work phone rang, and he answered. After speaking to the man, he stuck the cell back in his shirt pocket. "Flat tire on the interstate and no spare. Duty calls."

"I'll probably be here when you get back. I'm trying to line things up for a business trip, and there's something else I'd like to talk to you about."

"Okay. I'll be back in about an hour." He stowed his sandwich under the counter and went out to the wrecker.

He hated interstate calls. The chances of getting hit by a passing vehicle while hooking up a car were twice what they were for any other tow job, and it was even worse at night. The passing driver's attention swung toward the action on the side, and it only took a second for them to drift right into the stopped vehicles.

Derrick took the I-5 north and watched the mile markers pass by. Seeing the truck sitting on the side of the road on the southbound side, he went on to the next exit and turned around to head south, then pulled ahead of the vehicle to park and jumped out with the clipboard and forms. He approached the driver sitting in the truck. "You called for a tow?"

"Yeah. I been waitin' for damn near an hour." The guy's speech was slurred and he started to get out of the truck.

Derrick blocked the door to prevent him from opening it. He wasn't going to argue with the guy, even though it had only been about thirty minutes. And he wasn't going to drag him out of traffic to keep him from getting hit either. "You'll be safer in the vehicle, sir." He passed the guy the clipboard. "I need you to sign this before I tow you."

"What is it?" The man squinted at the form.

"It's permission for me to tow the vehicle. It'll be a hundred dollars."

"Fuck me, man. A hundred bucks to get me off this road?"

How many times had he heard the complaint? "It's a flat fee. I don't set the rates, sir."

The guy tugged the pen out of the top slot and scribbled a signature.

Derrick tossed the board into the front seat of the truck cab and lowered the bed, hooked the truck up to be dragged onto the bed, and approached the window again. "You'll have to ride inside with me, sir. You can't ride in your vehicle on the bed of the wrecker." He could just see the drunk getting out of his truck mid-drive, falling off the wrecker and getting killed.

The man opened the door and heaved himself out of the truck, weaving on his feet for a few moments, then leaning against the guardrail for support. Derrick went to the controls, and with one eye on the drunk and one on the vehicle, pushed the lever to roll the truck up on the bed.

It was a good thing the guy had a flat. It saved him from causing an accident. Crazy fucker.

Derrick followed him around the wrecker to make certain he didn't weave his way right into traffic. Once he was settled in the passenger seat, Derrick slammed the door shut and went around the front of the wrecker to the driver's side. The guy leaned back in his seat, tugged his denim jacket around him, and nodded off. Thank Christ he wasn't puking in the wrecker.

Arriving back at the garage, Derrick backed into the bay, tilted the wrecker's platform, got into the truck, and rolled it back into position. With the truck offloaded, he lowered the wrecker's bed and got back into the cab to pull it back out.

The drunk stirred, turned to face him…and brought up a Beretta and leveled it inches from his face. "Where's the cash?"

Derrick froze. It had been too many years since his SEAL days to expect the focused calm to kick in instantly. His heart pounded, its beat drumming in his ears. He looked past the barrel of the gun to the man's face. He stared back, calm, deliberate. The blurry-eyed drunk was gone, and a hard face with cold gray-green eyes stared back at him.

His mouth dry, Derrick said, "I don't carry any cash on me, and there's just enough to make change in the register in the office. Most everyone pays by credit card."

"Ease out. Try anything, I'll shoot you."

Derrick slid out of the wrecker, holding up his hands in a pose of surrender.

How many times had the guy done this? He was too practiced for it to be his first try. The twenty bucks Derrick had in his wallet weren't worth dying for. Or the three hundred they left in the cash drawer to make change.

The man climbed over the console and out without shifting

the gun off of him.

"Move. First, you're going to refill my tire. Then you're going to give me the cash."

Braced to feel the puncture of a bullet in his back, Derrick moved into the bay and knelt to get the air hose, tugged it over to the trunk's back flat tire, unscrewed the cap, and pushed the nozzle down on it. Air rushed in, filling the tire. He pretended to concentrate on what he was doing while he observed the man standing over him.

Late twenties to early thirties, five-nine, maybe a little less, medium brown hair, green eyes, scruffy beard, thin face with a narrow nose, an earring in his left ear, a tattoo on his gun hand. He could catch just the darkness of it on his skin, but not the shape. And the guy wasn't a druggie. There was nothing dull about his eyes now, and, now Derrick thought about it, the asshole had avoided making eye contact.

Goddammit, he should have had his mind on what he was doing instead of just going through the motions. But he was all in the game now. He finished filling the tire and rose, coiled the air hose, and hung it on the hook by the door.

The man waved the gun. "Let's go get the cash."

And then what? A bullet in the brain? Not happening. He steeled himself to do whatever was necessary to survive.

He preceded the man into the office and moved behind the counter. The guy followed, keeping the gun leveled at Derrick's back.

Derrick opened the cash drawer and reached for twenties.

The office door swung inward, and the guy swiveled toward it, the gun moving with him.

Certain he was going to fire, Derrick grabbed the barrel and pulled back. The gun went off like a cannon in the small room. The shooter screamed as his finger bent back, the pop of it breaking deadened by the ringing in Derrick's ears. He wrenched the gun free and slammed it against the man's head.

The tango hit the file cabinets with such force it sounded like kicking an empty trash can. He crumpled to the floor and lay still.

"Jesus H. Christ!" Roger's exclamation sounded distant.

Derrick bent to check the guy's pulse. It was strong and steady, but his head was bleeding and he was out cold. Derrick jerked his cell phone free and dialed nine-one-one. He identified himself, reported an armed robbery, and requested an ambulance and police. "Yes, the shooter is down."

"What the fuck happened?" Roger demanded.

Derrick placed the gun on the counter, but at the instructions of the dispatcher kept the phone close to his ear. "He's the guy who called me about a flat on the interstate. I towed the truck back, and as soon as we got here, he pulled a gun and held it on me until I refilled his tire. Then he brought me in here. I thought he was going to shoot you when you opened the door."

"He shot at me. The damn thing nearly parted my hair." Roger flopped down on the leather bench and took several deep breaths, his face pale.

The man at Derrick's feet started to come around as a siren screamed from outside the garage.

"The officers should be there." The dispatcher's voice broke into their conversation.

"Yes, they're here. Thanks."

"How the hell can you be so calm?" Roger asked.

Derrick disconnected his phone and stepped over the guy to lean against the far wall, away from the pistol. Derrick assessed the question and realized he was right. He'd shut down his emotions the moment the guy drew the gun on him. Some training never left you. "This was a cakewalk compared to some of the shit that went down when I was in the Navy. You keep your head or you die."

Two officers rushed into the office, guns drawn, and for the second time in the past twenty-five minutes he stared down the barrel of a gun.

CHAPTER 17

"**T**URN AND LOOK over your shoulder," Davis directed as he snapped another picture.

If she'd ever thought modeling was easy, she knew better now. Three hours of changing clothes and having her hair and makeup touched up wasn't bad. But the lights were hot and Carmella, Davis's assistant, kept handing her water in between sessions—a good thing, because she felt dehydrated.

Davis was fierce in his concentration. He had photographed her in every pose imaginable. Reclining, sitting, draping this here and that there, and now they'd gotten into the action shots where she actually had to move.

She tried to project herself into the mindset that she moved in a choreographed dance to music only she could hear. She threw her head back and embraced what they were doing. She ignored the camera and him, and struck poses as she walked around the small square screened in by the lights. Her hands before her, behind her, out to the side. Chin up, chin down, resting on her shoulder. She switched into dance moves that fanned the kaleidoscope-colored silk skirt out around her.

When she realized the camera wasn't clicking anymore, she froze and looked at him.

Davis grinned. "That was remarkable. You were smiling. And I didn't even have to direct you to do it."

"I do that on occasion."

He laughed. He handed off the camera to his assistant, Carmella. "We're done." He looked around the room at the makeup artist, wardrobe, and Carmella. "We're finished, everyone." He turned back to her. "Get changed and I'll take you out to lunch. I'm starving, and we need to talk about the screen test commercial you'll do on Friday."

Five minutes later, Carmella slipped into the dressing room. Her red hair stuck out in spikes atop her head, and her heavily made-up green eyes held a speculative light. Several earrings sparkled as she moved her head, and Ella was curious about the tattoo she'd caught a peek of when Carmella leaned down to adjust one of the lights. "Davis said he'd wait in his office for you. You did a good job today."

Ella tugged her thigh-length tunic down over her leggings. "Thanks. It always surprises me when someone says stuff like that. Because I don't really understand what it is that I've done."

Carmella laughed. "You don't poker up like some of the girls. And you don't try to sex things up. Your movements are like...watching the wind blow, kind of effortless and natural. And it doesn't matter what angle he shoots you from, you're gorgeous."

Ella blinked at her. "Wow. I don't know what to say to that."

Carmella shrugged one shoulder. "And you don't flirt with Davis. It's as though you're not aware of him behind the camera. I can't tell you how different that is."

Why was she saying this to her? Was she involved with Davis and warning her off? "Business is business. I've always found it isn't a good idea to get involved with anyone you work for." She reached for her shoulder bag and slipped her feet into ballet flats.

"I've been with him for five years. He's excited about you. He knows the ones who will make it big, and the ones who won't. Just keep doing what you're doing, and you'll be fine."

Was Carmella afraid Ella would disappoint him? Or was she just being sincerely complimentary? It was so hard to trust anyone. To look beyond their façade and know who and what they really were. "Thanks for the advice. Although this contract isn't a sure thing, and I'm trying hard not to count on it."

"I think you'll get it. Brigitte would be a fool to pass you up." Carmella slipped out the door.

Ella felt unsettled as she finger-combed her hair and stared into the mirror at the features still dramatized by the makeup the team applied. It was like donning a costume for a play or a ballet. She'd applied stage makeup before dancing. But it wasn't real. She went into the bathroom and washed her face, then applied her normal mascara and lip gloss.

She felt more herself as she walked down the hall to Davis's office.

He looked up from the computer screen. "Want to see some of the shots?"

He did seem excited, and she tried hard to suppress a response to it, the voice inside her that said, *"As long as you don't hope, you won't get hurt when things go south."*

He raised his brows, his expression inquiring.

"Of course, I'd love to see them."

He stood so she could sit down in his office chair.

She clicked on the first one. She sat on a park bench, her face turned three-quarters to look beyond the room where they'd taken the picture. The clothes and makeup were exquisite. She went on to the next and the next. Wearing dresses, suits, casual wear, up close, full body, with a backdrop, without one. They'd taken so many. She looked at a stranger. Yet it was her.

"Let me take you to the action shots."

He scooted the cursor down the list to the bottom of the screen. The silk dress flowed around her as she spun in a pirouette, the next shot was as if she'd stepped forward out of the move. Her head was up, her hand reaching out to grasp something while the silk skirt flowed around her legs like a colorful waterfall.

"They're gorgeous. I believe you could take anyone off the street and make them look beautiful, Davis." She rose and stepped around the chair, putting it between them.

"You have the bone structure, the coloring, the body shape, and the camera loves you."

He shut the laptop.

"Come on. Let's go to lunch. I'll explain to you what to expect tomorrow when you do the commercial."

"How much is all this costing you?"

"It isn't unusual for us to do these photos. I have two other models I'll be photographing this week. Both for the same campaign. They're our clients, too. We get reimbursed for the time and materials and paying our staff, if any of you are signed. Since I know the quality of my clientele, I can promise that one of you will be signed."

She relaxed a little. "I read somewhere that models are supposed to pay for stuff like this."

"It's a business expense. If we get the contract, we'll be the ones to photograph the one who gets the contract and do the commercials. That's thousands of dollars, Ella."

"Okay." She hesitated. "She'd be crazy to go with any other photographer but you."

He grinned again, and this time she acknowledged the tug of attraction she'd ignored every time they were together.

"Yeah, she would. Let's go eat, and we'll talk."

FOR THE FIRST time he could remember, he felt beat to shit when he went into class at seven in the morning. Being tired didn't ease the bitter hurt and rage stewing in his gut, but aggravated it. He'd tossed and turned, reliving every moment he spent trapped in Roger's office while the two detectives poked and prodded and did everything they could to get a rise out of him.

Would any amount of running rid him of this pain? If it would, he'd run a marathon to get away from it.

Once they discovered he had a record, they made the automatic leap to conclude he was in on the robbery. Until Roger played the security tapes and they were able to watch the guy hold him at gunpoint throughout the whole thing. They hadn't even apologized before leaving with the tapes.

He hadn't done time for stealing or robbery. He'd been arrested for breaking and entering, because he broke into Hawk's house, but he hadn't stolen anything. It didn't matter. He'd be guilty for the rest of his life, no matter what he did, because he couldn't change what he'd done.

Burk Straus, his instructor, paused by his station. "You okay today, Derrick?" The elder man had been kind to him. Had taken him on as a student when many other instructors wouldn't because of his record. He wouldn't allow these feelings inside him to jeopardize his relationship with the man.

"I'm fine, sir."

"Do you have any questions about the process?"

"No, sir. I'm just looking through my notes before I start."

"Ask for help if you need it."

"Thanks, I will." Once he got a job welding, he'd be on-site, his face hidden from the world while he did his job. There wouldn't be any reason for anyone to hassle him.

He fit the mask over his head, lowered the face shield, hit the switch to turn on the electric current, and started the weld.

An hour later he wandered outside to take his lunch break before his next class began. He settled on a bench by the back steps and took out his sandwich, apple and drink. He'd taken the first bite of his sandwich when a man sat down on the other end of the bench.

Derrick eyed him while he continued to chew the bread, cheese, and turkey. Wearing a suit, tie, and scuffed brown lace-ups, he had cop written all over him. His bland features and close-cropped hair further confirmed it.

"Derrick Armstrong?" he asked and flashed his badge. "Detective Ross Acampa."

"You guys harass me or fuck up things for me here, and I'll bring suit against the city and you. I'm keeping my nose clean, taking classes here to try and learn a new skill so I can make a decent living, and I'm not breaking any laws. Leave me the fuck alone."

"I'm not here to harass you, Derrick."

He knew how it worked. Use a suspect's first name to create rapport. "Don't try and be all buddy-buddy with me. You're here to fuck with me, just like those guys did last night." He grabbed for the plastic bag he'd packed his lunch in and crammed the uneaten sandwich into it, and every muscle in his body tightened when the guy jumped up to block his escape. Derrick barely managed to stifle the urge to lash out at him.

"I'm here to ask for your help."

"Fuck you." He gripped the bag hard.

"You took down a serial armed robbery suspect last night. He'd used the same routine to rob seven other wrecker services. The drivers of the other rigs have all identified him."

"Good."

"We appreciated your help."

There was a catch here. He wasn't here to thank him. Derrick continued to eye him, waiting for him to get to the point.

"There's another robbery suspect we've been investigating for the past two months, and we think you can help us bring in him and his partners, too."

"I don't know anything about any robberies. I've never stolen anything in my life. I just eat, sleep, work, and take classes."

"We know that. We've talked to your landlady and a few other people you associate with."

Had they talked to Ella? Did they tell her what he was, what he'd done? Panic gripped his throat for a moment.

No. They couldn't know about her. He hadn't told anyone about her but Mama, and she wouldn't tell the cops jack shit. His voice sounded hoarse around the breathiness of relief. "You have no right to fuck up my life."

"We were very discreet, and they know what happened last night. We've left them with the impression that you played the hero last night, which you did. Otherwise your boss would either be dead or in the hospital. That bullet barely missed him. While he's feeling grateful, we thought you might use some of that goodwill to maneuver yourself into a position where he'll ask you to join him and his partners in their illegal side business."

"You've got to be kidding me. Why the hell would Roger rob anyone? He owns two businesses."

"Which is a great front to launder the money. We're not talking about residential breaking and entering here, Derrick, though they may have started out that way. We're talking a highly organized, skilled group breaking into jewelry stores. They bypass the alarm systems like they're nothing."

The cops had to be wrong. But Roger did hire ex-cons, and some of them could have those special skills.

He'd hired Derrick because he had experience driving a wrecker.

"Roger knows I'm toeing the line. I just want a life now. I lost seven years, and I'll never get them back. I lost everything I cared about—my family, my team, being a SEAL. It's taken me a long time to believe I can build something else. So why would they take a chance on approaching me? And why would I want to take risk going back to prison to be a part of it?"

"Their last haul was three hundred thousand. That's a lot of incentive."

Jesus! "If it was ten times that it wouldn't be enough for me to risk ending up back in a cage."

"You wouldn't be at risk of going back. You'd be working *for* us, Derrick. We think they're interested in getting someone to train them in different ways to break into buildings and get in and out and gone in a hurry. Rappelling off the sides of buildings, setting explosives, that kind of thing."

He thought of the gantry crane he built and for half a second was tempted to say something. He checked his watch, gathered his books, and the crushed bag with his lunch in it. "I have a class."

"If he approaches you, contact me." Acampa offered him a business card.

"Why should I trust you? You could be trying to railroad me like those assholes last night. I had a guy holding a gun on me for twenty-five minutes. I expected him to shoot me just because he could. Once he had the money, he probably would have. He damn sure meant to shoot Roger.

"As soon as those assholes got a look at my record, they got busy trying to figure out a way to arrest me for it. They didn't even look at the security tapes before they started grilling me, trying to build a connection between me and that fucker. If the security cameras hadn't caught it all, I'd be in a cell now. And you expect me to put my ass on the line? For what? More of the same?"

"I'm sorry about what they did to you, Derrick."

"No, you're not. You'd do the same thing. I could stay clean for seven years instead of seven months, and I'd still be treated like I was guilty of something. Once a con, always a con. Right?"

"They were looking for leverage to force your cooperation."

Derrick felt heat flare in his face, and his blood began to pound in his temples. In that moment he wanted to rip Acampa's head off. He even imagined how good it would feel doing it.

Acampa took a step back, and Derrick shoved past him, went up the steps, and entered the building. Once he was inside, the walls seemed to close in on him, and he didn't trust himself not to punch something or someone.

He had the choice of the bathroom or the stairwell for privacy. He hit the stairwell and went down half a flight toward the basement. He braced an arm on the wall and rested his forehead on it while he took deep breaths to slow his heart rate.

As the rage eased and his heart rate came down, his emotions rose. He sat on the steps and rested his head in his hands. He'd been through worse than this. If he thought about it at all, he could come up with other things he'd been through ten times worse. *The only easy day was yesterday.*

And yesterday was wonderful. He and Ella made love for the first time, and it was fantastic. And he wasn't judging it through the eyes of a guy who hadn't had real sex in seven years. It was hot, and they'd connected. And he'd been able to hold on long enough to please her. He needed to concentrate on that. Not on the guy with the gun or the cops.

The only person who knew he'd seen a woman yesterday was Mama, and she would never share anything important with the cops. So the cops didn't know about Ella, and neither did Roger.

He needed to keep it that way.

Feeling more composed, he gathered his books and the bag and got to his feet. He could still have a life. He just needed to keep putting one foot in front of the other.

CHAPTER 18

ELLA SIPPED HER sweet tea and waited for the waiter to box up the rest of her club sandwich to take home. "Are you helping the other models like you're helping me?" she asked.

"No. But I have in the past." Davis leaned back in his chair and stretched out his legs in a relaxed pose that showed off the long, lean line of his body.

Was he aware of doing it, or was it just a habitual mannerism?

When he continued to speak, she dragged her attention back to his face. "They've been modeling for a while now and know how we work. You're the new kid on the block."

"I'm not sure I'll ever be so relaxed about this that it will become old hat. I have to pretend to be somewhere else to get through it."

His eyes narrowed. "What makes you so anxious?"

"I don't like to think you're discovering all my secrets when you look through the camera lens." Could he tell she was hiding things? And would her stripping end up being just a drop of water in the pond, or would it turn into a major ripple?

"I'm not. You're all buttoned up, and all your secrets are well hidden. That's what makes the photos I take of you so interesting. It's as though you're on the cusp of breaking out."

She already had with Derrick. And one man at a time was enough. Besides, Davis was too sophisticated for her. And she had no intention of following through on those small feelings of physical attraction. Her connection to Derrick was much stronger.

Was she trying to convince herself?

"Tell me about you, Ella."

She hesitated. "It isn't pretty. I ran off to Los Angeles with my boyfriend at seventeen. I had just graduated from high school, and we both had dreams that he would make it big as a songwriter and musician, and I would as a dancer. He even sold one of his songs after a few months, and he went out to celebrate with the guys he sold the song to... Trae had never done drugs, and they gave him something..." It was still hard to talk about. "He died of an overdose. He was nineteen."

"Jesus," Davis breathed.

"I went home to Salt Lake City for the funeral. My father's very dedicated to the Mormon church. An unwed daughter pregnant with her boyfriend's child didn't fit into his world, so I left and came here to have my baby and raise him. We don't have much contact with them.

"I've worked a lot of jobs to support us. I've run into a lot of kind people, like my neighbor Patsy, and a lot of hard ones out to take advantage, like my last boss. I've managed to keep me and my son together, despite the assholes and with the help of the others."

He remained silent for a moment, his expression carefully neutral." Are you wondering which kind I am?"

"I knew which kind you were when you asked me who put the bruises on my neck."

"That makes things easier and more difficult for me, Ella." He turned his water glass around and around, using his thumb and forefinger, watching it turn. "I'm interested in you as more than a model."

She'd known. The way he looked at her from behind the camera, the way he was careful not to touch her while they worked, as though he didn't quite trust himself to keep his distance. It was impossible to ignore the heat he projected when he looked at her now, or her physical response to it.

"I'm seeing someone."

His features tightened. "Is it serious?"

The eagerness on Derrick's face as he stood at the elevator after their first kiss flashed through her mind. "It has the possibility of being serious."

"We could have some possibilities too, Ella."

She remained silent for a moment. "And it could be both easier and harder with you. You're an established businessman, talented, successful. But what could I offer you that you really need, other than being another model?"

"We wouldn't know unless we explored it."

Her throat dry, she reached for her iced tea again. "I can't, Davis. The first thing is, the man I'm seeing deserves more than just half my attention. Dating two men at once is never a good thing, at least not for me. It would only create confusion and jealousy. And the second thing is, you're my boss. And romance and business are never a good combination. It might end up being difficult for us to work together. And I'd regret that, because I like working with you. I'd rather have you as my friend and mentor than have you as an angry ex."

"But you're tempted." It was a statement not a question.

Heat flared in her cheeks. "Well, duh."

He laughed, and drew the attention of several ladies around them.

"I hope this guy you're seeing is a nice guy."

"He's proven to be several times so far." But there was more to Derrick. There was trouble in his past. She didn't want to delve too deeply into her own thoughts about it, because if she did... As she kept ruling things out, bigger things kept coming to mind And she didn't want those bigger things to be true and stand in the way. Because he was special. Everything about him told her he was.

Davis leaned forward, and she was relieved to see his business face slide back on. "We need to talk about the commercial."

Relief washed over her.

"I'm not going to harass you Ella, but I'm a nice guy too. Not perfect by a long shot, but I recognize we have some heat between us. And if you were completely committed to this guy, you wouldn't be hedging at all."

She hadn't realized she had been.

THE SUN GLARED off the windshields in the parking lot when he came out of the building after class. A business card stood out beneath his windshield wiper, and he ground his teeth.

He needed to call Ella and tell her about the robbery last night, just in case it made the papers or the local news. He'd already gotten calls from both the newspapers and a television station. How the hell had they gotten his cell phone number? And the cops had released his name and Roger's.

What he'd done was nothing heroic, but simply self-preservation. Why they'd be interested in it was beyond him. But the aftermath of the attempted robbery and the way the cops had treated him still ate at him.

He had to let it go.

He tossed the business card into the floorboard of the car.

He needed to hear Ella's voice and feel a part of something good.

He grabbed his phone and dialed her number. At her hello he was hard in a millisecond. "Any chance I can see you today before I go to work?"

"I know you need to sleep, but you could come by on your way to the garage. I'm making parmesan chicken, and I can save you some for your dinner."

"Sounds perfect. How did the shoot go?"

"Good, I think. I saw some of the pictures on the computer, and they don't look like me at all. I'm a different person when they make me up. And the clothes are fabulous. I wore a silk skirt today that was heaven. I bet it costs at least three hundred dollars when you buy it in the stores."

"I bet you looked terrific." She'd turn heads wearing a pillow-case, a shower curtain, nothing at all. The thought had his raging erection aching for release. He needed to get his mind on something else. "Are you on your way to pick up the munchkin?"

"I'm sitting outside the school waiting for the release bell to ring."

"He's a killer on the motorcycle game we played."

"I noticed. And the two of you really had a colorful vocabulary while you were racing."

"But no swear words. Though it's sometimes hard for me to remember to be careful."

"My favorite was buttface. I've worried that being with just me and Patsy for so long I was somehow cheating him out of being boyish enough. I'd never actually heard Micah exchange insults with anyone before."

"You're doing a great job with him, Ella. He's a regular kid. And as for the insults, he and his buds probably do that all the time. Guys don't really outgrow it. We just get ruder and more graphic as we get older."

Her laughter made him smile. "Will nine-thirty be too late for me to come over?"

"No. Micah goes to bed at nine."

"If I come at nine it will probably get him revved up, so I'll keep to the schedule. I need to tell you about something that happened last night at work."

"Okay." The easy tone in her voice changed instantly.

"Some guy pulled a gun on me and tried to rob the garage last night." He quickly described what had happened in the shortest possible way. "I didn't want you to hear it first on the news."

"Are you okay?"

"Yeah. I'm okay." Better now he'd talked to her.

"I didn't realize how dangerous your job is until just now. I mean, you're out on the interstate with the cars rushing by like it's a racetrack, and you face off against angry assholes armed with baseball bats who want to beat up on cars. I don't know why it didn't dawn on me how dangerous it could be."

"I have to be careful, but it isn't too bad, Ella. I've had a far more dangerous job, and this one is a cakewalk by comparison."

He refused to even think about any of the stuff he'd done or seen in Iraq. He couldn't and stay on top of what was going on now.

"I'm sure it is, but… At least you got a serial robber off the street."

"Yeah." Not that the cops cared about that. Not really. "I'll just look forward to spending some time with you before I have to go to work."

"If you need a few days to get past this, I'm sure your boss will understand."

"No, it's better to get back on the horse than to put it off, Ella." But to be able to spend the night with her would be worth it. But then there was Micah, and she said she didn't have men spend the night with him there. He could understand.

"When is your neighbor getting married again?"

"They've set a date for June twenty-fourth. But she'll be moving out the end of this month. Her fiancé wants her with him."

He wondered how much rent and utilities would be there. It would be convenient to be next door. But Ella wasn't really ready for that kind of closeness, and he wasn't sure he was either. And how close to stalking would that be? Mama Hernandez had been good to him, and he'd signed the lease just seven months ago.

"Does Micah know?"

"Not yet."

"I know he's very attached to her."

"She's been the grandmother he's never had."

He heard a touch of worry and grief beneath the normal in her voice. Was it better to have family or not to have them? Both was were painful at times.

"Kids are resilient, Ella. He'll be okay."

"I'm searching for someone to keep an eye on him. Maybe some kind of program for kids his age after school."

He searched for some way to be supportive. "Talk to his teacher. She might know of something. It'll work out." He got another beep on his phone. "I need to go, this is my boss. I'll see you at nine-thirty tonight."

They said goodbye and he switched over to Roger.

"Can you come in for a few minutes now?"

"Sure. I can be there in twenty minutes."

"Okay. See you then."

Shit. His eyelids were getting heavy, and the sofa bed at the apartment was calling his name.

He made it to the garage in thirty-five because of a traffic accident holding up the flow, but was glad he wasn't the one having to tow the two cars in.

He took the office door into the building instead of cutting through the garage. The noise was enough to aggravate the headache pounding at his temples.

The bullet hole in the threshold of the office door was still visible when Roger opened it at his knock. "Hey. Come on in."

Derrick followed him back to his desk and slumped into a seat in front of it.

"You haven't been to bed yet?" Roger asked.

"No, I had class, and I was too wound up to sleep last night."

"Me too." Roger stuck his hands in his pockets. "I wanted to talk to you about how the police treated you last night."

Derrick leaned forward in his chair. "What about it?"

"They leaned on you pretty hard. You didn't let them get to you."

He'd thought about how the instructors had ridden them during BUD/S to try and stay calm. But that didn't mean it hadn't made him angry. He'd finally left it behind. Even he couldn't sustain his anger over an entire day.

"They were hoping you'd take a swing at one of them."

"Not happening. I'm not going back in a cage again."

"I can see that. What did you do in the Navy, Derrick?"

Moment of truth. Was Acampa right? "I was a SEAL."

Roger grinned. "I knew it."

Derrick studied his face.

"You're cool under fire. I was impressed."

He could play along with this and see what happened. "When you're in a dangerous situation, you don't really have any choice. And give yourself some credit. You opened the door and created a distraction, which was what saved me."

"I fell down on the job. I used to watch the security feeds all the time in my office. I stopped doing it. Had I known what was happening, I could have called the cops." His expression seemed sincerely apologetic.

"It worked out. Neither of us got shot. It was a good day."

"Yeah. Was that the way it was in the SEALs?"

"Sometimes." He didn't want to talk about the SEALs. "What was the job you were going to talk to me about last night before everything went to shit?"

"I want to see if you're willing to work on the suspension of one of the wreckers. I can take that one out of service until you get it fixed."

"Yeah. I can start on that tonight if you like. Air ride or spring?" He was relieved to know wrecker repairs were all Roger had in mind. He cursed Acampa for putting ideas and suspicions in his head. If Roger was dirty, Derrick didn't want to know. He needed this job. He even liked it. And he didn't have to put up with too much shit.

"Spring. I ordered the system, and it's ready to be installed."

Okay. "I'm not looking a gift horse in the mouth, but why me? You have plenty of guys on day shift who have more experience, and who can do it faster."

"I thought you could ignore some of the calls tonight and get it done. A break from towing for a night won't hurt business."

Surprised by Roger's sensitivity, Derrick continued to eye him.

"What happened last night is only part of it. It's been brought to my attention that you've been spreading our business card around, drumming up business at some of the bars and other businesses."

How had he found out about that?

"I figured a little extra pay on the side was warranted." Roger leaned forward and folded his arms on the desk. "Why did you go out of your way to do that?"

"I noticed a trend on certain nights of how many calls I was getting from certain places. So I just stopped by some of the other bars and strip clubs close to the same area and left a card."

Roger shook his head. "Why didn't you tell me what you were doing?"

"No particular reason."

"Jesus, Derrick. You're the most closemouthed son of a bitch I've ever met."

Derrick hitched up one shoulder in a shrug. "In prison you learn to keep your mouth shut and your nose out of everyone else's business."

"You know you've allowed that one experience to define your life."

"Yeah. It tends to do that when you lose your freedom for seven years."

"You need to break loose from that."

Shit! Here it comes. "How do you suggest I do it, beyond school and work?"

"Some friends and I are doing an obstacle course training thing this Friday for a couple of hours. It's been set up at one of their houses. Why don't you come join us since you have a few hours off on Friday from your classes?"

Fuck! This was looking more and more like Acampa was right. He could say no and walk away right now and not get involved. But Roger knew he worked out, lifted weights, and ran. He'd think it was strange if he didn't go. And he had buttered the deal with the night off from towing and the extra work fixing the wrecker. "What time?"

"Just meet me here before seven and I'll drive."

"Okay." What were they training for? And would he find out on Friday?

"IF SUPERMAN AND Thor were fighting, who do you think would win, Mom?" Micah asked as he put on his pajama top.

Ella gathered the school papers he'd dragged out of his backpack and thumbed through them. "I think they'd probably be pretty closely matched, and they'd beat each other senseless. But since they're both good guys, I can't imagine why they'd be fighting each other with so many bad guys to take down."

Micah's math and spelling papers looked great, but his handwriting still left a lot to be desired. They were going to have to practice.

She set the papers on his small desk. "Want me to read a chapter of our book to you tonight, or do you want to read a book to me?"

"I want to read to you." Micah got a library book off the small shelf next to the desk and climbed into bed.

Ella slipped in beside him and rested her head on the pillow next to his. "What are we reading?"

"Captain Underpants."

She enjoyed the books because he loved them so much and was so enthusiastic when he read them.

He finished one chapter with only one stumble and started the next before he started to flag and rub at his eyes.

"I think that's a good place to stop," she said as he ended the next chapter. "We can finish this one tomorrow night. How's that?"

"Okay."

She got his bookmark off the desk, marked his place, and put the book back on the shelf.

"Is Derrick your boyfriend, Mom?"

What was she supposed to say? "I suppose he is. I'm not dating anyone else."

"Does he kiss you like Charlie kisses Patsy?"

"Sometimes."

"Gross!"

Ella laughed. "Sometimes when you feel something special for someone, you kiss them." She drew the covers up to his chin. "I kiss you good night every night." She bent to press her lips to his forehead.

"That's different. Brian says his sister's boyfriend sticks his tongue in her mouth."

Oh, shit! She was not ready to deal with the birds and bees. "And how does Brian know he does?"

"Sharon babysits him when his parents go out to dinner sometimes. Her boyfriend comes over when they're not there. They were wrestling on the couch, and his sister told him to stop sticking his tongue down her throat."

Ella bit her lip, a little concerned because the sister was only fourteen and, from the sounds of it, gaining more experience than she should. If she brought the subject up with Brian's mom, would she shoot the messenger? Probably.

"You might want to tell Brian that he should tell his mom that Sharon's having her boyfriend over when she's babysitting. That's something her parents might want to know about."

"Okay." He rolled over on his side, turning his back. "Love you, Mom." She smoothed his hair and leaned down to kiss him again. He smelled of soap from his shower and minty toothpaste, but the underlying scent of active boy still lingered. She couldn't put her finger on anything it was similar to. It was just Micah.

She lingered for a moment, feeling blessed. Even if she'd done nothing else right, Micah was happy and well-adjusted, which was plenty to be grateful for.

As she shut the bedroom door the buzzer went off for the door downstairs. She rushed to the intercom and buzzed Derrick up. Her breathing quickened while she waited for him to knock on the door, and her body warmed, areas going sensitive as though her body remembered how they'd made love as well as she did.

Had her heart ever turned over for Davis? Maybe a little But nothing like this.

Opening the door, she took in Derrick's blond good looks, the sky blue of his eyes, and the strength of his jaw. She knew what lay beneath his clothes now, and just the thought of putting her hands on him shot a rush of desire straight to the intimate heart of her.

"Hey," he greeted her, his hands already on her, tugging her against him. Her fingers ran up the back of his neck. His mouth found hers, hungry, adamant with need. She groaned with relief.

They were both breathing hard by the time he broke the kiss. But with his hands firmly on her butt pressing her close, she felt his rampant response, and the urge to part her legs for him to come inside was hard to resist. But Micah lay sleeping in the next room, and if he woke and came out while they were in the middle of...

"I'm sorry we can't..."

"It's okay. We can catch a few hours at my apartment this weekend if you want to."

"Of course I do. I'll see if I can trade out with Regina upstairs. She can take the boys for a few hours on Sunday, and I'll take them on Saturday. All they do is play video games or go skateboarding in the courtyard behind the apartment complex."

"Let me heat up your food while you tell me more about what happened last night."

He wandered into the kitchen with her and sat on one of the barstools while she heated his food. "There isn't that much to tell, Ella."

She set a folded paper towel on the counter and arranged a knife, fork and spoon next to his plate. She studied his expression. "You don't have to protect me from things, Derrick. It was on the six o'clock news. His name is Mark Tyler Weston."

"Why do you think they always list their middle name like that? Does this guy really warrant that kind of recognition?"

"They might do it to keep people from mistaking the bad guys for someone else. And he did hold up seven other wrecker services and pistol-whipped a couple of the other drivers. He could have done that to you, too."

"He kept his distance."

"He probably didn't want to chance triggering a fight with you. Your size would be intimidating."

"I think he'd made up his mind he was going to shoot me before we ever got to the garage."

"Why do you think that?"

"His body language, the look in his eyes as I looked past the gun to his face. The first couple of times he held up drivers, he just took the money. Then he pistol-whipped the last three. I think he was working his way up to killing someone.

"Roger was in his office, and when he heard us come into the outer office, he opened the door to step out. The guy turned toward him with the gun and I grabbed it. It went off, and the shot hit the doorframe just above Roger's head. I jerked the pistol free, hit him with it, and knocked him into the filing cabinets. He was out, so I dialed nine-one-one...and that was it."

Ella's stomach quivered as she filled two glasses of iced tea and set them on the counter. He was right. The guy would probably have killed him once he had the money. He was growing bolder with each robbery. She placed the hot food in front of Derrick.

She went around to sit next to him, but paused to rest her head against his shoulder and put an arm around him. What would have happened if he had been injured...or killed? Had he told his friends he was seeing someone? "You're sure you're all right?"

"Yeah. I didn't sleep much last night, but after I got home today I managed about four hours. I'm good."

She ran a smoothing hand over his button-up shirt. "No flashbacks or anything like that?"

"No. I haven't had one of those in at least four years. And I rarely dream about things anymore. I'm solid, Ella. You don't have to worry."

"Okay. I know we just started seeing each other, but if something had happened to you...would anyone have called to tell me?"

He fell silent for a moment. "I'll make sure there's someone. Maybe Mama can do it, okay? But it isn't going to happen. This was a fluke."

She hiked herself upon the barstool to sip her tea while he ate.

"Will you have to testify against this man in court?"

"I don't know. Since most of the drivers he held up have identified him, he'd be smart to plea it out. Because his weapon discharged this time, and because the violence of his attacks has escalated, he'd run the risk of serving more time."

He sliced the chicken and forked up another bite. "This is really good, Ella."

"I'm glad you like it."

"When do you film the commercial?" he asked.

"Friday." She bit her lip. "I'm not sure I want it, Derrick."

He stopped eating. "I think you're going to be fantastic, and they're going to offer you a contract. It'll give you some financial security. Knowing that, what are you afraid of?"

Was she so transparent? "I don't know what the hell I'm doing. I haven't been trained like the other models."

"You must be good at it, otherwise they wouldn't keep calling you back. I can tell from my observations that the way you move is sexy as hell. And you're going to sell a hell of a lot of clothes."

"I have to do more than just show off the clothes on Friday. I have to speak."

He smiled. "One of my buds used to date this woman who could break glass with her voice. You don't have that issue, so I'm sure you'll be fine."

Ella laughed. "She could break glass with her voice?"

"Well, her voice was kind of high, and when she got excited you could hear her for a city block. Kind of a screech."

Ella covered her mouth to stifle her laughter. "What kind of excited?"

He looked over his iced tea glass, laughter in his gaze. "Any kind." He covered her hand with his. "You're going to be fine, Ella. You're smart, beautiful, and graceful. This job was made for you."

The tight feeling in the pit of her stomach relaxed. "Thanks, Derrick."

"At first I didn't want to admit it. I knew right off, the minute you signed up for this modeling gig, that things would start happening for you. You're too unique for it not to happen. And I thought, 'she'll jet off somewhere, right out of my life, before I get a chance to know her.' But you have Micah, and you both deserve a life without such constant struggle."

Her eyes stung. "There's no guarantee I'll get this."

"If you don't, you'll get the next one. And if you decide you don't like it, you can always get your own food truck and sell that chicken out of it." He pointed at his clean plate. "The rice was terrific too."

On impulse she kissed his cheek.

His smile held a hint of sadness and he pushed aside his plate to turn and face her. "If you think this is your dream, go for it. Don't let the chains of the past hold you back from a future."

"This isn't my dream, Derrick. My dream died years ago, and I haven't had time to figure out if I even have another. I just want us to be safe, fed, housed."

"Sit down and make a plan in writing, with ideas outlining how you can achieve that. If it's in writing, you'll have something tangible to work toward."

She could see him doing that.

"And it will help you know what you want to ask for when they offer you this contract. If they pay you, and you have to pay for all the travel expenses and housing, it's going to cut into your bottom line big time."

"Someone mentioned that I might need an agent."

"And he'll take his cut."

She'd known all this, but she hadn't wanted to think beyond getting the money they needed to live. Why hadn't she? Because she'd been in survival mode too long, living from month to month for the past seven years.

"Is this what you do?" she asked.

"Yeah, it is. I left Louisiana with the clothes on my back and my Jeep. I had to sell the Jeep to make first and last month's rent, Mama didn't charge me a security deposit, and the utilities are in her name and included in the rent. It saved me the cost of hook-ups. I bought the junker from my boss to replace the car so I could get to and from work. I'd saved the money for my classes working along the way, and part of it was left over from the car As soon as I got settled, I signed up for the classes. I have two more semesters, and I'll be able to apply for work on construction sites.

"Once I get settled into a job, I'll move to a better apartment and save for a home. But I think I'll keep the junker."

"It won't look like a junker much longer, and you'll have to find something else to call it."

"That will depend on what it looks like once I'm done." His blue eyes leaped to her face. "Think I should ask Micah to name it?"

His thoughtfulness had her eyes stinging again. "I think he'd love it if you did."

He took another drink of his iced tea. "My boss has invited me to do an obstacle course with him and a couple of buddies on Friday morning."

"Are you going?"

"I couldn't really say no since he gave me some extra work to do on one of the wreckers and extra pay for it."

"There are several here in San Diego."

"I think they've set something up on their own."

"Are they training for something? Competing against each other?"

"I don't know. But when your boss invites you to join him, you don't really have the option of saying no. Especially since he's offered you extra money for a side job." He didn't look happy about it, though. "I've lost count of the number of times I've done military obstacle courses. He knows I was a SEAL."

"I hope they're not inviting you because they think if one of them beats you at whatever they've set up, it will be some kind of one-upmanship."

"It isn't really important if one of the guys beats me, Ella. I've been beaten by the best. During the real deal, you don't really compete against other people, you compete against yourself, because it's timed. That makes it a mind game as much as a physical challenge."

She studied the careful composure of his expression. Even he suspected there was more to this than just a few guys running a course. All her protective instincts were pinging away like a metal detector that had hit the motherlode. "In my experience, guys look at everything as a competition. You'll be careful?"

He rested his hand on her thigh and gave it a light squeeze.

"I'll be careful.

They moved to the couch, and Derrick tucked her against his side.

"Did you do the same kind of job when you lived in Baton Rouge?"

"Yes. I worked for my father until I left for college. Then, when I lost my scholarship, I worked for him again until I finished my degree. I was offered some good jobs, but the Navy recruiter gave me the idea that I'd make a good naval officer. Because of my mathematics degree, I could be a pilot and go into military intelligence later.

"The thing about the military is they sign you up and then they give you the job they need you to do as soon as you come out of boot camp. I was waiting for an opportunity to become a pilot when I learned about the SEALs. The more I found out about them, the more I wanted to be one of them. More than I ever wanted anything.

"My CO signed off for me to try for them, thinking I'd probably wash out and come back with my tail between my legs. But I made it. There were a hundred and nineteen guys who started training, only twenty-two finished. It was worth making the team to see his face when I made it."

His world stopped with the loss of his SEAL career, just as hers ended when Trae died. It seemed they both needed to figure out what their dreams were now those were closed off to them.

She caressed the curve of his jaw. At the look of loss and longing in his expression, the tenderness she'd always reserved for Micah rose in her. She wanted to hold him and protect him. To wipe that look of loss from his expression.

She moved to sit in his lap. "You could get your pilot's license now, Derrick. That could be your dream. If you can do what you did to be a SEAL, you can be whatever you set your mind to."

He cupped her cheek and his expression cleared. "I wish…"

He kissed her with such sweetness and longing, she clung to him. When the kiss grew more heated, she forgot all the lost opportunities, and just thought of him.

CHAPTER 19

ELLA PEERED DOWN the busy street and wondered how they would possibly film her weaving among the mob of people on the street. The Gaslamp Quarter was alive with tourists ambling along, talking, window-shopping, going into the restaurants and boutiques, and just generally enjoying the day.

After two weeks of delays and a couple of her regular shoots for magazine ads, it was happening. What if her voice shook with nerves? What if she tripped over something and fell on her face?

She adjusted the belt around her waist for the hundredth time, fretting because she hadn't been able to eat anything with nerves cramping her stomach one minute and rolling it into nausea the next. At least Carmella said the belt made her waist look tiny.

They'd played up the Audrey Hepburn look Davis insisted she had, and dressed her in a bright red silk blouse tucked into a white skirt, generously gathered at the waist and flowing down to just beneath her kneecaps. She loved the hidden pockets on each side because they gave her somewhere to put her trembling, sweaty hands.

Davis and the cameraman stood twenty feet away, deep in discussion. It seemed they'd been going over every inch of the space they'd use on the street. After a final, all-set nod from the cameraman, they both turned and approached her.

Ella's breathing hitched and her mouth got even drier. She

could do this. If she could walk out onstage nearly naked, she could wander down a city street and talk about how glamourous she felt wearing a Brigitte Simpson design. Or were they going to dub her voice after they filmed? That would be easier.

And why the hell did she judge everything good that happened to her by how hard and terrible it was?

While the hairdresser dealt with her hair, which took all of two seconds, she ran her lines through in her mind.

"Remember to speak directly into the camera, Ella." Davis instructed. "You're going to walk down the sidewalk, but the camera will be the friend you're sharing with about how wonderful Brigitte Simpson's clothes are. How much you enjoy wearing them."

"I've got it. Let's do it."

Despite her nerves, Davis's quick grin triggered that small, niggling feeling of connection.

He was turning away even as she was trying to figure it out.

"All right people, let's do it."

The cameraman took his position behind a camera mounted on two metal tracks. "Whenever you're ready, Ella."

She looked into the camera...and for a moment the words wouldn't come. She took a breath, then started forward. The cameraman walked backward in front of her, sliding the camera along with her.

"I like being a woman. I like dressing like one." She flashed a smile and caressed the collar of the silk blouse. "With a Brigitte Simpson design, you not only look fantastic, you're comfortable, too." She flipped the skirt, letting it flow around her legs. "So if you're looking for style, beauty, and comfort, look no further than Brigitte Simpson." She flashed another smile, "I never do."

She reached the man they'd chosen to act as her boyfriend, walked up to him, and he held her off to take in her appearance before slipping an arm around her waist and guiding her toward one of the restaurants.

"Cut!"

"That was damn near perfect, Ella," Davis said. "But let's do it a couple more times just to be certain."

She was sweating bullets and he wanted her to do it again. She sucked in a breath and said, "Okay."

The whole company walked back up the street to the starting point while a group of tourists lingered across the street taking pictures. She tried to ignore them and concentrate on what she needed to do.

DERRICK EYED THE setup.

It wasn't an obstacle course. It was exactly what Acampa warned him it would be. There were several areas where they'd run, crawled, and climbed. They'd used ropes anchored to the rafters inside the two-story garage to climb to the loft, then ridden a zip line down to the ground. And the biggie, the rappelling line that ran from the top of this hill to the bottom.

"You've done some rappelling before?" Roger asked.

"Yeah." It had been a while since he'd done any climbing or rappelling, but it was impossible to forget the things that saved your life, especially when they'd been drummed into you over and over with practice and used in more than one dangerous situation.

He pulled as hard as he could on the anchor, testing it. It was stable. He checked the ropes and the harnesses for any wear. One or two of the carabiners were beginning to show some wear, and he pointed them out. He checked his rappelling device to make certain it was working properly, glad to see they'd provided a cord called an autoblock for the friction hitch. They were all going to be using the same doubled rope to rappel, but he wondered if they intended to use the same equipment when they did the job they were planning.

He recognized the itchy feeling between his shoulder blades. It meant he was in the crosshairs. He wanted to get this over with and leave.

But first he took time to study each one of the men. Martin, Sam, Roger and Hank. He didn't know last names other than

Roger's, but he'd recognize their faces if he saw them again.

Every one of them had a wary hardness about them he recognized. They were all ex-cons. Martin was the youngest at eighteen. Short but muscular, he was built like a baseball player. With his streaked blond hair and tanned skin, he looked like a surfer. Sam was at least thirty, heavy with muscle, and already balding. And then there was Hank—muscled, tattooed, with an attitude.

Turning his back, Derrick set up his extension. The safety line made of webbing with a carabiner at each end locked him to the anchor so he could look over the edge and study the terrain below.

"Everything okay?" Hank asked. Derrick eased away from the edge. Hank reminded him of himself seven years earlier. If the guy wasn't careful, he'd end up back in prison. He had anger issues, and every word sounded like a challenge. If they were planning another robbery, he'd probably end up in the same place regardless.

"Yes, everything's okay. My only suggestion is that you put a stopper knot on the end of each rope to insure you don't rappel right off the end of the line."

"The rope is long enough to reach the bottom with lots to spare. They aren't needed."

"The bank is steep at the bottom, and if someone loses their footing it might save them from sliding down."

"It's not needed, man."

He could see where this was going, and it wasn't worth fighting over.

Derrick fastened his safety helmet and tugged on his gloves. Since his rappel extension was already hitched to the anchor, he shouted *rope* and tossed the doubled coil over the edge of the drop-off He threaded both strands of the main rope through his rappelling device, captured it with the carabiner, and locked it to his harness.

Next he wound the free end of his autoblock around both strands of the rope and locked it to his harness with the carabiner, creating his friction hitch. If he fell, the coils of cord would tighten around the rope and act as a safety lock, holding him in place. He tested it by pulling the rope sharply upward, and saw the cord tighten around it just as it should. Confident it would catch him if he fell, he checked to make sure everything else was as it should be, and, holding the double strands of the rope tightly in one hand, he unhooked his extension and clipped it to his harness, out of the way.

The rock bowed out away from the face of the hill. Feet braced a little farther than shoulder width apart, knees bent, the rope in front of him in one hand, the free rope in the other against his hip, he said, "See you below," and backed over the edge.

The preparation for rappelling was always way more time-consuming than the drop. It had taken him two and half, maybe three minutes to get rigged for the drop, and thirty seconds to make it, where he unhooked himself from the line and shouted, "Clear."

Bracing a hand on the rocky edge of the bank, he walked along it and out of the way of the next rappeler. He removed his helmet, gloves, and harness and, finding a clump of the harsh yellow grass to act as a cushion, sat down and watched while Roger lowered himself over the edge and down. He turned to look outward toward the city and the distant flicker of the water beyond. He'd have never guessed any of this was here. And he bet the neighbors weren't aware either.

"You have to ignore Hank. He's a little rough around the edges," Roger said as he approached him.

"No problem."

"Did his attitude roll off of you as easily as it seemed?"

"If I want to fight about something, I make sure it's important enough to shed blood. Things rarely are. Tying knots in the end of rope isn't significant enough to worry about."

Roger removed his harness and other gear and took a seat next to him. "This stuff we did today was a cakewalk for you."

Derrick shrugged one shoulder. "I do a lot of running and weight lifting to stay in shape." He changed the subject. "Who told you about me leaving business cards at some of the bars?"

Sam came over the edge and lowered himself with more caution than he or Roger had.

"I happen to have a small investment in one of the clubs you went to. The guy who owns the place happened to mention you stopped by and left the card."

He wondered if it was Larry and was tempted to ask. Naw, it couldn't have been him. He'd have said something to Roger about being extorted for sabotaging Ella's vehicle.

"Why am I here?" he asked. He figured it was so the other guys could get a look at him and decide whether they wanted him to be a part of their team.

Roger shrugged. "I just thought you'd like doing something physical. I kind of guessed you work out regularly. It's pretty obvious."

"It keeps me from having an attitude like Hank's."

Roger laughed. "I'm not sure there would be enough exercise in the world to take care of Hank's issues, but he's a good mechanic."

Sam joined them, and they watched while Martin rappelled like a pro down the drop-off, wandering over as he tugged off his gloves.

The four of them waited for Hank to appear.

Like the rest of them, he rappelled down the embankment with flawless technique and unhooked himself. Then started toward them. As though in slow motion, he lost his footing and slid belly-down on the edge of the slope.

All four of them turned aside, pretending they hadn't seen anything.

"Karma," Martin commented.

Derrick glanced away to hide his amusement, got to his feet, and gathered his gear. They all started walking to the garage, leaving Hank to catch up.

THANK GOD DAVIS was satisfied. It had taken longer than she expected, because somewhere in the middle of the next take something went wrong with the sound and the cameraman had to deal with it.

Ella was shaky with hunger, but had no time to eat since she was going to be late picking Micah up. Carmella handed off her clothes, and she rushed to the nearest restaurant to borrow their restroom and change.

Davis was waiting for her as she exited the restroom. "You'll need to sign a separate release for the video, Ella. They might want to use it as an actual commercial."

"I will, but I'll have to come in tomorrow and do it. I've got to get Micah." She bundled the skirt and blouse into his arms.

Davis fell into step with her. "You're going to have to find someone responsible to get him when things run late, Ella."

"I've been trying to, Davis. But I can't trust my kid to just anyone. And we don't have that many people we can depend on in our lives."

"You'll never make it across town in time to pick him up."

He was right. She pulled out her cell phone and dialed Patsy's number. It went directly to voice mail. She batted away the panicky feelings. She could call the school and tell them she'd be late. She'd only had to do that once before. She tried that and the phone went to a busy signal.

Could Derrick pick him up? She could trust him. He'd protected her, and he'd protect Micah. Would he be back from the obstacle thing he was doing with his boss? Please, God, let him be close enough to do it. She punched his number and the phone rang.

At the sound of his voice, her panic level eased. "Can you do me a huge favor?"

"Yeah, sure."

"I need you to pick Micah up for me at school. I'm stuck across town, and I can't get there in time, and I can't get through to the school on the phone."

"What's the address?"

She rattled it off.

"I'm on it. I'll call you when I've got him."

"Thanks, Derrick. I'll see you at the apartment."

Her heart was still beating high in her throat when she dialed the school once again and finally got a person. Five minutes on the phone with the school secretary and Micah's teacher cleared Derrick to pick Micah up for her this one time. She promised to come in tomorrow morning and fill out the paperwork to put him on the list of people allowed to pick Micah up, just in case.

She looked up to find Davis watching her.

"I've never been married, never had a child. I've had relationships and even lived with a woman for two years, but I never had to put her ahead of my work."

"It's different when you have a child, Davis. They have to come first. Ahead of your job, ahead of everything else in your life. Micah depends on me to keep him safe. Everything else takes a back seat to that."

"Not according to most of the models I've dealt with, but very few of them have children. At least until they're ready to retire. Why don't you bring him into the office sometime so I can meet him, and he can see where you work."

Where she worked? "If I get this contract, how will it be? Will it be one big marketing campaign and then that's it?"

"You'll be exclusive to them for the clothing line, but you can do other things outside of fashion."

She'd be at their beck and call. "I need full-time work, Davis. I need stability. Micah needs stability."

"If you get this contract, you will make enough money to be stable for a while."

And then what?

"Once you've built a name for yourself, Ella, there'll be other contracts."

She still had no steady job. For every application she filled out, there were a minimum of fifteen people looking to fill it, and this job depended too much on the whim of the client.

She'd get this, and she'd never know when she could work another job because she'd never know when they were going to call and need her. And no boss would hire her on a flexible schedule.

She needed to know how much she was going to make every week so she could budget and make it stretch as far as possible.

"You don't believe in any of this do you?" Davis said.

"You guys live in a fairy-tale world where you take the pictures and sign the contracts. Your models are at your mercy, waiting for that phone call, afraid to get full-time employment because there's no way your boss is going to let you take a day off to do your side job. Where your dream is your side job and it doesn't pay the bills.

"When Micah was a newborn, we lived out of our car for three weeks until I could find an apartment for us. There have been times we've eaten ramen noodles three times a day because it was the only food we could afford. I've gone hungry so my child could eat.

"If I sign a contract, it will be for an entire year, with a regular salary attached that I can depend on. And if this doesn't pan out, I'm walking away as soon as I find something full-time. Because I don't live in a fairy-tale, I live in the real world, where I worry how I'm going to pay for new pajamas or blue jeans or sneakers for my seven-year-old. Where I've worked jobs that would have turned your stomach just to make sure we had a roof over our heads. I have to go now."

She walked away because the tears were building, and she was *not* going to cry. Crying didn't solve a damn thing.

CHAPTER 20

I T WAS A big deal for Ella to trust him with Micah. He knew that, understood it. Micah was her world, the world he'd begun to share.

He'd been stopping over to see her every night before going to work, and they were continuing to get to know each other, getting closer, and it would continue if he didn't fuck it up. But the feeling he already had lay low in the pit of his stomach. He should never have accepted Roger's invitation.

By going to that dilapidated garage and joining in with whatever they had been training for, he'd opened a door. A door he hadn't wanted to open.

Goddamn that detective. Damn him to hell. This was going to fuck up his life. Fuck up his chances with Ella. He could feel it.

Was a chance to be loved too much to ask? Was having a normal life after seven years of stagnation too much to ask?

Traffic coming from the school crept by while buses whipped through and turned off in different directions. Around a curve, he fell in behind a minivan and crept along, following the flow of traffic.

He spotted Micah standing with a woman in front of the school. He let a Toyota, its blinker going like mad, ease out in front of him and took its place along the curb. He braved having his door hit to get out and walk over to identify himself.

The woman, mid-thirties with a pleasant face, eyed him up and down and must have decided he looked trustworthy, because she smiled.

"Derrick Armstrong," he introduced himself and offered his hand.

The woman's cheeks flushed a little when she shook it. "Shelley Lamm. I'm Micah's teacher."

"Nice to meet you. Hey, munchkin," he greeted Micah and offered his fist. Micah bumped it with his own.

"Do you need to see my driver's license or anything?" he asked the teacher.

"If you wouldn't mind."

He reached for his wallet and slipped the license out.

After taking down the number, she handed it back. "Ms. Bailey said she'd come in to fill out the paperwork to put you on the list of people allowed to pick up Micah in future. Remind her, if you wouldn't mind."

"I'll do that." He tucked the license back in place. "Ready to go, Micah? Your mom will meet us at the apartment."

Micah picked up his backpack and slung one strap over his shoulder. "Yeah, I'm ready."

Derrick opened the back door of the car. Micah climbed in, dumped his backpack on the floorboard between his feet, and fastened his seatbelt without him having to ask.

Derrick keyed in the password into his phone and handed it back to him. "I promised your mom I'd call as soon as I picked you up. Why don't you do that for me while I drive?"

"Okay."

Derrick eased into traffic. She was going to put him on the trusted list to pick up her kid. The thought irritated the burn in his stomach. She trusted him because he hadn't been honest with her. He'd tried to tell her a couple of times this week, but...Ella was a worrier. If he told her, she might try to give him a chance, but it would be too much for her.

If the school ran a background check on him...

He listened to Micah's conversation with Ella and it made the burn worse.

When Micah ended the call, Derrick asked, "Are you hungry, bud?"

"Yeah."

Maybe if he ate something the hollow feeling eating at his gut would ease. "We'll stop at a drive-through and pick up some burgers."

"And a milkshake?"

The hopeful gleam in Micah's eyes was impossible to resist. "What flavor?"

"Chocolate."

Of course. "Okay."

Twenty-five minutes later, after debating who was stronger, Aquaman or Thor, they arrived at the apartment. Micah keyed in the security code, and they went inside and rode the elevator up. Micah produced a key on a string from beneath his shirt and unlocked the door.

Ella sat at the bar, a glass of sweet tea before her and her head in her hands. She attempted a smile and slipped off the stool when she saw them. "I thought you might have swung through somewhere for something to eat."

"We got you a cheeseburger and fries, Mom."

"Thanks for thinking of me." Her gaze went from Micah to him. "Thanks for picking Micah up for me."

"No problem." He set the bag on the bar.

She put her arms around him and leaned in to be held. Something must have happened at the shoot. This was more than being late picking up Micah. When she looked up at him, he brushed his lips over her forehead then pressed his lips to hers.

Micah made a gagging noise. "Gross."

Derrick laughed. "Get over it, kid. One day, when you're a little older, you won't think it's gross at all."

"Yeah, I will," Micah argued, his nose wrinkled in disgust.

"You'll be trying to lock lips with every girl in school," Derrick teased.

"Yuck."

"All right you two, have a seat, and I'll get us some plates." Ella flashed him a smile.

After eating, they lingered at the table while Micah did homework in his room.

"How did the meeting with your boss go?" she asked.

"It was okay. I got along with most of the guys."

"Most?"

"There's always one asshole in every crowd. The key to getting along with them is to not respond to their assholery."

"Is that a word?" Ella asked, laughing.

He was glad to hear her laugh. Something had upset her. "My word for it. There's one guy who's bad news. I won't have to worry about him, though. This was a one-time deal." He hoped it was. If he was lucky, Roger would drop it, and he wouldn't hear anything else about what they were doing.

He changed the subject. "How was the shoot today?"

"It went okay. But I may have shot myself in the foot. I had a meltdown afterwards. I was tired, and I didn't have anything to eat before we started because I was too nervous to even nibble on crackers.

"And we had to do seven takes. One because some asshole blew his horn in the middle of it, and then another decided to shout across the street to someone on purpose. He grinned at me like an idiot afterwards. I wanted to give him a good view of my middle finger, but I controlled myself."

Derrick laughed.

"Then I'm rushing to change clothes to pick up Micah, because the blouse and skirt are worth more than half a week's pay, and Davis starts talking to me about another release I need to sign. And I told him I'd sign it tomorrow, but I needed to pick up Micah. Then I realized it was too late and I wouldn't make it in time.

"He started saying I needed to find someone to keep him during times like this, like I haven't already. And I snapped and told him he lived in a fairy-tale world with models at his mercy. And how if I didn't get a regular paycheck out of this marketing thing, I was walking away because I needed a full-time job, not something that leaves me hanging in between jobs."

"What did he say?"

"I didn't give him a chance to say anything. I just walked away. I'd been there since eight, and I was tired and hungry."

"And worried. Worried about Micah. And Micah was fine. He was standing with his teacher, waiting. He's a good kid, Ella, and has a good head on his shoulders. Sometimes when he looks at me, I can even see the adult he's going to be."

"Sometimes he even sounds like one," she agreed.

"Having social services on your ass that one time has made you hypersensitive. They aren't going to take Micah because you were a few minutes late picking him up at school. You'd called the school, talked to his teacher. You took all the right steps. Shit happens to everyone now and then. His teacher wasn't upset."

"You talked to her?"

"Yeah. Introduced myself and let her look at my driver's license."

"It seems you did all the right things, too."

He shrugged one shoulder. "I wanted her to know Micah would be safe with me."

"I knew he would be, too."

If he really wanted to keep them safe, keep their lives from being turned upside down, he'd walk away. He clasped her hand and held it against his cheek for a moment then kissed it.

"I wouldn't worry too much about the meltdown. I'm sure this Davis guy has dealt with worse than that."

She sighed, and didn't look too convinced. "I'll have to apologize tomorrow when I go in to sign the release."

She'd been put through as much shit as he had dealing with asshole bosses. She'd stood up for herself the first night they met. Why wasn't she doing it with this guy? "Did you mean what you said?"

"Yes. Every word."

"Then don't apologize. If you apologize, he'll think you didn't mean it. Or you're backing down. Stand by it."

After a brief pause, she gave a definite nod. "I will."

"I have to go, Ella. I need to sleep before work. I'll be replacing the suspension system on one of the wreckers tonight instead of doing tows."

"Is that a good thing or bad?"

"I'll let you know if I get the wrecker fixed. I'm going to tell Micah bye." He went to the Micah's bedroom door and tapped on the doorframe. "Gotta go, Bud."

Micah looked up from the book he was reading. "Thanks for the milkshake and burgers."

"You're welcome."

"You and mom are going together, right?".

"Yeah, we are." They called it hooking up these days, didn't they? But then that wasn't right either, because they had more than sex between them, though they had enough of that when they could steal away for a couple of hours on Saturday or Sunday.

And they talked. In fact, he couldn't remember ever talking to a woman so much, other than his therapist. But he still hadn't told her...

Micah looked like he wanted to say more, and Derrick stepped into the room. He went to the window next to the desk and glanced out at the courtyard to give Micah time to work up to it.

The sidewalks led to a mulched playground area with swings, slides, teeter-totters, and weird animals on springs for the smaller kids to ride. Two boys rode skateboards along a stretch of sidewalk behind the swings. While he waited for Micah to spit out what he wanted to say, he wondered why there wasn't a basketball court for the older kids.

When he turned back, Micah spoke in a rush, "There's this breakfast for parents next week. Mom's supposed to come and eat with me in the cafeteria. You can come with her if you want."

The hope in Micah's gaze was like a punch in the chest, and, overwhelmed with emotion, Derrick fought hard to catch his breath. He swallowed in an effort to ease the tightness of his throat. He'd fallen for the kid just like he had for Ella. "What time does it start?"

"I have the thing in my backpack." He bailed out of his chair with a twist and went to his bed to unzip his pack, returning with the letter.

He felt Micah's eyes on his face as he read the pamphlet. Next Friday at eight a.m. "You ask your mom to make sure it's okay with her, and I'll meet you both at school and eat with you."

Micah grinned. "Okay."

Derrick rested his hand on Micah's shoulder and gave it a light squeeze. "Thanks for asking me."

"Sure."

CHAPTER 21

Ella studied Jasmine's features. She looked more worn, almost haggard, since the last time they'd spoken. She could only imagine the dreams she had. She'd had a few herself since her experience with Larry. How much worse it must be for Jasmine since he'd succeeded in his intent.

The breeze seemed a little warmer this time as they sat at the picnic table, but Jasmine kept rubbing her arms, as though she was cold.

"We have a new girl working now. She's young, Ella. Barely legal to serve liquor. The first day one of the customers patted her on the ass, and she nearly freaked out. She's virgin territory, and Larry's homing in on her like a wolf on a sheep."

Dear God. "Take her aside and tell her what he's like. Warn her so she can quit before it happens. Get the other women to stick with her so they can protect her, and you can protect each other."

"We've been doing that for weeks. He's getting wise to it, and he's getting bolder. Making threats."

"Has anyone thought about calling his wife and letting her know what he's doing?"

Silence hung between them.

"If he found out which one of us did it…"

Ella could do it. She could play the audio file over the phone.

But she'd have to call from a prepaid phone that couldn't be traced.

"I've sent the cops everything, Jasmine. I don't know why they aren't investigating him." She gripped Jasmine's hand. "Why can't you walk away?"

"My mom got laid off six months ago and hasn't been able to find anything but a waitressing job. She and my little sister had to move in with me. I have to have this job."

Ella understood being stuck between a rock and a hard place. But to put up with rape to eat...

"Talk to this girl and tell her straight-up that he's a rapist. At least then you won't have anything to feel guilty about if she doesn't leave."

"Call the cops, Ella. Ask them if they got the letter you sent." Jasmine sounded like she'd almost reached her limit.

Ella gripped her hand again. "I will, I promise."

"I don't think I can bear it if he touches me again." Jasmine shuddered and looked like she might be sick.

The desperation she heard in Jasmine's voice gripped her by the throat. "Throw up on him. That will kill his mood."

Jasmine laughed, but it sounded more like a sob.

"I'll try to come up with something more I can do to help you. I promise."

"Just having someone to talk to... The other girls just want to block it out. If they don't talk about it, it can go away for a while. One of them said she goes to another place until it's over. Why should we have to do that, Ella?"

"You shouldn't. Can you videotape him threatening you? You could take it to a lawyer and sue him for damages. The whole group could go to a lawyer and sue him. There's strength in banding together, Jasmine. If you all stood together, it would be five—or however many of you there are—against one.

"Tell me you'll do that. I'll make you a list of good attorneys if you'll do it."

"Make the list, and I'll try to get him on tape like you did. If I do, will you go with me?"

"Yes, I'll go with you." Finally, Jasmine was thinking proactively.

She gathered her purse. "I have to go. Thank you for being my support system."

"Stand strong, Jasmine. And talk to the others. I'll get on that list for you."

"Okay. Can I call you?"

"Yes, any time you need to." Ella walked with her to her car.

"Thanks, Ella." She sounded so young, as young as the girl she was trying to protect.

"I'll send you that list tonight."

Jasmine hugged her. "Thanks."

Ella slid behind the wheel and locked the doors, but didn't start her car. She wanted to help the women, but she couldn't leave herself open to the public scrutiny of a trial, if it even went that far.

A hard hand of guilt clamped around the back of her neck. She could call the cops if she got the prepaid phone, and see if they'd investigate. Someone had to help these women.

She started the car and drove around aimlessly, trying to build up her nerve. If she was going to do something, she had to do it before she picked up Micah. She drove to College Avenue and sat in the Walmart parking lot for a moment. She could call the cops and report it. She could play them the audio file. She could call his wife and play it for her. She could do this.

Twenty minutes later she bought the phone. Once in the car, she started the engine, attached the phone to the car charger, and used her regular cell phone to look up the non-emergency number for the police. Impatient and fearful she'd back down, she muttered "fuck it" and dialed nine-one-one.

Ten minutes later she was still trembling when she ended the call. She'd played the audio file for the dispatcher, given her all the information. She'd done everything she could.

Next, she looked up Larry's home address and phone number. She dialed it. "Mrs. Leland. Am I speaking to the wife of the Larry Leland, the owner of the Honey Pot?"

"Yes, you are. What's this about?"

"Mrs. Leland, I'm calling about your husband. I know this will be a shock and I'm really sorry, but I need to tell you something. Larry's molesting the girls who work for him at the Honey Pot. He corners them in the back room and forces them to have sex with him.

"You're crazy. How dare you tell such lies? My husband just runs that place to keep you and the other girls off the street. All you are is a bunch of hookers anyway."

"Is that how he describes us? We're not. We're just regular women with families, children, trying to keep our families together and safe. Your husband threatens to blackball the women to keep them from quitting and getting other jobs. He's treating them like his own personal harem."

She placed the track phone to the speaker of the other phone and hit the play button.

When she brought the track phone back to her ear all she heard was silence. Mrs. Leland had hung up.

Ella didn't know if she'd listened long enough to hear any of it, but at least she tried. She turned off the phone and slipped it into her purse.

"Please don't let any of this backfire." Uncertain if she was speaking to herself or the Powers that Be, she put the idling car in gear and pulled away.

DERRICK FELL FACEDOWN on the bed with a groan. He'd been up seventeen hours. He managed to catch a couple of hours of sleep sometime before six, but any benefit had long ago run out. His whole body ached.

But he only had two more weeks to go before the end of the semester. He could do this... He was out before any other thoughts could take hold.

He woke to several knocks on the door and staggered to his feet in his boxer briefs. He'd been asleep less than thirty minutes.

Whoever it was, he was going to rip off their head and jam it up their ass. They'd be talking out their asshole for the rest of their days. He jerked open the door.

Ella jumped startled.

His rage disintegrated as thoughts of why she would be here rushed in.

"I'm sorry for waking you, but I want to see you, and Micah is with one of his friends upstairs until after dinner. He'll be there until at least seven."

He held open the door and stood to the side so she could come in. Would she have braved this neighborhood just to see him? "Is something wrong?"

"Nothing. You can lie back down, and I'll lie down with you. I brought you dinner so you can nuke it in the microwave before you leave for work." She set the bag in the refrigerator and started bailing out of her clothes. When she reached a pale green bra and a matching thong, he was already rock hard.

She crawled up from the end of the bed and curled against him. "I just want to be close. I wish we could be together like this more. I want to know what it's like to sleep with you, Derrick. To go to sleep with you holding me and waking up the same way. Think you could learn to be a cuddler?"

His sleep-deprived brain stumbled to find something to say. "I could work on it."

Jesus, he was still asleep. He was dreaming, he had to be.

He turned on his side to hold her closer. The feel of her warm skin, the way her body nestled against his gave his hard on a boost. "If I ever start working days, what do you think Micah might think about me sleeping over?"

"I don't know. I've never had anyone stay over."

Pleased with that, heat flushed his face. He had to be careful he didn't get too possessive, though. God, he was so tired of second-guessing his own feelings. "Did he ask you about the breakfast this Friday?"

"Yes. If you want to come, we'd both be glad to have you join us."

He needed to tell her now, while they were together alone. He'd encouraged her to trust him, encouraged Micah. He'd destroy that trust if he didn't own up to his past and she found out somehow from someone else.

"It's special that he asked me, Ella"

"I know."

"Damn near brought me to my knees."

She started to draw back to look at him but he curled his fingers along the back of her neck and played with the thick, hair that lay against it while his lips brushed her forehead.

"Ella…"

Her lips moved along his collarbone, her breath heating his skin. He dragged in enough air to groan and slid downward to find her mouth with his own and palm one round, muscular cheek of her ass while he moved against her. He slid down farther to ease down her bra and latch onto one of her breasts to suck at the nipple.

Ella raked her fingers through his hair and massaged the back of his neck. They'd been together a lot lately, talking, kissing, touching each other, without being able to make love, and it had sharpened his hunger for her.

He slipped his fingers under the tiny scrap of fabric covering her mound and found the moist heat of her, coating his fingers while she moved.

"It's been a week, Derrick. God, please come inside me."

He shucked his boxer briefs while she shed her bra and slipped the thong down. He reached for his pants on the floor and found the condom he'd put in his wallet.

"You been saving that for anyone special?" she asked with a smile while he slipped on the condom.

"Only you. I don't see anyone but you, Ella. From the time I open my eyes at night until I go to bed in the afternoon, you're the only woman I think about."

Her features softened. "Show me what you think about."

"I think about that first time we were together. How you took me in, and how you moved over me."

He turned to slide between her legs and rubbed the head of his penis against her.

Ella's eyes fluttered and she spread her legs in invitation. He eased inside her, and when his body covered hers, she ran her hands up his back. "I don't think of anyone else like this, either," she murmured, cupping his cheek. Her answering response was eager, giving, building his need and hers. Had he ever felt this way about a woman? Had he ever shared this much with one?

Her hands trailed up and down his back, then down over his ass. He eased back and thrust forward, slow, easy, and her body rose to meet him. They set an unhurried rhythm, building slowly, stretching it out. Until his control broke and he had to quicken the pace.

The ragged sound of her breathing, and the small, breathy sound she made when she found her release, sent him over the edge.

He muscles felt lax, his eye lids heavy as he rolled to one side and rose to take care of the condom. He returned to the bed to cuddle against Ella's back and hold her.

"Go to sleep. I'll just lie here with you until you go under. You need to rest." She stroked the arm he put around her waist.

"You're way more than a booty call to me, Ella."

"I know. You are to me, too."

He managed a chuckle.

"Sleep a little longer tonight. I'll see you tomorrow." She lifted his hand and pressed it to her cheek. He kissed her shoulder.

With the soft, warm feel of her in his arms, he drifted back to sleep.

ELLA TURNED IN his arms to watch him. She'd seen the exhaustion in his face when he opened the door, and couldn't bring herself to dump anything else on him just so he could comfort her. And he would have. But he had enough on his plate without shouldering more.

She'd turned to sex for the comfort, for the closeness she needed. Which wasn't fair to Derrick. He deserved better than that from her.

Guilt drove her out of the bed, and she eased out from under the weight of his arm and quietly slipped back into her clothes.

He was beginning to lose the lonely, lost look she'd caught glimpses of when they first met. The way his features softened when he saw her, the way he smiled... It gave her heart a turn every time. She was beginning to care for him. Or was it already more?

Something inside him touched her and soothed the empty, needy space inside her. She hadn't realized how vast that space was until she let him in.

Pulling the covers over him, and resisting the urge to kiss him, she dressed and slipped out of the apartment, securing the door behind her.

CHAPTER 22

THREE CARS PULLED into the parking lot outside the garage and Derrick returned the wave of a guy on the day crew, He'd had a conversation with the guy a few days ago in passing, him coming on shift and Derrick going off. Roger exited one of the vehicles and jogged his direction.

"How are things going?"

"Fine." Derrick nodded. "I have class in forty-five minutes, and I'd like a cup of coffee, so I better go."

"Classes going okay?"

"Good. We've moved on to TIG welding and are doing some larger projects for the school."

"Great." Roger's brows rose. "I may have to get you to do some welding for me at the body shop at the other garage. On occasion we have repairs that require welds. I'll let you know."

"Okay."

"The wrecker is riding good. The new suspension system is working just like it's supposed to."

"Good."

"Are you up for another Friday with the guys this week?"

God, he'd hoped Roger wouldn't ask. "I have a standing appointment with my counselor this Friday." Not to mention his promise to Micah to go to school and eat breakfast with him.

Roger started to say something, then seemed to change his

mind. "Maybe next week."

"Sure. Talk to you later." He slid behind the wheel and started the engine. He looked toward the floorboard where the detective's business card lay on the mat, staring at him accusingly.

Fuck, he needed to call the man.

Arriving at the college, he retrieved the business card and checked his watch. He had five minutes, which was all he was going to spare for this shit anyway. He dialed the number written on the back of the card and waited for Acampa to answer.

"Acampa."

"Armstrong."

"What can I do for you, Derrick?"

"Not a damn thing, but I have some information for you. They're training for something. Roger invited me to come out and hang with them a week ago. Told me it was an obstacle course, but it wasn't. They're building upper body strength, climbing ropes and rappelling off an embankment. The house where they meet to practice is in University City."

"Do you know the address?"

"No. But I think I can take you to it. They'll be there this Friday. It'll be up to you what you do with the information."

"Where will you be?"

"I won't be with them. I have my own life to lead. Meet me after class today." He chose the Chuck E. Cheese where he and Ella met. "I'll take you there, then I'm out of it."

"We could really use your help Derrick."

"I want a clean record, a home, and a decent car. We all want things we can't have. I'm not getting involved"

Acampa sighed. "Okay. I'll be there at three thirty, waiting in the parking lot."

Derrick hung up and got out of the car. Running late, he broke into a jog and took the front steps two at a time. He was running toward his life, not being stalled again by something that wasn't his business.

★

ELLA OPENED THE door to Patsy. She'd just gotten home from taking Micah to school, and she and Patsy shared breakfast frequently. "Would you like something to eat?"

Patsy shook her head. "Hot tea maybe?"

"Okay." She put on the teakettle and got out a mug and tea bag and set it in front of her.

"I miss Micah." Patsy said as she toyed with her spoon.

For someone who had been so happy only a couple of weeks ago, planning a wedding and a move, she seemed…stressed and…sad.

"Since you've been home so much, he hasn't spent more than an hour with me. I know I've been busy with my family and Charlie's, but you two are family too. Think it would be okay if I invite him over to my apartment for dinner tonight and we go to a seven o'clock movie? We'd be home by nine thirty, and I'd see he goes straight to bed when we get back."

Ella had to work hard to suppress a grin as she turned on the oven and set the temperature. "I don't mind at all if you want to invite him for dinner, and he's always up for a movie. I think he'd be thrilled to go on a school night. It will be a treat."

"I thought you and Derrick could use some alone time, though I notice he gets here around nine-fifteen every night and stays until ten thirty. That isn't much time for you two to spend together."

Ella grabbed the whistling tea kettle, poured hot water in Patsy's cup, and set the cup and a squeeze bottle of honey next to her.

"We make plans for Fridays because he doesn't have class and Micah's in school. He's off on Sundays, but tries to sleep in to make up for the little sleep he gets during the week, but we get the afternoon together with Micah. Monday through Thursday he works eleven to seven, then has classes from seven to three. He naps at about four and sleeps for about five hours, comes over to see me, then goes to work."

Patsy dunked the tea bag up and down, then added some honey. "I don't know how he survives like that."

Having promised Micah a cake, Ella got a mixing bowl and measuring cup from the upper cabinet next to the stove and retrieved a bottle of oil from below. "He says he catnaps between tow jobs at night. Some nights he only gets a couple of calls all night. It's the only way he can take classes and work at the same time."

"That can't be healthy, Ella."

She agreed, but it was what it was. She worried he might fall asleep at the wheel of the tow truck. "It's only for this semester. He'll drop down to one class next semester and be able to sleep more." She folded the eggs into the cake batter, poured it into the greased and flowered pan, and popped it in the oven.

"If I take Micah tonight, will the two of you get to share some alone time together?"

"Yes, I'm sure we will."

"Then consider it done."

Anticipation fired through her. "How's the family stuff going?"

Patsy's smile was only halfhearted. "I think the kids are finally getting used to the idea of me remarrying. They like Charlie, and they want me to be happy. I believe they think that when you're in your sixties you're already on your way out, so what's the point?"

Ella laughed. "They obviously haven't gone shopping with you lately. You run rings around me. But at least they're accepting things."

"Charlie's children are a different matter. They think I'm marrying him for financial security and that he's going to write them out of his will, leaving everything to me."

"Well, shit." Why were people so selfish they lost sight of what was important?

"That just about says it."

"What does Charlie say?"

"He's devastated. He feels like they care more about the money than they do him. He's talking about putting the money in a trust for his grandchildren to be divided equally among them and leaving each one of his children one dollar each."

Wow! "Well, that will certainly make a statement."

"I told him we could do a prenuptial saying that I don't get anything, but he thinks it's an insult to me to have to sign a legal document to pacify them."

"And what if something happened to you?"

"We talked it out, and we were going to keep our finances separate, and we would write a will that whatever we brought into the marriage would remain separate and would go to our children. We both thought that was good enough, but Karen and Charles Jr. don't think that's binding enough."

She read stress and pain on Patsy's face. Ella moved around the counter to put her arms around her. "I'm sorry you're going through this, Patsy. You and Charlie make a wonderful couple. He's crazy about you."

"I know he is. But his children don't want him to remarry. He's going to meet with them one more time tonight to try and change their minds. I never thought this would happen. Never dreamed it might cause a rift between him and his children. And it has already.

"They've hurt him. He's worked his entire life for what he has, and they want to reap the rewards because they feel entitled to it. They don't care about his happiness at all. That's how it feels to him—and to me." She sounded as weary as she did hurt.

It seemed money was the center of every issue. When you had it, it caused problems, and when you didn't, it did the same.

"I'm sorry for you both. But Charlie is his own man, and he can't allow his children to dictate how he should live his life. And they need to take care of their own business. He'll make them see that. He loves you."

"It's hard to go against your children when you love them, Ella. But you're right. They're adults, and they need to live their lives and let us live ours." She straightened her shoulders. "I thought Micah might take my mind off of it while I wait to hear what they have to say. My apartment has been so quiet without him."

"We've been trying to give you time to arrange everything. We thought you were busy."

"I have been. But I don't want us to grow apart, Ella." Patsy's eyes sheened with tears.

"I don't either. You're the closest thing we have to family." She hugged her again. "Micah's been a little worried about you moving. But Derrick and I have both reassured him you'll only be a few minutes away." She wiggled up into one of the barstools.

"How does Micah get along with him?"

"They're bonding over his football and motorcycle video games. He's good with Micah. Patient." She thought about mentioning his childhood but thought better of it. Derrick was very private. But then again, so was she. "He doesn't try to force things between them. He waits for Micah to initiate things."

"That's good. You haven't really dated since you've lived here."

"Guys are strange about women with kids. They figure one of three things if you're raising a child alone—one, you'll put out without much effort because you're as sex-starved as they are, or two, you're a ho and you're as sex-starved as they are, or three, you're good to be a friend with benefits, but they don't want to get too deeply involved because the kid is too much baggage.

"I've dealt with all three kinds by showing them the door. But Derrick isn't like that. He accepts that Micah and I are a package deal. Our first meal together was at Chuck E. Cheese. We talked while Micah played some games, then he played arcade games with Micah after we ate.

"And he respects my no-sex rule while Micah's in the apartment. I really wish I could afford a two bedroom with a door to lock..." She sighed. "I've arranged to switch out babysitting duty with Regina from upstairs on Saturday so Derrick and I can have some alone time on Sunday."

"You'll have some alone time tonight, and I'll try not to think about what you're doing while I'm watching the movie." Patsy put both hands over her eyes.

Ella laughed. "We may not be doing anything. He may be too tired and need to sleep."

"I doubt that."

He hadn't been yesterday, even though he was clearly exhausted. "You could be right."

"Have you heard anything about the contract with Brigitte Simpson?"

"Not yet. There were two other models who were doing photos and screen tests. It will probably take some time for Brigitte to make a decision." And they hadn't called her to do any more photography work in over a week. If she'd messed things up by speaking her mind, she'd have to live with it.

"They'll call, Ella. You're gorgeous, and you'll be a fresh face. With your dark hair and eyes, you'll beat out all those tall, leggy blonds."

"I'd settle for a nine-to-five job, Patsy, if I could find one. But at least I still have a couple of months before I have to start worrying." Or start stripping again.

"It's going to work out, Ella. I have good feelings about this." Patsy slipped off the barstool. "I have some errands to run and a pizza to make for Micah. He loves my homemade pizza."

"*I* love your homemade pizza."

"I'll make two, and you and Derrick can share one."

"You don't have to go to all that trouble. But I'll have Micah bring you half the cake in the oven when he joins you. After I frost it."

"Sounds like a good trade. I'll just add a little more flour and yeast to the bowl. It's no trouble." She hugged Ella hard. "Send Micah over at five so you can primp a little before Derrick comes. Thanks for making me feel better."

"I didn't do anything but lend a little moral support." It seemed that was her job the past couple of days.

While she gathered laundry to wash, Ella pondered the behavior of Charlie's children for a moment. It was hard for her to understand why they'd even try telling to their father whether he could marry or not. She felt outraged on both Patsy's and Charlie's behalf.

Then her thoughts turned to Derrick, and she got out her

phone to shoot him a text about Micah's surprise movie date with Patsy.

His answer of *What time can I come over?* made her smile.

When she mentioned he had to sleep, his answer, *Sleep is overrated.* She laughed.

She wouldn't be able to primp until Micah was gone. If they wore each other out, they could sleep before he had to leave for work. Fingers flying, she typed. *How's five thirty?*

I'll be there.

She dusted furniture and washed laundry, iced the cake, and boxed up half of it to send to Patsy when she sent Micah over. The whole time the feeling of anticipation warmed her and made the numerous chores fly by.

It had been so long since she'd felt like this.

At the sound of the intercom, she wandered into the living room and pushed the button. "Yes."

"Ella Bailey?" A woman's voice came over the device.

"Yes."

"This is Detective Kelly Turner. I'm here about a recording and letter you sent to our sex crimes unit. I'd like to speak to you about it."

She'd often read about someone's heart dropping, and knew it couldn't happen, but the sensation she experienced was close.

CHAPTER 23

GRIPPING HER CELL phone, Ella caught the elevator down to the first floor. Exiting on the main floor, she walked to the front entrance and studied the woman through the window, wary of opening the door. She was an attractive five-foot-five, slim but solidly built, with sun-streaked brown hair pulled into a bun at the back of her head. She was wearing dark blue slacks, a white blouse with thin, pale blue stripes, and a dark blue blazer. Her blue eyes were cop eyes, taking Ella in even as she was studying the detective.

The detective pulled back the edge of the jacket to unhook her badge from her belt and in the process flashed her holstered weapon. She held the badge up against the window.

Ella really had no choice. She'd started this by mailing them the information and by calling the dispatch yesterday, but how the hell had they found her? Ella opened the door.

"Thanks for seeing me."

Ella couldn't say you're welcome. "How did you find me?"

"You gave the school your fingerprints for them to do a background check so you could volunteer there. Your prints were on the packaging, the flash drive, and the letter you sent us, so they popped up in the system."

Two women entered the building, and they had to move aside to let them by.

They couldn't really discuss anything in the entrance foyer of the apartment building. "Come upstairs and we'll talk."

"My partner is in the car. Do you mind if he comes up as well?"

It was too late to take everything back. She'd made the decision to send them the information. "No, that will be okay."

Nerves weakened her legs, and her breathing hitched like she'd been exercising too hard. She'd hoped to avoid any involvement, but it seemed it wasn't to be.

It took just a moment for the detective to text her partner and another for him to show up at the door. Five foot-nine, dark hair, Hispanic, with a wide, handsome face, he carried himself with a grace she'd seen in some male dancers.

He smiled and extended his hand. "Detective Vincent Sanchez."

She shook his hand, then turned toward the elevator.

Once inside the apartment, she offered them a seat and something to drink. "We're fine, Ms. Bailey," Sanchez said.

Ella settled in the only living room chair she had and tucked her hands between her knees. Her stomach jittered with nerves.

"Why didn't you report the assault?" he asked.

"Because I had no witnesses other than the audio file, and I didn't want my work history coming out. I have a seven-year-old. People today like to make themselves feel better by tearing other people down, by sitting in judgement on them. I don't want Micah knowing I stripped. And if anyone at his school found out, it would spread. Besides, if Larry was arrested and it went to trial, every juror would think, 'with her history, she deserves to be treated like a piece of trash.'"

Detective Turner was quick to say, "Not everyone would. We don't believe that."

"I never turned tricks. But they'd still think it. And Micah'd suffer for it."

Detective Sanchez leaned forward to rest his elbows on his knees. "And what about the other women you mentioned?"

"I went to one of them and tried to talk to some of the others.

I wanted them to come with me and report him. If we bonded as a group to stand against him, we'd be stronger. But Jasmine refused because she has a history, and the others wouldn't return my calls."

"So, you sent the audio file and the letter, hoping we'd investigate him?"

"Yes. A month ago."

"Then yesterday you called dispatch."

"Yes. One of the girls came to see me. Larry's hired a new girl, very young, and this girl who contacted me said Larry is doing the same thing to her that he's done to most the women he hires. He starts out by touching you. Nothing intimate at first…resting a hand on your shoulder, that kind of thing, then he progresses to brushing your breasts or patting you on the ass. If you tell him to stop, he ignores it. Then he starts crowding into your space. I told him I was a lesbian, hoping he'd stop, but he didn't.

"I called the dispatch yesterday, hoping someone would step in before he had a chance to attack anyone else."

She needed to tell them about the money. "I was afraid to go back to pick up my final week's paycheck, and later he sent me a letter and a check for five thousand dollars. It was hush money. I banked the check, but I still have the letter if you want it."

"We'd like to see it," Turner said.

She retrieved the envelope from her kitchen bill drawer and took it to her.

Turner removed the letter from the envelope and scanned it, then passed it on to her partner. "You didn't write him back or call him to tell him you'd stay quiet?"

"No, because I didn't have any intention of staying quiet if someone came around asking questions. His actions cost me my job. I thought of the check as severance pay for putting up with his harassment." She shuddered and rubbed her arms.

"When did this come?" Sanchez asked, raising the envelope.

"About a week after I quit."

"And what have you been doing since?" he asked.

"I've been doing modeling jobs. I'm working for the Morgan-

Tolliver Agency." Oh, Jesus. If all this came out... But Davis already knew about the attempted assault. "Mr. Morgan took pictures of me two days after the assault and asked me about the bruises on my neck. He may still have them."

"We'll check with him." Turner said.

"Has someone else come forward? Are you going to arrest him?"

The detectives shared a look. It was Turner who spoke. "No, we won't be arresting him."

After all this and they weren't going to do anything? "You have to. He's a sexual predator, a rapist. Why aren't you going after him?"

"Because Larry Leland is dead."

Oh, my God popped into her mind. Her vocal chords froze, preventing her from voicing it. The next moment fear ricocheted through her. It had to be murder. Did they think she did it?

"We need to ask you where you were last night about eleven."

She couldn't seem to take her eyes off them. It was like looking at two big snakes about to strike. Every muscle in her body went rigid.

She'd thought they were here to help, but they came only to accuse. "You came here under false pretenses, led me to believe you were here to investigate Larry, and now you're investigating me?"

"We believe Mr. Leland was killed because of his actions. We're attempting to rule you out as a suspect." Turner's tone was soothing.

Damn them. "I was with my son. I don't leave him here alone. Ever. He's only seven." Of all the days for her to tell Derrick not to come over.

"Do you have any proof you were here? A phone call? Did you go online on any social media sites?"

"Derrick, my boyfriend, called at ten thirty on his way to work to check in. We talked about ten minutes. He has to clock in at eleven."

"Where does your boyfriend work?" Turner asked.

"Carpenter Towing. His name is Derrick Armstrong. He leaves just in time for the late shift at the towing yard to go off at eleven and he takes over from there."

"We need to take the letter, Ms. Bailey."

"Take it." She rose, her heart beating hard, her legs feeling like rubber. Oh God, she'd called Larry's wife yesterday. Would she have been angry enough...? Had she listened to the file she'd played? "I have to go pick up my son from school."

The ride down in the elevator was tense and silent.

"If we need more information, we'll be back," Sanchez said.

She didn't reply, just strode to her vehicle, got behind the wheel, whipped out of her parking spot, and drove away. She couldn't get away from them fast enough.

DERRICK LEANED FORWARD in his seat and studied the house below. "That's the house and garage. They'll be meeting here this Friday. You could set up surveillance here and watch most of what they're doing." The scent of pine wafted through the window.

Acampa retrieved binoculars from the glove box and focused on the area below. "They're working their way up to asking you to join them. They need you to train them to do something."

"You don't know that." He was not getting involved.

"They just lost one of their team. He shattered his elbow in a fall and will be laid up for at least three months."

The guy that was building the gantry crane, maybe. "Why would they want to add someone else to the team? They'd have to give the new guy a cut Or get rid of him." He turned to look at Acampa. "These guys have a record of violence?"

Acampa lowered the binoculars. "Why do you ask?"

"Because Roger's boy, Hank, has an anger management issue. He's dangerous, and I think Roger keeps him on a short leash...until he doesn't."

"You're talking about Hank Petrey, then yes, he went to prison for four years for assault with a deadly weapon. It should have been attempted murder but was pled down."

"What about Sam and Martin?"

"Sam Bogart and Martin Lester. We believe Sam is the getaway driver. He ran his own chop shop and can boost any car. Martin is definitely the B and E guy. He has a history."

"If you have all the pieces, why don't you have them behind bars?"

"We haven't got any evidence. No fingerprints, no digital images on the cameras, they're covered from head to toe in black, no DNA. Nothing. We haven't even been able to trace any of the stolen merchandise. We think they must ship it out of state to sell."

"Then how the hell did you home in on these guys?"

"After the fourth robbery, we started looking at guys who had records for robbery and weeded through them. Martin's name came up. The jobs had some of the hallmarks of his technique. Then we started looking at some of the cons he worked with at the garage. But we didn't have the funding to stay on them twenty-four seven.

"Your boss hires a lot of ex-cons. And he knows a number of the parole officers who are in charge of them. He's been very smart. These guys don't miss a single meeting with their parole officer.

"We need you to work with us, Derrick. We need someone inside to let us know what their plans are."

"No. I'm trying to build a life, and I've already waited seven years to do that. Waited until I felt I could make it if I did. I've met a woman, and she cares about me." He was sure of it. "When I was a SEAL, I couldn't have that. I was too fucked up to sustain a relationship. This might be my only chance at normal and I have to take it."

"If they approach you and want you to teach them about something specific...."

"I'll let you know. I'll try to keep my ear to the ground, and if I hear anything, I'll let you know. But I can't be a part of what they're about, not even for you."

Acampa started the car. The green scent of pine and salvia from where they'd been sitting was whisked away as he moved forward and the breeze whipped through the car.

"Who was the guy who broke an arm?"

"Why?"

"Because Roger had me build a gantry crane for him. He'd already had the pieces machine cut. He mentioned that the guy who was supposed to build it broke his arm and couldn't finish it. He had me put a motorized pully on top of it."

"How do you suppose it could be used during a heist?"

"I don't know, but it can be used numerous ways at the garage and the body shop." And he'd given him extra pay.

Derrick's cell phone dinged with a text and he smiled. Ella's neighbor Patsy was going to take Micah for the evening, and they could have some alone time. He was all over that. He typed in his answer to her text.

Ten minutes later his phone rang with an unfamiliar number. "Hello."

"Derrick Armstrong?"

"Yes."

"This is Detective Vincent Sanchez with SDPD. I'd like to speak to you about a man named Larry Leland."

"What about him?"

"We have a few questions about what happened between him and your girlfriend."

"You should talk to her if you want the story."

"We already have, but we'd like to talk to you too."

"So, you're going to finally arrest him?"

He was aware of Detective Acampa's quick glance in his direction.

"We're investigating everything that's been going on at the Honey Pot."

"From what Ella's told me, it's about time."

"Can you meet us at your apartment?"

"Tomorrow at four would be better for me. I have an appointment at five thirty today."

"Can you change it?"

He wasn't going to. "No, I can't."

"It will only take a few minutes."

"I'll be getting ready for my appointment. If you're there at four on the dot you can have fifteen minutes."

"We'll be there."

Fifteen minutes would give him just enough time to shower and get ready to go over to Ella's apartment. He ended the call.

"Care to share?" Acampa asked.

What could it hurt? The cops were already investigating Larry.

Derrick gave him a quick rundown of the night he met Ella.

Acampa's features hardened. "And your girlfriend sent them a letter about all this?"

"Yeah. Over a month ago."

The phone rang again. It was Ella. Her breathing was uneven, and he could tell she was upset. "The police were here. Larry's dead, and they wanted to know where I was last night."

Jesus!

Everything had just gone to hell.

CHAPTER 24

THE TWO DETECTIVES were waiting in their car across the street from Mama's house. He spotted them as soon as he pulled in. They exited their vehicle, walked up the drive, and introduced themselves.

The woman was attractive but buttoned-up. The man would be trouble for him. His body language projected wariness, and he eyed him with the look that said, *I'm just waiting for you to make a move.*

Derrick led the way up the stairs and unlocked the door, noticing Detective Sanchez rested his hand on his gun, and Derrick gave him a steady look.

"I don't own a weapon of any kind. I'm following the guidelines of my release to the letter." He opened the door and stood aside so they could enter. He gestured to the only upholstered chair he had for Detective Turner while he took a seat on the end of his bed. Turner grabbed a kitchen chair from under the small kitchen table and moved it so they bracketed him.

"We checked you out on our way over." Sanchez said.

"I'm sure you did."

"How did you meet, Ella Bailey?" Turner asked.

"She called me from the Honey Pot for a tow. Just as I arrived, she came running out of the building like the place was on fire. She was shaking, upset, and looking over her shoulder every few seconds, and gripping a hair spray can for all she was worth. She asked if she could sit in the wrecker while I assessed the car. Someone had punctured both her front tires.

"A few minutes later her boss came out with a baseball bat, and his eyes were red and he was wheezing a little. He took a swing at the back-quarter panel of the car and dented it, and was about to take another when I took his picture with my phone and threatened to call the cops.

"That settled him down. The cleaning crew came out and got in their cars to leave, and I put two and two together. He'd punctured her tires to leave her stranded with him alone so he could make his move.

"He had the whole thing down pretty good, like he'd done it before. I guessed what he'd done and ran the whole thing for him. Pointed out the cleaning crew had seen her run out just like I had. Said if I were him, I'd try to make some restitution for the trouble he'd caused her. He gave me five hundred dollars to pay for the two tires, the tow and the front-end alignment. And a thousand dollars to keep my mouth shut."

It was probably better not to tell them he and Ella had split the money.

"So I towed her car in and replaced the tires. She had to bring the car back in the next morning because I had another tow job and couldn't get to the front-end alignment. The day crew did that for her."

"I gave her the company business card and wrote my number on the back. Told her if she decided to press charges to give me a call and I'd testify to his behavior that night. She'd hid in the cab out of sight the whole time.

"Five days later she called me, and I met her at Chuck E. Cheese for pizza. She brought her son, Micah. We started seeing each other. I go over to see her most nights during the week between nine and nine-thirty, and stay until ten thirty. I have to be at work by eleven. We try and get together after I get off on Fridays and have breakfast before I have to sleep. It's the only time I don't have class."

"Class?" Turner asked.

He explained about his welding classes, his schedule.

"But you didn't go over last night."

"No, I was pretty exhausted. I've been going on four and five hours of sleep for weeks. I needed the extra hours sleep."

"Does she know you have a record?" Sanchez asked.

"Not yet." He clenched his hands. Would they tell her? If she became afraid of him... She'd dump him. Or would she?

"What time did you leave for work last night?" Turner asked.

"Ten thirty. It takes twenty-five minutes for me to get from here to the garage. I called Ella to check in with her, and talked to her for a little while on the way. I clocked in at eleven and started taking tow calls as soon as I arrived."

"Has she ever left her son alone at home while she runs errands?"

So they were looking at her, not him. Relief and concern— then outrage—warred inside him. Ella had fought back that night, but she wasn't a killer. "She would never leave Micah alone. She's very protective of him. Her next-door neighbor, Patsy, babysits if she needs someone to keep him."

"How has she been since the attack?" Turner continued the questioning while Sanchez wandered the room, sliding open the kitchen drawers and opening doors. Did they really think he'd leave any kind of weapon out for them to find? Since he didn't have anything but a paring knife in the house, he probably didn't have much to worry about.

"She was shaken that night, but the next time I saw her she'd found her balance and she was moving on, talking about finding a new job. Then she started modeling. She's up for a big contract with a clothing designer."

"And if her name comes up in the paper associated with a lowlife like Larry Leland?" Sanchez asked, moving back to them and sitting down again.

He studied the detective through narrowed eyes. "They could make her the poster girl for the #metoo movement if they slanted the story right. A brave woman escaping from a sexual predator who's made sexual slaves out of his employees and continued to molest them while holding hostage their ability to make a living.

"Ella didn't kill Larry Leland. But there are several women still working for him with a stronger reason to." And in his opinion, whoever had done it deserved a medal.

"So you talked to Ella before we arrived?"

"Yeah. She was upset about being accused when she'd gone out of her way to try and point you in the direction of a rapist."

"We might have gotten on it quicker if she'd come in and reported it face-to-face. We can't gather evidence if people aren't willing to talk to us."

He studied Sanchez. "You can't gather anything if you don't show up to ask the questions, either. You've had a month. Are we done?" He addressed Turner.

"Yes, we're done." She rose and shot her partner a look.

Sanchez stood. "We'll be checking on the time you reported to work and looking into the towing jobs you did last night."

"Let me help you with that. I have my work phone, I answered the calls, the numbers will still be on there." He stood and moved across the room to the table he usually dropped his change on. He brought back the phone and keyed in the password. "The time I received the call will be on there, and you can call the customer back while we're sitting here." Because he didn't trust the son of a bitch.

He handed Sanchez the phone. "I had two back-to-back tows, one at eleven, one at twelve fifteen. The first was a flat tire, and I was able to fix it and get them back on the road. The second was an accident, and the vehicle is still there in the yard waiting for the insurance adjuster to take a look at it." *Fuck you very much, asshole.*

As soon as the two detectives left, he climbed in the shower, but even there thoughts kept rolling around in his head. They'd tell Ella about his record. Sanchez or his partner would be on the phone to her at the first opportunity. He needed to get out in front of it if he could.

But how could you get out in front of something like a seven-year prison sentence?

CHAPTER 25

WHILE ELLA PACKED Micah's overnight bag, she stewed over every question the cops had asked her. They couldn't really believe she'd done anything to Larry. He'd attempted to rape her but hadn't succeeded. He'd given her money to stay quiet. And she hadn't been back to the Honey Pot since she left.

Her visit with Jasmine yesterday morning... Could she have killed Larry? She'd certainly been on the edge. If Jasmine had taken the law into her own hands, as much as Ella abhorred violence, she hoped she got away with it. But she didn't believe Jasmine had done it.

Why hadn't the police looked into things when they received her letter? All they had to do was listen to the audio file. Why hadn't they done it?

Why had they waited? Larry would be in a cage, alive, the girls would be safe, and she wouldn't be worried they were going to come here and arrest her.

"Are you done yet, Mom?" Micah broke into her thoughts as he stood at the bedroom door. He was excited about the movie, since he rarely got to go during the week. And then they had the breakfast tomorrow morning at school.

"Yes, I'm done." She held out his bag. "What movie are you and Patsy going to see?"

"Aquaman." He grabbed the bag.

"Another superhero. That's right up your alley."

"Yeah. Derrick's almost as big as him."

"Is he?"

"I bet he could arm wrestle Aquaman and win."

Ella bit her lip to keep from smiling. "Maybe he could. He's pretty strong." He'd lifted the tires to put on her car without any trouble.

The phone rang, and she followed Micah out of the room to answer it. "Patsy has your pizza in the oven, and she wants you to bring one back here for me and Derrick."

"Okay." He raced off to run the short errand while she waited for him at the open door.

He walked back down the hallway with the pizza at a more sedate pace. "You think Derrick's coming to breakfast tomorrow?" he asked as he handed over the round pan.

She breathed in the aroma of sauce and peperoni as she placed the pizza on the stove. "He'll be there. He's looking forward to it." She handed him the plastic cake container with half the cake she'd baked for him.

Micah's grinned and shuffled with exaggerated care back down the hall to Patsy's apartment.

She got out the dusty bottle of wine she'd been saving to go with the pizza, rinsed it, and put it in the refrigerator to chill. She'd also bought a six-pack of beer in case Derrick wanted to drink a beer with his pizza.

Anxiety had her pacing. She wanted to know everything the cops said to him. Would they think he'd done something? God, she hoped she hadn't brought trouble to his door.

She should never have called Larry's wife.

Her cell phone rang and she picked it up off the island. It was Davis.

"Hello."

"Hi. I wanted to let you know right away. You've got the contract, Ella. Brigitte wants you for the marketing campaign. Congratulations."

"Oh." Stunned she stared into space, her mind a blank. Hearing any kind of good news on top of everything that had transpired just seemed…ironic. "I didn't really think she'd give it to me. I thought she'd pick someone well-known who could bring her more recognition."

"You have to watch the commercial we made. You've got to see how you look, how you sound. I'll show it to you when you come in to sign the contract."

"I'm just…" She couldn't get enough air in her lungs. "I just never dreamed she'd give me a chance."

"I told her what you said about the salary. I know it wasn't my place, but she thought it was totally reasonable. It'll be up to the two of you to hammer that out. But she's already hired us to do the photography for magazine layouts, shows, and a number of other things.

"Congratulations, Davis. I'm really happy for you."

"Thanks. I hope you're excited."

She lowered herself to the couch, her legs feeling a little weak. "I think I'm having a panic attack."

He laughed. "No, you're not, Ella. You're going to be great. Can you come in tomorrow?"

"Yes, of course. What time?"

"Eleven. I have another client I'll be taking some quick shots for, but afterwards I've set up a small celebration for the crew and us."

He had every right to be excited. She might be getting excited after all. "Okay. Thanks, Davis. I'm sure she realizes it's the genius behind the camera who makes me look good and doesn't want to screw up a good thing."

He laughed again. "You're giving me way too much credit. It's all about you, Ella."

She didn't know what to say to that and managed a, "Thanks."

"See you tomorrow." He hung up just as the intercom buzzed.

She had something positive to tell Derrick. She rushed to the door and swung it open. He wore a pale blue knit pullover shirt tucked into khakis, the color making his eyes look startlingly blue.

His hair had managed to grow out enough so he actually had to brush it back off his forehead, and now streaks of pale color overlaid the sandy blond. He looked so handsome, and he smelled delicious.

She'd seen him in his work clothes often, in dressier clothes rarely. She wanted to just gaze at him for a moment. It also made her glad she'd taken the time to clean up a little too. The spring-weight sweater of cream, gold, and burnt sienna had been a gift from Patsy. She'd said she had to buy it for her because it reflected the colors in her eyes. Cream-colored pants and black flats completed the outfit.

"For you." He produced flowers from behind his back, the icing on the cake.

No one had ever given her flowers. And her eyes burned. The pink, orange, and yellow Gerbera daisies mixed with some baby's breath lay nestled in a bed of green tissue.

"Thank you, Derrick." She held them against her and stepped back to let him in. When she looked up from admiring the flowers he murmured, "God, Ella." He cupped her face and kissed her.

She rested against him and brushed at the tears that ran down her cheeks. "No one's ever given me flowers before."

He gave her waist a squeeze. "That's a damn shame. You've been dating the wrong guys."

She laughed. "Meaning you're the right guy?"

"Yeah."

He was. He touched her in so many ways. She tilted her head to look up at him. "I have some news."

His expression shifted to concern. "Good or bad?"

"Good. I got the contract to do the marketing thing for Brigitte Simpson's Designs."

His smile lit up. "That's great, honey."

"And she's going to give me a monthly salary. We're going to talk about it when we do contract negotiations. Mr. Tolliver is going to represent me."

"That's wonderful." He gave her a squeeze.

"I'll be at her beck and call for as long as that lasts."

"That's the way it works. I'm tied to the phone for seven hours. You'll get used to it."

"I don't know if I'm happy or terrified."

"You'll be able to decide once you stop worrying about the other things that happened today." His hands moved restlessly up and down her arms.

"I don't know if they suspected me or not."

"They know you were on the phone with me between ten thirty and eleven, Ella. All they have to do is check the cell towers and they'll be able to pinpoint where you were at that time."

"I was right here with Micah all night."

"I know, honey."

"I need to get this off my mind, and I need to put these in water." She moved to the kitchen, got a pale green tea pitcher out of the cabinet and filled it with water. She unfolded the tissue paper and carefully removed each flower and placed it in the pitcher. It made a perfect centerpiece for the small kitchen table.

"Patsy made us a pizza. She and Micah are sharing one right now. They'll be leaving for the movie at six thirty."

"Maybe I can go over and say hello before they leave."

Twice in five minutes he'd done something thoughtful that touched her. "Micah would love it. He's so excited you'll be joining us for breakfast. And I got some beer in case you want one with your pizza. Or I have wine."

"A beer will be great. I used to be a big beer drinker, but I think I've outgrown it. I rarely drink anything but water or sweet tea anymore. Can we go for a drive before we eat?"

"Sure."

"Let's swing by Patsy's on the way out."

"Okay."

PATSY STUDIED DERRICK with the sharp gaze of a protective grandmother, but he quickly won her over with the easy way he spoke to and interacted with Micah. The two were using the computer to look up all the Marvel superheroes and having a deep discussion about who was the strongest, smartest, and who had the coolest superpowers.

Then Patsy leaned over and whispered in her ear, "He's hot."

Ella laughed. "Yeah, he is. He brought me flowers."

"Good. It's time someone noticed you're worth a little extra attention."

"He gives me that. And it was his idea to come over and see Micah before we went for a drive."

"That's nice."

"Does he have children?"

"No, and he's never been married." He'd never talked about any of his ex-girlfriends except the dancer. She wanted to ask about them, about why he'd never married. But would it sound like she was hinting for something more permanent than either one of them were ready for?

Once they were in the car, Derrick pulled out and headed south.

It always seemed she was dumping things on him, but she couldn't share all this with Patsy. "I want to tell you two things I did yesterday. One the police know about and one they don't. I had a good reason for doing both."

Derrick glanced away from the road to her, then right back. "All right. Let 'er rip."

"I bought a prepaid phone so no one could track my number, and so I could call the police dispatch and report Larry."

He remained silent for a moment. "Why did you do that?"

"Because I didn't want them to know it was me calling."

"They don't know you have two phones yet."

"They have the transcript of the call, and they'll eventually notice it came from a different number."

Derrick's features remained carefully blank which only served to make her stomach do cartwheels.

"I called Larry's wife and told her everything."

Derrick glanced at her again, his expression concerned. "Why did you do that, Ella?"

"Jasmine said Larry hired a new girl who's very young and inexperienced. He's been stalking her at work like he does them all. I just wanted someone to stop him."

"You'd gotten out of that situation. And now…" He whipped into the parking lot of a strip mall. "You have to throw that phone away. Do you have it with you?"

"No. I left it in a drawer at the apartment."

He's blue eyes had never looked so intent. "Ella, they might try to say you forwarded your calls from your phone to the other one. You could be anywhere, doing anything with two phones, and they wouldn't be able to pinpoint your location. Even taking Larry out."

She felt the blood drain from her head. He whipped back into traffic and started back to the apartment.

"You're going to go in and get it, and we'll go somewhere and throw it away."

"I didn't kill him, Derrick. There won't be any DNA or anything from me there to say I did."

"You worked there three weeks, Ella. And do you really think they clean that place well enough to have wiped away all your fingerprints, not to mention all the other stuff people shed and leave behind everywhere they go?"

Probably not. Her mouth was dry and her heart was trying to climb its way up into her throat.

HE DROVE BACK into the parking lot and leaned over to grip her hand. It was ice cold. "It'll be okay."

He tried to keep his tone soothing in spite of his insides jumping like he'd just been in a firefight. "Go get it, and we'll take care of it. Did you turn it off once you'd made the calls?"

"Yes. I only charged the battery enough with my car charger to make the calls, then I turned it off."

She slid out of the car, keyed in the code and entered the building.

Her heart was too tender. It was going to get her into more trouble than she could deal with. Jesus, she'd been protecting someone she'd never even met. He rubbed at his temples.

Dear God. Just the thought of Ella behind bars had him gasping for air. She'd never make it in a cage. Never.

Ella appeared in the doorway wearing a heavier sweater. She walked with her hands in her pockets. She slipped back into the car and dropped the phone in the cupholder between them. Derrick pulled out of the parking space and out onto the street.

"Where did you buy it?"

"Walmart on University. I didn't do anything wrong, Derrick."

"I know you didn't." He gripped her hand.

"Where are we going?"

"We're going to Ocean Beach Pier, and we're going to drop that sucker into the ocean. When they come back to you and ask where the phone is you called from, you tell them you threw it away after you made the calls, which is technically correct."

"What made you think about the call forwarding?"

"I knew a guy who was a whiz with phones, computers, any kind of technology. The things he did weren't always on the up-and-up. He was a little bit of a screwup, but you couldn't help but like him. He said he'd never own anything the police or government could track him with again. He'd gone AWOL—that means he left his post, was a deserter.

"He wanted to see his girl, and they tracked him down using his cellphone. She dumped him, and he'd been drowning his sorrows for about a month, and they tossed him into the brig. He said he lost track of time. I guess you have a tendency to do that if you stay drunk for days at a time."

"Poor fellow. Were you...there with him?"

"Yeah. He got out after a month."

Ella sat motionless, her white-knuckled hands gripping each other. "How long were you...there?"

"I was only there a few months. I was in Miramar Military Prison for seven years."

He glanced in her direction. It had been a shitty way to tell her, but she needed to know before he went to the school tomorrow. If he was still welcome. He needed to tell her before the detectives did.

The silence built as he wove his way toward the pier. The longer it stretched, the harder it was for him to break it. The pain grew, filling him, solid, immovable, making it hard for him to breathe. He beat it back, though it cost him a burning stomach and the beginnings of a headache.

He found a parking space and whipped into it, then turned the car off. He got the burner phone, took off the back, popped out the battery, and put it back together. Wind buffeted the car, and the sky out to sea looked gray and sulky.

"I knew. I just didn't want it to be true." She grabbed one of the napkins in the console as tears streamed down her cheeks. "You never talked about any time after your SEAL career. You never mentioned a girlfriend other than the dancer or the one you hit. Or told stories about anything that happened after you left the Navy. There was a void."

He gripped his forehead where the headache pounded at his temples. "One day is much like any other when you're behind bars, Ella. I worked in the laundry, or did maintenance on the building, or put stuff together in the machine shop. And the years dragged by until I thought I might go crazy if I had to hear the cage doors slam one more time.

"I ached to hear a friendly voice over the phone. My mom was the only one who called. I hungered for an affectionate touch that never came, because none of my family visited.

"During the summer, when the air conditioning wasn't working, I'd lie on the concrete floor to sleep because just having sheets against my skin made me sweat so much I'd feel weak when we were called down for breakfast. The smell of sweat permeated everything in the cell. I'd drink as much as I could during the day, hoping to offset the effects of dehydration later.

"I read as much as I could to escape. And I read lots of self-help books on anger management. I'd play cards with some of the guys in the common area, or lift weights, or I'd exercise, hoping I'd be too exhausted to lie awake wishing for a free breath that wasn't shared with a hundred other guys on my block."

"There was a program where we trained dogs, and I took one, but when I had to give him up… I knew I'd have to, but to have another living thing in the cell with me…" The unexpected rush of emotion caught him and his voice broke. "I'd grown attached. I didn't do another. Couldn't.

"I'd look forward to meetings with my psychologist because she was the only female voice I heard for days. When we had a female on the floor, she'd have to be a cast-iron bitch or a cardboard cutout on a recruiting poster to keep the guys in line. If she got too friendly, the guys would take advantage."

He raised his head to look at her. "The first time we made love was the first time I'd been with a woman in seven years."

Seeing the pity in her expression, he released his seat belt and reached for the door handle.

She grabbed his arm. "Stop, Derrick." She drew a deep breath. "Let's walk along the pier."

CHAPTER 26

THE WIND RIPPED and tugged at their clothes as the afternoon turned to evening. Ella narrowed her eyes against the breeze and wrapped her sweater around her more closely. As carefully as Derrick always touched her, he was avoiding it now, though he raised a hand to take hers as they walked onto the pier, then withdrew it.

He'd just given her a glimpse of seven years of his life. Being trapped in her apartment with nothing to do was driving her crazy, and she couldn't even begin to imagine what seven years of it would do to her.

He'd said he was violent. He said he'd been messed up. She should have connected the dots, but she hadn't wanted to. Because she'd been as tired of being alone as he was. He'd been charming, thoughtful, attentive and…seven years. How had he borne it?

Micah was bonding with him. And if she was going to end things, she needed to do it now, before he and her son got any closer.

They were midway down the pier when she stopped to look down at the water and lean against the railing. Derrick extended the phone to her. She slipped it into her pocket. She'd drop it in one of the trash receptacles nearby.

"I need time to think about this, Derrick."

"I know."

She couldn't stand still. She had the driving need to keep moving, because to stop would mean she'd start crying again, and crying solved nothing.

But the need to weep and wail for hours squatted on her chest like a two-ton boulder. She turned to walk farther down the pier.

He'd been trying to tell her for days. She remembered several instances where he'd started to say things and had drawn back at the last minute.

She wished he hadn't told her. She'd been happy. He'd made her happy. Even just watching television with him had been enough.

But how much more upset would she be if he hadn't told her and she found out later? A thought occurred to her. "The police yesterday... How were they with you?"

"Sanchez was a minor asshole. Turner was okay. They ran me, and Sanchez treated me like I was going to attack them at any minute, strutting around with his hand on the butt of his sidearm. Once he was in my apartment, he prowled around peeking in the drawers in my kitchen, looking in the refrigerator, and checking out the bathroom.

"Turner just seemed to want to get the job done. They contacted the two people I towed after I got to work, and Roger said they'd contacted him to see when I clocked in. They'll probably check with Mama about the time I left for work."

Because of her. "I'm sorry."

"For what?"

"The only thing you've done to be dragged into this is be with me."

"Because I have a record, they'll always be trying to prove I've done something wrong, even if I haven't. When I took the guy down who tried to hold me up, they were holding guns on me while trying to tie me to him, like we were in on the robbery together. If the garage security cameras hadn't been there, had my boss not been there, they'd have arrested me that night."

"Why?"

"Because I've been in prison, and because I did something once that put me there, and cops assume I must be doing something I deserve to be put back in for."

She couldn't picture what it could be. He wouldn't. He was working too hard to make a new life.

He started to say more, then looked off into the distance.

"Say it, Derrick. You've hidden things from me, just like I hid what I did a couple of days ago, and here we are."

"There's a cop who wants to use me to get information about my boss and some of his employees. He believes Roger is using the garage and body shop as a front to launder money from jewelry heists, and believes Roger's using some of the other cons he's hired to pull the jobs."

"How does he want you to help him?"

"He wants me to become part of their gang so when they make their next move, he can be waiting for them."

"Don't do it." She caught his arm. "If they suspect you have ties to the police, they'll kill you."

"I told him no, Ella. I was locked up with drug addicts and sex offenders, crooks, thieves, and violent offenders like me. I deserved to be there then, but I won't ever do anything to be put back in again."

"Don't let them drag you into something that will cost you one moment of your life. It's only property that's being taken. It isn't worth the risk."

She looked away at the hope she read in his eyes. She had to think of Micah. Tears rose up again and she blinked them away.

"I'm going to start looking for another job as soon as the semester ends, since it looks like eventually I'll be out of a job. And now I know what's going on, I don't want to hang around too much longer." He grimaced.

He touched her arm and brought her attention back to his face. "I know what I'm asking of you, Ella."

He probably did. He might have paid the debt the court had given him, but society would continue to make him pay for the rest of his life.

Was she strong enough to take that on? "I don't know, Derrick. I have to think."

"Yeah, I know."

She stepped away from the railing and turned back to retrace their steps. Her fingers brushed the phone, and she stopped, used the hem of her sweater to wipe off both their fingerprints and dropped it over the railing into the water below.

"You're not afraid of me now, are you?"

The question gripped her by the throat, and triggered more tears. "No, Derrick, I'm not afraid." Not of him, but of what his past would do to them.

He slipped an arm around her and held her against his side. She turned into him. He had protected her from Larry, but he couldn't protect her from this.

CHAPTER 27

DERRICK SLAMMED CN his breaks and swore as the driver of a red pickup truck suddenly swerved in front of him. Son of a bitch. That would be all he'd need, a traffic accident to keep him from reaching the school.

In the old days he'd have been railing at the guy and ready to run him off the road. At least he was making progress with controlling his emotions.

He blinked to moisten eyeballs that felt gritty as sandpaper and concentrated on keeping a safe distance between him and the erratic driver.

The catnaps he could usually catch while working had been few and far between, not because he had a bunch of tows the night before, but because keeping his mind off Ella had been an exercise in futility. She hadn't cut him out of her life, but she hadn't offered him a deadline for how long she needed to think about it either.

But she'd agreed he needed to keep his promise to Micah. If this was going to be the last thing he did with the kid, he wanted him to remember he'd kept his word. He cared about Micah, just like he did Ella.

Aw, hell. Who was he kidding? He was crazy about them both. When he was with them, they were the family he hadn't had the opportunity to have They couldn't give him back the sever.

years he'd lost, but they gave him more.

The parking area of the school was packed. He squeaked into a space so small he had a hard time getting out of the car. Ella and Micah were to meet him in the entrance foyer of the school, so he fell in with several people walking that way and held the door for two ladies entering behind him.

He spotted Ella standing to one side talking to Micah's teacher. Her relaxed posture and easy smile offered him some reassurance that Mrs. Lamm hadn't run the background check. He dodged several women with their children in tow and cut across to join them.

Micah grinned when he spotted him and broke away to come to him. "Hey."

"Are you hungry?"

"Starving." He said the word like he was going to keel over any minute.

Derrick laughed.

"You're here, and Mom's still talking to my teacher."

"As long as their talking about good stuff, you're in the clear."

Micah rolled his eyes. "Maybe if you come, we'll get to eat." He grabbed Derrick's hand and gave a tug.

Micah's teacher smiled as he approached.

"It's nice to see you again, Mr. Armstrong."

"You too, Mrs. Lamm."

"You three better get to the cafeteria. It will be a little crowded in there, and it may take a few minutes to get your food. I'll see you later, Micah."

Micah caught Ella's hand, and for several moments the three of them were bridged together as they walked down the wide hallway. The sound built as they approached to just below a roar.

When they fell into line behind other parents, Micah grinned at him. "The eggs suck, but the bacon's good."

"Just like the chow halls."

"Chow halls?"

"That's what you call cafeterias in the military."

"That's sick."

Derrick looked up.

"New slang for something he likes," Ella explained. "Micah heard it on television, and it's now his favorite expression. He told Patsy her pizza was sick and it upset her. He's always loved her pizza. I had to explain to her this morning it means the opposite of what it sounds like."

He shook his head.

The eggs were real mixed with powdered, but the bacon was good. Yep, just like the Navy.

Micah's constant chatter about the school and his friends filled in the silence that lingered between him and Ella.

Micah pointed to a boy the same height and build as himself. "That's my friend JT. His real name is John Taylor, but so's his dad's and his grandpa's, and they call him JT 'cause it's too confusing having three Johns at their house."

"That makes sense. If his mom yelled John, there'd be too many people answering."

Micah giggled.

They finished eating and wandered down to Micah's classroom. He pointed out the papers on the wall his teacher had mounted, a class assignment everyone had done well on. Derrick paused to look at Micah's. Though the handwriting was a little messy, there was an A+ at the top.

"Good job, buddy," Derrick presented his fist and Micah bumped it with his own

"Will you come over earlier tonight so we can play *Ride*?" he asked.

"I don't know if I can come over tonight. I have to do some things today that might keep me tied up. We'll see."

Micah nodded.

He knelt so he could talk to him eye-to-eye. He wanted very much to take him into his arms and hold him close for a moment. He'd allowed the mind-set of prison and his father's abuse had forged to keep him from getting too close. Regret hit him hard. "I really appreciate you inviting me to come today, Micah."

"You haven't been to breakfast at school before?"

"Not since I was really young." Derrick forced a smile. "You have a good day." He touched Micah's shoulder.

"Okay."

He turned aside while Ella gave Micah a kiss on the forehead and sent him into his room. He stuffed his hands in his pockets as they walked.

"You wanted to hug him," Ella said, when they had almost reached the outer doors.

"Yeah."

"Why didn't you?"

"I didn't know whether it would be okay with you, with him. My father was more apt to give us his belt than a pat on the back. I never learned how to give affection freely. I can't read the signals."

"You have with me."

"You made the first move, Ella. You made it easy for me." His throat felt like he'd swallowed crushed glass and he looked away. "Why did you do that?"

"Because you made me feel safe."

He held the door for her. At least that was something he'd gotten right. He hesitated next to her car a few slots away from his and waited for her to make the last move and send him on his way.

ELLA RESTED A hand on his arm, drawing his eyes to her face.

The night had been long. She hadn't slept more than an hour all night. She'd run a background check and read everything about him that was listed. The man it described was a stranger to her, nothing like the one who stood before her, with heavy, sleep-deprived eyes. The man afraid to embrace her child for fear she wouldn't want him to.

But his past was a roadblock that would affect them both, and affect Micah if anyone at his school found out about it. It was something neither of them could hide or hide from.

"Is there anything you can do to have your record sealed?"

He shook his head. "It's military, Ella. What's done is done.

"I'm not required by law to put it on my resume, but I have to put it on a job application if they ask if I've ever been convicted of a felony. I could lie, but once they do the background check it's there.

"I know I'm not a good bet Ella, but I love you and Micah. When I'm with the two of you, I feel like we could be a family."

She'd felt that way too.

But looking down the road... It would be a struggle, and she was so tired of struggling.

She loved him. But she had Micah to think about.

Tears rolled down her cheeks.

Derrick moved to hold her. A piece of her died, knowing this would be the last time she felt his arms around her. The people walking to their cars, giving them curious looks, didn't mean a thing when her life would be forever damaged by this.

He deserved better. He'd worked for something better.

"I can't, Derrick."

His arms tightened around her, and he cupped the back of her head, holding her, offering her comfort even while his breathing hitched and his muscles tensed. He brushed his lips against her cheek. "I love you, Ella."

He released her and took a step back. Tears trailed down his cheeks. He turned and walked away.

CHAPTER 28

THE POP OF the champagne bottle broke into Ella's thoughts and she jerked. Her head felt heavy from her hours-long crying jag, the skin beneath her eyes raw. It had taken the makeup expert, Susan, ten minutes to cover up the evidence. She'd been understanding and comforting, kind.

The cameraman, Ed, was cradling a plate laden with finger foods and was using a finger sandwich to underline something he was saying to Carmella, Davis's assistant. Susan sipped a glass of the champagne while Davis poured, then handed the bottle off to Angela, the receptionist, to finish filling the glasses.

The rest of the people milling around lined up for food and champagne. She didn't know all of them, but she'd seen some of them at different jobs.

All these people, working, living their lives, caring for their families. That's all Derrick and she had wanted. Would he ever have that? She fought back more tears.

Davis approached with two champagne glasses, and she forced a smile.

"You're quiet," he said. "Everything okay?"

"Yeah. Everything's fine. I'm just a little stunned right now. I'm sure it'll sink in when I start doing the work."

"We'll need to start that in a few weeks, but I'll have some jobs for you to do until you and Brigitte settle everything."

"Thanks, Davis. This whole experience has been a little surreal. I'm not an actress or a model, and for her to choose me..." She shook her head.

"You have the look she's going for, Ella. You wear the clothes she designs like they were made for you. And everyone has to start somewhere."

"She could go bigger, she has the contacts."

"Maybe that isn't what she wants. If she went bigger, someone would be sniffing around wanting to buy her out and blow things up. She might be like me. I want to be the master of my own destiny. I want to enjoy the things I do. And if it got any bigger, I wouldn't enjoy it anymore because I'd have to give up some of the creativity to deal with the business part of it.

"I'm content to let Justin, my partner, deal with all that. He enjoys writing up the contracts and dealing with all the money. And he likes investing it in talented people like you."

She'd never believed she had a talent other than dancing.

"He'll want to talk to you about what kind of salary you'll want to shoot for with Brigitte. And he'll want you to sign the contracts he's drawn up to represent you."

"I know I already signed the contract that said if I got this gig, I'd allow him to represent me...."

"You know the picture in my office you admired the first day you came in?"

"Yeah."

"He represents her."

"Oh."

Davis laughed. "Don't ever lose that innocent quality you have, Ella. It draws people to you."

"It isn't innocence, it's stupidity."

He laughed.

"I'm just stumbling along here, finding my way. I never thought this would go so far."

And like Derrick, she was always braced for when her past might bite her.

Derrick had been brave enough to come clean with her, and

been punished for it. She flinched at the thought and pushed on.

She needed to come clean with Davis. "I'm not that innocent. I used to strip for a living, Davis. Will that screw this up for me?" She hazarded an upward glance, but read no shock in his expression.

"I realized that the first day, when you asked me if you'd have to take your clothes off. We all have a past, Ella. And we all have to own it. And no, it won't screw things up for you.

His lean, masculine face was solemn. "Twenty-five years ago, I was a heroin addict."

He might not have been shocked by her admission, but she had to forcibly close her mouth at his.

He grimaced at her expression. "I was a functioning addict. I thought I could handle the drugs and still make a living with my photography, and I did. For a while. But you're never in charge of drugs, they're in charge of you. I lost control, and I pawned my cameras to buy drugs. Then one day I woke up in the hospital from an overdose, and Justin was standing over me. He said he wanted me to sign a contract to work with him. I was the best damned photographer he'd ever seen, and if I was that good on drugs, he could only imagine how good I'd be if I got off them. But I had to get clean before I signed the contract."

"I had to make a choice between my photography, the one thing I loved, or letting that monkey ride my back until I died. And obviously I chose what I love. It was the hardest thing I've ever done, but it's given me my life."

It had to be a sign, or she was just in the right place at the right time. Like she'd been for the past month. Tears rolled down her cheeks, and she brushed at them. "I wish you'd told me this story when we first met."

"You wouldn't have trusted me, Ella."

"No, you're right, I wouldn't have. But I trust you now." She tipped her glass of champagne up and drank it. She wanted to go to Derrick right now, but she needed to take care of this first. "I need to see Mr. Tolliver now, because there's something I need to do before Micah gets out of school."

"Okay." He glanced at his watch. "I'll take you to his office. He had some appointments earlier and couldn't join us, but he should be free now."

SWEAT STREAMED DOWN Derrick's bare torso and his arms shook as he raised the weight. He'd pushed himself to exhaustion in the hopes of deadening the pain still gnawing at him.

Part of healing was acknowledging the pain, recognizing it for what it was and letting it go, but this was going to stick with him for a long time. He set the weight in the support and lay on the bench, panting, breathing in the smell of oil and dirt that lingered inside the old garage.

His phone buzzed for the third time in the past ten minutes. He reached for it and saw Acampa's name and number for the third time. He reached for the towel looped over the stand and dried his hair. Acampa left him a voice mail this time.

The detective's message was rushed, like he couldn't get the words out fast enough. "We picked up your boss and his accomplices last night, during a robbery, but Hank Petrey slipped past us. He's been telling Roger he thought you were working for us. He may have seen us together that day we drove up to the house. Anyway, he's been following you, so I'm just giving you a heads-up. Be on guard, Derrick."

Jesus! He'd probably seen the cops who'd come to see him about Ella's situation. And he'd followed him. Why hadn't he seen the fucker?

The bastard probably knew about Ella and Micah.

Derrick pushed Ella's number. Would she answer after they'd just broken up? It went immediately to voice mail, and he swore. She was probably at the agency signing her contract.

He dried his chest and slung the towel over his shoulder. He'd go to her apartment and wait for her. He rushed out of the garage, ran up the stairs. He turned at the sound of a car pulling in the drive, recognized Ella's vehicle, and rushed back down.

She shoved open the car door and broke out into a graceful run to meet him at the bottom of the steps. "I made a mistake Derrick. I want us to try."

Relief coursed through him and he wrapped his arms around her. "Thank God." She clung to him as tightly as he did her. When she pulled back to look up at him, he kissed her.

When they came up for air, he murmured. "Sorry I'm all hot and sweaty."

"It doesn't matter, I love you. You've been hot and sweaty before and I didn't mind." She ran the backs of her fingers down beneath the waistband of his gym shorts.

He laughed. After the last few hours, it felt good. And making love with her would feel even better, but they needed to talk.

"Last night they arrested my boss and the men he had pulling the jewelry store robberies. Hank, the angry guy I told you about, got away. Acampa just called to warn me he's been following me, and he told Roger I was working for the police. He either saw me with Acampa, or he saw Sanchez and Miller here the other day."

"You should stay with me and Micah until they catch him, Derrick. We have better security in our building."

"Think Micah would be okay with that?"

"I think he'll be fine with it."

"Let's go up so I can take a shower, and we'll pick up Micah after school. If Roger's in jail, there may be no reason for me to go in to work." He held her hand as they went up the stairs.

Another car pulled into the driveway and he turned. It was a police car. Glass from the apartment door spit at him, and he felt a blow like a punch in his side. He stumbled, dragging Ella down with him onto the steps, curving his body protectively around hers.

The cops below drew their guns. Gasping for air, he nudged her to the side. "He's in the apartment, Ella. Go off the side of the steps. I'll lower you down." His muscles felt like cooked spaghetti after all the lifting, but the adrenaline coursing through him would give him the strength he needed.

Her face looked ghostly white against her black hair.

"Go, Ella."

She slipped her legs through the rungs of the banister and eased down. It would only be about twelve feet.

Another bullet hit the steps, shooting up wood near where she hung, and Derrick released her, then swung his own legs through and gripped the banister with one hand as he swung through.

Blood splattered his face as a bullet ripped through his forearm, and he lost his grip, landing on his back on the hard-packed dirt. What air he was able to drag in was forced out, and he struggled to draw another breath.

Ella crawled to him and ripped her blouse off to wrap around his arm, knotting it tight. Then she pulled the towel out from under him and put pressure on his side.

"It'll be okay, honey." His words were slurred, it was getting harder to get the air in and out, and the pain was starting to break through the adrenaline rush and the numbness brought on by the initial trauma.

Ella's tears were hot against his face. "I love you. Don't leave me."

"Won't." Things grew gray around the edges, then darker, until he couldn't see anything at all.

HE WAS DYING. He had to be. She'd never seen so much blood.

She looked toward the two police officers who were pinned down behind their doors. More sirens screamed in the distance. The pop of an occasional shot came from upstairs.

They had to do something. *She* had to do something. She looked toward the side yard where a rickety wooden fence separated Mama's yard from the neighbors. Keeping low, she crawled to it. The fence was actually part wire fence and part wood, hodge-podged together as a boundary line and clogged with weeds. She braced one foot against one of the posts and pulled against the picket closest to it. It gave way, and she fell back, then tossed it aside. She worked on the next one. Then the next.

A man suddenly appeared on the other side of the fence, his Hispanic heritage written in his straight dark hair and wide-cheeked face.

"Please help us," she gasped. "He's been shot. I think he's dying."

"Move away, señora." He began to kick the wooden pickets free of the structure.

Ella ran back to Derrick and touched his throat, seeking a pulse. It beat weakly against her fingers, and his breathing was labored. She forced herself to keep breathing, to cry later, because right now he needed her. He was strong, he had to live.

She grabbed one of Derrick's wrists, braced her feet, and, using all her weight hauled back on his arm. His limp weight moved only inches.

The man's head popped through the fence, and he looked up at the side window of the apartment above, then crawled to her. "We will drag him through together."

She took one wrist, he the other, and they pulled.

The police fired several shots at the apartment, drawing the man's attention as other police cars skidded to a stop on the street and officers rushed up the drive.

Another man appeared through the fence. "Move," he ordered, and pushed her aside. The two made swift progress dragging Derrick to the fence, then pulling him through.

"There's an ambulance at the end of the street. Get him into the car, and we'll take him to the EMTs," the second man said. They manhandled Derrick's limp body into the back seat while Ella jumped into the front seat next to them. The engine revved, and they tore out of the driveway and down the street.

CHAPTER 29

T HE SURGICAL WAITING room at the UC San Diego trauma
center smelled like the cleaning agents and alcohol had bonded
to create the distinctive smell of sickness held at bay.

Ella held Micah close and stroked his hair, over and over. The
movement soothed her and him. He'd cried and clung to her
when he and Patsy arrived, but now seemed to have calmed.

"No one's come out to tell you anything?" Patsy asked.

"No. And h-he's been in surgery for nearly four hours." But,
as she kept reminding herself, as long as he was there, he was
alive.

"His neighbors came and got us while the two policemen held
the shooter off. They kicked through the fence and hauled Derrick
out through the hole. Then they put us in a car and took us down
to the end of the street where the ambulance waited. If they hadn't
done it, he'd probably have bled to death."

"I brought you some clothes if you'd like to change. I can stay
with Micah." Patsy held up a plastic bag.

Ella looked down at the green scrubs they'd given her to wear.
"Okay. I'll be right back. If they come, tell them where I am." She
kissed Micah's forehead and got to her feet.

Once in the ladies' room, she closed herself into one of the
stalls to undress. The nurses had taken her to the shower to scrub
down and change while the doctors prepared Derrick for surgery.

The water had run pink while she rinsed away the blood.

She shuddered and stepped out of the stall. Her face, washed-out and drawn, stared back at her from the mirror, reminding her of how pale he'd been, how still. She started to tear up again but managed to halt the mounting grief.

Because he was going to be okay. He had to be. They were going to get through this. They were going to build a life together.

She folded the scrubs and, pausing at the nurse's station, returned them, then went back into the waiting room. Detectives Sanchez and Miller were waiting at the door, and she stopped.

"The nurse said you'd gone to the restroom. Detective Acampa wanted you to know the shooter, Hank Petrey, has been taken into custody," Miller said.

"Thank you."

"Also, you're no longer a person of interest in our investigation."

She was too exhausted to react. Maybe she'd feel the proper relief later. "Have you made an arrest?"

"Yes. Two people have come forward. Jasmine Carr and Lisa Garrett. Lisa is claiming it was self-defense. And Jasmine is claiming she witnessed what happened."

"I'd take them at their word. Larry was a violent man, and he didn't take no for an answer. I was lucky I'd been warned and was able to get away."

"Your boyfriend is a violent man, too," Sanchez said. "You may want to rethink things."

Ella studied him for a moment. Derrick was right. All anyone saw was the piece of paper with his past on it. "I know all about what Derrick did, and how long his sentence was. That was his past, Detective, and he owns it.

"He protected me with his body today, even though he was shot and bleeding profusely and struggling to breathe. And when he lowered me over the side of the steps and dropped me while bullets were hitting so close to him, he got splinters in his skin."

She leaned closer, looking right in Sanchez's eyes. "He saved my life today, and all he's ever shown me is respect and gentleness.

So don't act like you know him because you read a piece of paper printed with the charges he was convicted of seven years ago. He isn't that man any longer. He's the man he's made himself since then."

She saw a man in scrubs walking toward her and braced herself.

"Are you Derrick Armstrong's family?"

She started to tear up again and clenched her fists against it. "Yes."

"Derrick's out of surgery. He lost a lot of blood, and had to be transfused, and we had some difficulty repairing the lung and getting it to inflate, but he's stable now. He's got a chest tube for drainage, but he has a fair chance of making it as long as he doesn't develop an infection. I'll do another assessment in a few hours to see how he's doing. The arm will be fine. The bullet damaged a vessel, and we had to do a graft, but it will heal."

He grasped her arm briefly. "He's in recovery, and you can see him as soon as he's moved to a room."

"Thank you." The relief she hadn't experienced before hit her and she swayed. Miller grasped her arm to steady her.

Ella opened her eyes to the other woman's face. "Thank you for coming to let me know about Petrey. I need to go tell Micah Derrick is out of surgery."

He was going to be okay. He had to be. He would be.

CHAPTER 30

"**Y**OU'RE NOT SUPPOSED to be doing that." Ella fell into step with Derrick as he pulled the loaded dolly toward Patsy's now empty apartment one-handed. The five days he'd lain in the hospital with the drainage tube in his side had seemed a lifetime. That he was up and moving with any kind of ease was a miracle.

"I'm not straining anything. Micah and Patsy loaded it. I'm just delivering it to his room. Besides, a little exercise is good for me. My breathing is better, and this is a hell of a lot easier than the PT they had me doing this past week."

He opened and closed his free hand, and the muscle in his forearm bulged, the scar from his surgery a thin, red, five-inch line that still looked a little raw. "See? Almost good as new."

"I had some good news earlier. Detective Acampa contacted the college and they're going to let me take the end of the semester exams so I'll earn credit for my classes."

"Oh, Derrick. That's wonderful." Ella teared up as she paused to embrace him.

Micah zipped past them, his hands working the imaginary throttle of a motorcycle as he zoomed into the apartment in order to beat Derrick to his room.

Ella smiled. "He's really excited about the bigger apartment, even though his room is the same size as the one next door."

"It was really great you were able to work it out with the super to take Patsy's apartment after she moved out. Micah told me he felt bad about you having to sleep on a sofa bed."

She smiled. "Well, I won't be anymore. Think you'll be up to breaking in the new mattress later?" She bumped her hip against his.

"Oh, yeah. You have room, a door, *and* a lock."

"And a real bed. Don't forget the bed."

"Now you've pointed that out, I won't be about to think of anything else but the bed and what we might do in it."

She laughed. She stopped to watch him maneuver the dolly with its load through the door and across the living room to Micah's room.

She took the box she carried to the kitchen and put it on the island, cabinet doors already wide open where she worked to put dishes away.

At a loud tap on the door, she turned to see a tall man with hair nearly as dark as her own standing at the opening. His pale gray eyes studied her with interest.

"Can I help you?"

"I'm looking for Derrick Armstrong. The lady next door let us up and said he was here."

"Yes. I'll get him."

She started toward the bedroom, but Derrick was already standing in the bedroom doorway. "There's someone here to see you."

He focused on the man, expression intent, watching him with a mixture of surprise and something else she couldn't read.

"Hawk."

"Derrick." He nodded. "Looks like you're busy." He stepped into the room.

"I'm helping Ella move." Derrick gestured toward her.

Hawk nodded to her. "I can see that. I heard you're walking wounded."

"Some, yeah."

"Your landlady told us where we could find you, so we decided to drop on by. There are six guys out here who can help get this done in about half an hour. What do you say?"

He spoke to Ella. She stared at him, uncertain of what to say. "That would be…good. Um. Thank you."

She studied each of the men and the way they greeted Derrick, not exactly friendly, but not hostile either. They were all muscular and fit, all had the same walk, and moved with the physical grace of the extremely fit. The tallest one in the group, Hawk, was definitely the leader.

They carried furniture and boxes like professional movers, rolling the dolly with a lot more speed and efficiency than she and Derrick had. Working as a team, they had the furniture in place in a jiffy, and the only thing left to do was to unpack the stuff in the bathroom and finish the kitchen.

When Derrick said, "Ella, the guys and I are going to go next door and talk for a few minutes," Her stomach did a little jig, but she had no way of judging what was going on.

All he'd told her was they were his old SEAL team. After all he had told her about what he had done, how they felt about him, and after she'd witnessed his ex-captain's behavior, her stomach cramped with anxious tension.

"How about some iced tea? Or I have some soft drinks."

He smiled and gave her arm a reassuring squeeze. "That would be good."

She passed out the cans of coke, and they wandered out the door with Derrick in the lead.

THE EMPTY ROOM echoed with their footsteps. There weren't any chairs, but he didn't think they'd wanted to take a seat with him anyway.

"I appreciate your help getting Ella moved."

"No problem," Greenback said and sipped the coke.

"You about healed up?" Langley asked, his expression neutral.

"Still hurts like hell to breathe too deeply, and I'm doing PT for the arm, but I'm getting there."

His eyes moved from face to face. They were harder than he remembered. But then so was he. They'd been younger then, more idealistic, and high on themselves and what they could accomplish.

Even after all the therapy and self-analysis, his emotions still ran rampant, but he knew how to direct them now.

Bowie and Doc were still joined at the hip. Greenback still seemed the mildest-mannered of the group. And he could barely bring himself to look Brett in the eye, but he did. Flash leaned against the bedroom doorframe his eyes moving from one to the other, as though he thought there might be a fight and he was going to have to act as referee.

And Hawk leaned against the wall, arms crossed, but he scanned the space with as much attention as they had in the rooms they cleared in Iraq.

Langley pinned Derrick with a glance. Lang hadn't been with them on the mission, but he'd betrayed him all the same.

"I just want to tell you all that I'm sorry. I know it probably doesn't mean much, but I am. If I could go back and change it all, I would.

"I didn't just mess up, I imploded my life and my career, and I almost took some of you with me." He closed his eyes against the accusations he read in every face.

"I spent the first year in therapy and in and out of the hospital. When I finally got my shit together, I worked on a lot of stuff from when I was a kid, all the way up to the moment I broke into your house, Hawk. I own everything I did. And I have to live with it all, I haven't just shrugged it aside like it's nothing.

"You guys were my friends and my family, and I betrayed you all. I hope one day you can forgive me."

"Is that all?" Brett challenged.

"No." Derrick stepped forward to face him. "I went back in for you, Brett."

"That's a lie," Bowie said, his voice hard with challenge.

Before Derrick had time to rebut it, Doc said, "No it's not."

His auburn hair seemed redder than Derrick remembered, and was it possible he had more freckles?

"He climbed through a window on the east side and dropped

his Boonie hat on the way in. Then Hawk went in the front. I wrote it in my report."

Derrick needed to finish this. "There were tangos in the back, and they passed the room I wired earlier. And once they heard the M-5, they rushed into the hall toward the front of the house. I held them off, then once Hawk went out the front, I dove back out a window and ran like hell, but the blast almost got me anyway. Threw me up in the air like a ping-pong ball and straight into a wall. Knocked the wind out of me and bruised my shoulder. Then I heard Hawk on the radio and knew he made it out with Brett, so I stumbled through the dust in the direction of his position and fell in with the rest of you."

"You almost cost us all our lives," Flash said, his eyes flaring with rage. He raked his fingers through his sun-streaked hair, then looked away.

They all knew what he had done, and one word from any of them and he'd be right back in prison.

And he'd deserve it. He had no defense.

Ella and Micah leapt instantly to mind. Being back in a cage, losing them, would kill him this time.

"You were messed up, Strong Man." Brett's voice cut through the tension and Derrick's chaotic emotions. "We all knew you were. You weren't sleeping. You were on edge, and your temper was out of control. You even talked in your sleep. What little of it you got.

"And none of us wanted to address any of it, because we saw some of the same things in ourselves. All any of us had to do was report it to Hawk, and he'd have ordered you to sick bay. But we covered for you instead. It was the wrong call. And we all learned from it. You most of all."

Derrick's throat thickened with emotion. "You almost died because of it."

"Almost is the operative word. We have close calls all the time and we don't even acknowledge them." Brett moved forward to stand even closer, his gaze steady. "We both had a close call, and we're both past it."

Brett looked around the room at each man. "We've carried this weight long enough as individuals, as a team. We all need to move on.

"It's time to forget and forgive." Brett offered Derrick his hand.

It took every ounce of courage Derrick had to grasp it. And once he did, more courage to maintain his composure. Brett was offering him a priceless gift—a free pass and forgiveness. He'd never forget it. "Thanks, Brett."

"Good luck. I wish you well, Derrick."

Each man in his team filed forward to grip his hand and offer similar sentiments, even Hawk, until Flash stood before him. Flash gripped his hand and asked, "How'd you get a woman that lovely and sweet, Strong Man?"

Derrick laughed. "It was a fucking miracle, Flash."

"Mine was too. Good luck."

As their footsteps in the hall grew distant, he drifted to the window. He'd never see them again, and if he did, they'd more than likely just nod and keep on moving.

He had grieved their loss for seven years. Their forgiveness had eased the pain in one way, and sharpened it in another. But the weight he'd carried for so long seemed lighter.

Ella appeared in the doorway, a worried expression clouding her face. Relief spilled across to clear it, and she sauntered to him with her ballerina-like grace. "Is everything all right?"

"Yeah. Everything's fine." He tugged her in close. "They were once my family, Ella. We never got to say goodbye, and now we have."

Her arms tightened around him. "And now you have us, Derrick."

"I'll never stop feeling grateful for it, either." He kissed her, infusing the kiss with all his pent-up relief and joy. It really was a miracle. He'd always be grateful for her and Micah. He finally had a family.

THE END

FOR MORE INFORMATION ABOUT TERESA REASOR

Website: www.teresareasor.com

MILITARY ROMANTIC SUSPENSE
BREAKING FREE (Book 1 of the SEAL Team Heartbreakers)
BREAKING THROUGH (Book 2 of the SEAL Team Heartbreakers)
BREAKING AWAY (Book 3 of the SEAL Team Heartbreakers)
BREAKING TIES (A SEAL Team Heartbreakers Novella)
BUILDING TIES (Book 4 of the SEAL Team Heartbreakers)
BREAKING BOUNDARIES (Book 5 of the SEAL Team Heartbreakers)
BREAKING OUT (BOOK 6 of the SEAL Team Heartbreakers)
BREAKING POINT (A SEAL Team Heartbreakers Novella)
BREAKING HEARTS (Book 7 of the SEAL Team Heartbreakers)
BREAKING CHAINS (Book 8 of the SEAL Team Heartbreakers)

SEALS IN PARADISE SERIES
HOT SEAL, RUSTY NAIL

PARANORMAL ROMANCE
TIMELESS
DEEP WITHIN THE SHADOWS (Book 1 of the Superstition Series)
DEEP WITHIN THE STONE (Book 2 of the Superstition Series)
WHISPER IN MY EAR
HAVE WAND, WILL TRAVEL (Book 1 Have Wand, Will Travel)
ONCE BITTEN, TWICE SHY (Book 2 Have Wand, Will Travel)
ADVENTURES OF A WITCHY WALLFLOWER (Book 3 Have Wand, Will Travel)